"Why are you back?"

Callie didn't answer and Gabe realized it was because she wore earbuds. He could hear strains of music.

He touched her shoulder, startling her.

She yanked the buds out of her ears. "You scared the ever-living daylights out of me."

The cap pulled low on her forehead covered her red hair today. Her flawless skin glowed in the bright sunlight as though lit from within.

Had he ever been that…new? That clean and carefree?

"You're the most taciturn man I've ever met," she said. "Say something already."

He was trying to, but she rattled him, scattered his thoughts. "Told you not to come back."

"Technically, you didn't. You just told me that I couldn't *be* here. Nick says that I can." She lifted her narrow chin on that perfect heart-shaped face.

Don't want this woman. Don't desire her.

I already do

D1408882

Dear Reader,

Welcome to my fictional town of Accord, Colorado, and say hello to the three Jordan brothers, Gabriel, Tyler and Nick. The eldest, Gabe, runs a dogsledding business on the family's land. He loves his dogs as much as he loves the land.

A few years ago, while going through a difficult time in my life, I decided to do something outside of the box for me. I'd always wanted to try an Outward Bound course, so I headed off to beautiful Algonquin Park in northern Ontario in the middle of February. There, amid deep snow and stunning scenery, I went dogsledding for four days.

I'm not much of an athlete, but it was one of the best things I've ever done. The dogs made the challenge so, so much fun. They are eager and willing to put their hearts into the job for you. Once harnessed to the sled, they yip and jump in the air because they are so eager to just *go*. To *do*. You can't help but laugh at their infectious energy.

It turned out to be a wonderful experience.

I was happy to put my experience with the dogs and dogsledding to good use in Gabe's story. He's been through some tough times. Dogsledding is a healing and calming event for him, enriched by his relationship with his dogs. Whooshing through silent, snow-laden forests, he feels closer to the father who died when he was young.

I hope you enjoy Gabe's story.

Mary Sullivan

P.S. I enjoy hearing from readers! Contact me through my website at www.marysullivanbooks.com.

In from the Cold

MARY SULLIVAN

⟨H⟩**HARLEQUIN**®SUPER ROMANCE®

Recycling programs
for this product may
not exist in your area.

ISBN-13: 978-0-373-71831-3

IN FROM THE COLD

Copyright © 2013 by Mary Sullivan

All rights reserved. Except for use in any review, the reproduction or utilization of this work in whole or in part in any form by any electronic, mechanical or other means, now known or hereafter invented, including xerography, photocopying and recording, or in any information storage or retrieval system, is forbidden without the written permission of the publisher, Harlequin Enterprises Limited, 225 Duncan Mill Road, Don Mills, Ontario, Canada M3B 3K9.

This is a work of fiction. Names, characters, places and incidents are either the product of the author's imagination or are used fictitiously, and any resemblance to actual persons, living or dead, business establishments, events or locales is entirely coincidental.

This edition published by arrangement with Harlequin Books S.A.

For questions and comments about the quality of this book, please contact us at CustomerService@Harlequin.com.

® and TM are trademarks of Harlequin Enterprises Limited or its corporate affiliates. Trademarks indicated with ® are registered in the United States Patent and Trademark Office, the Canadian Trade Marks Office and in other countries.

Printed in U.S.A.

HARLEQUIN®
www.Harlequin.com

ABOUT THE AUTHOR

Mary Sullivan likes to challenge herself at times to try new and different things. If that happens to include trying to be an athlete, she's game. Athleticism doesn't come naturally, though, so don't expect great results. It's the effort that counts, and the willingness to try. Her dogsledding trip was one of those challenges that was worth every single speck of energy expended. It included moments of thoughtful solitude in a gorgeous pristine forest—a beautiful blessing.

Books by Mary Sullivan

HARLEQUIN SUPERROMANCE

Other titles by this author available in ebook format.

Don't miss any of our special offers. Write to us at the following address for information on our newest releases.

Harlequin Reader Service
U.S.: 3010 Walden Ave., P.O. Box 1325, Buffalo, NY 14269
Canadian: P.O. Box 609, Fort Erie, Ont. L2A 5X3

CHAPTER ONE

CALLISTA MACKINTOSH DIDN'T believe in beating around the bush. Gabriel Jordan had ignored the eight phone messages she had left in the past three days, and she was running out of patience. Hence, here she was on Jordan land to beard the lion in his den.

The curtain at the front window of the house fluttered.

Must be Gabe. No one else lived here.

"He's a recluse," some of the townsfolk confided.

"He's crazy," others whispered.

Wood smoke scented the air. If not for the aging house—tired and grumpy against the snowy beauty of a Colorado forest—the scene would be idyllic. The house needed to be demolished. Her boss had been right about that.

Callie didn't know nearly enough about its inhabitant. She'd done her research before driving out here but knew little more than facts.

Thirty-seven-year-old Gabe had served in the army for eight years, including a couple of tours in Afghanistan, and then had come home to start a dogsledding business. He lived alone in the old family house that neither his youngest brother, Nick, nor the middle brother, Tyler, wanted. The land, though…that was worth a lot.

Their mother died four years ago. Apparently, their father died when they were children.

Despite Callie's research, *who* Gabe was remained as elusive as that shadow lurking behind the curtain.

She girded her proverbial loins and knocked on the door, rubbing her arms through her wool jacket. Cripes, it was cold in Colorado.

At last, the door opened and a dog peeked out, a Lab with a coat as glossy as melted chocolate. Then the door swung wide and the man she had all but stalked by phone stood in the entrance. For an instant, Callie couldn't think.

Her first thought stunned her. *He's beautiful.*

Wild dark hair framed a face with granite planes that mimicked the mountain behind the sky-kissing trees of the forest.

I should have brought my camera. She could shoot that face all day. Dark eyes, deep-set and alert, studied her without blinking.

Nick no longer knows his older brother. Her boss had warned that Gabe would put up resistance to their plan, but not to worry, that Nick had ways to get around him. Seeing Gabe in person, Callie wasn't so sure. He didn't look like the pushover Nick had described. This man had substance, presence.

Handsome in a rugged mountain-man way, the antithesis of lean and refined Nick, Gabe wore a plaid shirt and blue jeans, the shirt wrinkled in spots that weren't stretched tautly over muscle, and the blue jeans old and pale with wear on his thighs. Not only did Gabe look as though he could eat a bear, but he could probably wrestle it into submission with his bare hands.

His unruly beard and moustache, his black eyes and high cheekbones in a stone-chiseled face spoke of hard-earned character. But what kind? Was he as devious as Nick, as willing to do whatever it took to get a job done?

Maybe not, but Callie had the sense that he would fight for this land tooth and nail, and that her job had just become a whole lot harder.

He watched her with shadowed eyes.

He has baggage. If Callie could peek inside his head at the contents of those suitcases, she would know better how to approach this man.

Still he said nothing, simply stared with mute wariness, held by a deep, unnaturally quiet...*waiting.*

He had a right to be wary.

Callie was about to blow his world apart.

"I'm Callista MacKintosh," she said in the confident voice that put people at their ease. "Callie. I'm here to talk about your land."

"What about my land?" His voice sounded rusty, probably par for the course with recluses, but how would she know? She'd never met one before.

"Perhaps it would be best if I come in?"

"No." He slammed the door.

Her smile vanished. She stared at paint peeling from the old wood, stunned. People liked her. They didn't close doors in her face.

She raised her fist to knock again, but the door swung open and he barged out so quickly her hand hit his chest. And stayed there.

Heat radiated through her fingers and up her arm as though the man were an oven. For the first time since arriving in the state two days ago, a small part of her warmed.

She looked up. Way up. He stared at her fingers glued to the flannel of his shirt and then at her face. His stillness came alive, resonated with a new awareness. She knew that look. He found her attractive. Men often did.

Good.

Even so, she jerked her hand away.

Normally, she would use his awareness of her as a woman to her advantage, but an attraction to him resonated inside her, disturbing her. How could she control him if she let her emotions lead the way?

She didn't mix emotion and business.

Nick Jordan built developments that made oodles of money. Callie came in ahead of time and laid the foundation before the work started. She counseled, cajoled and convinced until home or business owners finally sold, gave in or gave up their spaces so Nick could have what he wanted.

To do that, she couldn't think of them as men or women, only as clients and, when necessary, as obstacles.

No doubt about it, Gabe would be an obstacle. She couldn't possibly think of him as a man.

Oh, but Callie, you already do.

"We'll walk." Gabe shrugged into a beige rancher's coat, setting muscles rippling and flowing.

Callie stared, then registered what he'd said. *He wants to walk? Really? In this cold?*

Why didn't he want her inside the house? What was he hiding?

The dog stepped out. Gabe reached inside, retrieved a beige cowboy hat from a hook and snugged it onto his head, then closed the door.

When he stepped from the veranda, the dog followed.

"He doesn't need a leash?" Callie asked.

He flicked a quick glance over her, then took huge mittens from his pockets. "You have gloves?"

"In the car. I didn't think I'd need them *inside* the house."

He didn't acknowledge her sarcasm. "Get them."

She retrieved her leather gloves from the passenger seat but his lips flattened when she put them on. Before she could close the car door, he stepped close, took one of her hands in his and pulled the thin glove off. He tossed it into the car.

She should object to his presumption that he had the right to touch her, especially given what it was doing to her nerves, but his fingers were warm and hers too cold. He slipped one of his big mittens on her hand and then did the same with the other, his actions gentle, almost tender. A lot of restraint for such a big man.

"Won't you need these?" she asked.

He shook his head and walked away. She caught up to him easily. With his long legs, she expected long strides, so he must have shortened them to accommodate her. Soon enough, she realized it had nothing to do with her.

The chocolate Lab walked with a slow stiff gait and the man checked his stride for the dog's sake.

"What's wrong with him?" she asked.

She almost thought he wouldn't answer, then he said, "She. Arthritis."

"Oh. How old is she?"

Callie waited. *He had to think about it?*

Finally, Gabe said, "Fifteen."

Hmm. Not too talkative.

He led her along a path through a wood of tall pines behind the house. A carpet of snow hushed their footsteps. Sun shone through the pines, sending Jacob's ladders to the forest floor. A soft breeze whispered through the tops of the trees, dropping dollops of snowflakes through the sunbeams.

Callie stopped and stared. Lovely. Charming. She so rarely had the opportunity to appreciate nature. Maybe it was time to take a vacation. Ha! As if Nick would let her.

Gabe pulled too far ahead. The woods might be charming, but she didn't want to be alone in them and ran to catch up to Gabe and the Lab.

You're going to have to get comfortable alone here, girl. Nick wants shots of every part of this land.

Without warning, the dense forest opened into a huge clearing. There, in amongst the trees, were the trappings of Gabe's dogsledding business.

In the center of the clearing, a low brick fire pit held a

couple of huge stewpots on a grate. Steam rose out of them. That explained the source of the burning wood smell.

A large white tent sat at the far end—a squat rectangle maybe eighteen by twenty feet at a guess. Ropes running along the sides anchored it into the ground. A stovepipe broke through the snow-topped roof.

"Do people actually camp here?" He ignored her. "They sleep in that tent?"

Still he didn't respond. "Yes," he said finally.

Did the man really have to think that long to answer? Her questions were only going to get harder.

On one side of the clearing, a thick chain lined a row of trees, with dogs attached at regular intervals, each lying in a bed of straw. When they saw Gabe, they jumped to their feet.

He tore a hank of straw from a nearby bale and made a nest of it near the fire pit. The Lab curled onto the straw, her motions jerky.

Tired of waiting for Gabe to turn his attention to her, Callie asked, "Can we talk?"

She waited for his answer, but Gabe seemed completely absorbed in his task of pouring the steaming liquid from the pots into a row of stainless steel bowls. It smelled like chicken soup.

"Why were you in the house when I got here?" she asked. "Why would you leave a fire untended in the middle of the woods?"

This time, since the question was specific, she knew that if she waited long enough, he would eventually answer. She thought she was beginning to understand the man. He wasn't ignoring her questions with these tactics. Rather, he seemed to be composing appropriate responses. At least, that's what she suspected was happening. But why did it take him so long to do that? She could see in his eyes that he was an intelligent man.

"The can," he said, not making eye contact.

The can? What did that mean? A blush tinged his tanned cheeks above his beard. *Oh.* He'd needed to use the bathroom. It seemed significant and revealing that Gabe would actually go indoors when other men would have simply used the woods. Of course, it was frigid out here. So maybe going to the cabin was merely a matter of practicality rather than any great revelation about his character.

And why was she overanalyzing this? Surely there were other ways she could learn the character of this man.

One thing was already obvious to her—he had his own timetable, his own clock.

Maybe he thought if he made her wait enough before responding to her queries, she would get tired and leave. Never. Rather than waste her breath, she watched while, one by one, he delivered the filled bowls to his dogs.

Curiosity got the better of her. "Won't that burn their tongues?"

She'd never spent much time with animals, but to her untrained eye, these dogs appeared excited and happy—whether for the food or to see Gabe was unclear. Their sincere reactions put Callie in a good mood for some reason.

"Stainless steel." He carried bowls to the next couple of dogs.

"So?"

"It's cold out."

God, it was like pulling teeth getting a complete explanation out of him. "And?"

Several moments passed. "They cool fast."

Oh. That made sense.

After the last dog was fed, Gabe opened a pair of large picnic coolers and took out blocks of something frozen. He walked down the line and filled the now empty bowls with the frozen chunks.

"What are those?"

He didn't respond. She might as well not be there for all the attention he paid her.

And for reasons she didn't care to examine, his disregard bothered her. "What are you doing?"

Over his shoulder, he looked at her as though she had a screw loose. "Feeding my dogs."

"I can see that," she snapped. This interview wasn't going as planned. "Why are you ignoring me? Can you please stand still long enough for us to have a conversation?"

"In five minutes." A glint appeared in his eyes. Was it— Was he *laughing* at her? As quickly as it appeared, it was gone, and she wasn't certain she'd truly seen it.

While she crossed her arms over her chest to ward off the cold, he continued about his business.

"You need good clothes." The suddenness of his words, in the silence of the snow-shrouded forest, startled her.

She glanced at her jacket and boots. "What's wrong with my clothes?" They were from this season's collection.

He picked up a couple of empty bowls. "You're shivering."

Yes, of course she was shivering. She was frozen. "I hadn't planned on spending time in the woods today."

He took a moment as if to digest her sarcasm. "Buy a warm jacket. Boots. Gloves." He glanced at her red hair and she touched it self-consciously. "Get a hat."

He had a point. She planned to be in town long enough to walk every inch of this property. She should be prepared to spend hours out in these low temperatures.

"Don't go to the Willow Branch or that other fancy boutique," he said. "They'll sell you useless shit. Go to the Army Surplus. Noah will give you the right stuff."

"A speech. I'm honored."

That humor gleamed again—she *hadn't* imagined it—and as quickly disappeared.

"For a recluse, you sure know a lot about Accord."

He stopped walking and his innate stillness deepened. "Who said I'm a recluse?"

Had she said something wrong? "Everyone in town."

"Everyone?"

"Most people," she amended. He didn't respond. "Well? Are you one?"

He dumped the last bowl into a pot of clean water. "I'm myself. No more. No less."

He approached her, moving in too closely, taking her breath and hovering over her as though to intimidate her. Fat chance.

"Back off, Chewbacca. You're in my space."

Another glimmer of amusement in his eyes. It didn't reach his lips, though. Or did it? Hard to tell through that much facial hair.

He eased away from her. "Why are you here?"

The moment of truth. In her gut, she knew she would have a fight on her hands. For the briefest of seconds, she considered lying, then quickly abandoned the thought. Best to get it out into the open. Nick might be devious. She was not.

"I work for your brother Nick."

Gabe startled at his brother's name. "So? What does he want?"

"He wants to build a ski resort on this land."

His face turned to stone. "Never."

"Can't we discuss it?"

"No." There was no hesitation now. "Boo," he shouted and spun away.

She jumped. What the hell? "Hey! You can't scare me off that easily."

"I was talking to the dog." He tossed the words over his shoulder as he stalked into the woods.

The Lab accompanied him.

Callie followed, keeping only a small distance between them.

Once they'd reached the house, he opened a door. "Go sit by the fire, Boo." After Boo entered he closed it, then took Callie by the elbow, steering her toward her car, surprising her again with his gentle touch. Gentle, maybe, but also relentless.

"It's time," he said, taking no care now to keep his strides small. She had to skip to keep up.

"Time?"

"You can't be here."

Not *leave,* or *go,* but *you can't be here.* Why phrase it like that?

He opened her car door and urged her into her seat. How he did it without making her feel manhandled baffled her. She never let men control her, but he did it with such restraint that she acquiesced. He shut the door, again with a leashed touch and, without another word, disappeared around the side of the house.

"Well," Callie huffed. "That was that."

She removed Gabe's oversize mittens, got out of the car and left them on the veranda. She had no choice but to leave. There was nothing else for her to do here today. Anger would be useless. Instead she would go back to the B and B and regroup.

CALLIE MADE GABE LAUGH, made him want to give his rusty smile muscles a workout, made him want to be happy again.

That wasn't going to happen. He, Billy, Billy's dad and Monica all knew that was something he didn't deserve.

Callie had breezed onto his land like an augur of the worst tidings, here to blow his world apart.

He didn't like women on his land, didn't want them here. Didn't need them.

It wasn't that he disliked them—lord, no, he loved them—but when a man experiences profound betrayal it colors every relationship, even the most casual.

Callista. The woman had a name almost as pretty as she was.

Gabe stared at the impressions her boots had made in the snow. She wore fashionable boots that pushed all of her weight forward into the pointed toes, the impression from that part of the sole heavier than the dot left in the newly fallen snow by the ridiculously small heel. Too feminine.

He heard her car door open. *Get back in the car. Don't come back here. Go. Please.* He couldn't possibly look at her again today.

A second later, he heard her door close, followed by the engine starting. She drove out of his driveway and he sighed. *Thank God.*

He followed her boot prints to the safety and predictability of his dogs, and to the comfort of his routines, washing the dogs' dishes and gathering wood and water for their next meal, but his nerves jumped and sizzled.

Damn her.

Damn Nick.

Gabe stood a chunk of wood on its end on a tree stump and brought his ax down hard. The log split in two. He did it again with more wood, and again and again.

She was here as his brother's emissary.

Happiness was never going to be in the cards for a man like Gabe. If there was one person on this earth who would agree, in fact who would do everything in his power to deny Gabe happiness, it was his youngest brother.

Gabe split more logs.

Nick knew what this land meant to Gabe, knew that it was part of his soul. Nick wouldn't care about that. Whatever Nick wanted, Nick got. It had been that way since their dad died. Their mother had seen to that.

Gabe's biceps burned. With a roar, he picked up a block of wood and threw it across the clearing, wishing he could send his brother to hell.

Gabe wanted to howl, "The house is *mine*. The land is *mine*. The mountain is *mine*."

Here, in Accord, Colorado, where he'd thought he would find sanctuary on his return from Afghanistan, he'd found changes, and alienation from the townspeople, and his world had grown smaller and smaller until these acres that he owned had become the entire thing.

Now it was threatened. By his own brother.

His jaw hurt. He tried to relax, but couldn't. Nick might as well tear out Gabe's soul. Was that Nick's real goal? Sure, he held a grudge, but even he couldn't be that cruel. Could he?

Gabe whipped out his cell phone. Nick had shaken the dirt of Accord off his shoes the moment he'd turned eighteen. His brother Tyler, on the other hand, had stuck around. Gabe phoned him now. When he answered, Gabe said, "Ty, get out here," then hung up.

CHAPTER TWO

CHILLED BY BOTH the weather and the man's stubbornness, Callie couldn't wait to get out of this wintry backwater to sit by the fire in the B and B in Accord.

Just before turning onto Main Street into town, she passed the sheriff's SUV driving toward the Jordan land.

The sheriff was the third member of the Jordan trinity, the middle brother, Tyler. At some point she would have to get to know him, but Gabe was the one who worried her with his recalcitrance.

In town, she parked on Main Street and called her mom, as she did every day.

No answer. Maybe Sophie had taken her out shopping or to a coffee shop. A few months ago, Callie had hired a caregiver for Mom, to protect her from herself. These days, Mom was her own worst enemy.

Callie dialed Sophie's cell number.

Sophie picked up right away. When Callie heard the tension in her voice, the skin on the back of her neck crawled.

"What's wrong?" She couldn't get the words out quickly enough.

"Johanna is missing," Sophie said.

"What?" Callie sat bolt upright. Images of her mom lost, alone and confused in Seattle, bombarded her. "Since when? Have you called the police?"

"Yes. When I got up this morning she was already gone and the front door wide open."

It was now afternoon. "You're supposed to lock the door."

"I did. Somehow, she figured out how to undo all three locks."

"*Three* locks?"

"I added another one on the weekend. She figured out all of them. You know how determined she is."

Yes, Callie knew that firsthand. That's why she'd hired a full-time caregiver for Mom. Oh lord, where was she?

"She's wily," Callie admitted. For a woman who was losing her mind, how could Mom be so clever sometimes?

"Like you wouldn't believe," Sophie continued. "The police are here. They've set up a neighborhood search. Lots of volunteers are out there looking for her."

Nausea rose in Callie's throat. What would she do if—

"Callie." Sophie sounded hesitant. "It might be time to consider other options."

"You mean a home?" Callie asked dully.

"Yes. You knew it would come to this eventually."

"Not so soon."

For the first few years after Mom developed odd symptoms of apathy and memory loss, Callie had blamed the changes on menopause. When depression set in, Callie urged Johanna to see a therapist. The therapist had suspicions and had sent her for tests. At last, a diagnosis had been reached—early-onset Alzheimer's. Early, all right. Mom had been only fifty-three. Two years later, she was deteriorating more rapidly than anyone could have predicted.

Now this woman who barely remembered her own name was out on the streets of Seattle alone.

"I'll come home," Callie blurted.

"No, you won't," Sophie ordered. "There's nothing you can do that we aren't already doing."

"I can't stay here."

"You have to. Haven't you just started a new assignment for Mr. Jordan?"

"Yes. Nick needs the proposal to present to the investors next week. He wants everything done yesterday. You know how he is."

"Concentrate on your work. I'll keep you posted. Okay?"

How could Callie sit here while Mom was lost?

"Okay, Callie?" Sophie's tone became forceful. "Call me the second you find her. Promise?"

"I promise."

Callie ended the call and tossed the phone onto the passenger seat. She should fly to Seattle this instant.

She could do nothing from here and that would drive her crazy. Sitting still here in Colorado wasn't an option. At least if she was in Seattle, she could join the search. Maybe her mother would respond to her voice calling out for her where she'd ignored other people.

The hell with it. Despite what she'd told Sophie, she was going home. She phoned Nick to tell him.

"What do you have for me?" he asked without preamble.

"Nick, I have a problem. I'm coming home. Today. As soon as I can book a flight. I have to. I—"

"Callie, you're rambling. Calm down. What's happening?"

She never lost control. Nick had to be surprised.

"It's my mom."

"What about her?"

Nick could be cold, but right now Callie treasured the sound of his composed voice.

"She left the house sometime during the night. Sophie doesn't know when exactly or how long she's been gone. And Sophie can't find her." Her voice cracked. "She's outside alone, Nick."

"Just a minute."

When he put her on hold, the line seemed to throb with

the pounding of her own pulse. A moment later, Nick spoke. "I'm taking care of it. Stop worrying."

"An order from you can't make that happen. I can't stop."

"I know." Nick's normally cool tone was sympathetic, which said a lot about how much he valued Callie. Nick was *never* sympathetic.

"I'm here in Seattle," he said. "I'll keep on top of this until she's found."

"But—"

"Take a deep breath, Callie. Have I ever failed you?"

No. He hadn't. She pulled her unruly emotions under control.

"I've set wheels in motion here. I've got people on this," he said, and his strength seeped into Callie. If Nick said he had it under control, he did. "How are you doing there? Anything to report?"

Before she could tell him of her visit with Gabe, she had to draw a deep breath. "Not yet. I went to talk to your brother before invading his land."

"It isn't his land. It belongs to all three of us."

"He doesn't feel that way."

"Gabe wouldn't. He's stubborn."

Pot calling the kettle black.

"Why didn't you just photograph the mountain first and to hell with Gabe?"

"Nick, you trust me to do preliminary work on these developments. I like the straightforward approach. Let me do my job the way I see fit."

"I need results, Callie."

"You'll get them. Have I ever failed *you?*"

Silence. What could he say? She hadn't let him down— ever.

"When you go back out there," Nick said, "don't let Gabe intimidate you."

"I won't."

"Legally, you have a right to be on that land because I've given you permission to be there."

"I know, but I'd like to see you brazen it out with a six-foot Chewbacca looming over you."

"Chewbacca? What are you talking about?"

"Your brother is huge and hairy."

"Hairy? I didn't know that."

"When was the last time you saw him?"

"Close to twelve years ago."

That surprised her. She had sensed an estrangement, but it was more profound than she'd suspected. That situation would impact her job here.

"What's wrong between the two of you?"

"Nothing. We're different people. We don't have much in common."

Instinct told her there was a whole lot more going on, but sensed she'd get no more out of Nick at the moment.

"He didn't attend your mom's funeral?" She had been working for Nick for only a couple of years when his mother passed away and had been the one to order the flower arrangement for him and his daughter, Emily.

Nick had attended the funeral, but had returned to work a couple of days later, subdued and not quite himself. He had been working harder than ever in the four years since then, as difficult as that was to believe. Her boss had already been the quintessential workaholic.

Callie had a strong suspicion that his mom's death had started the wheels turning on this whole Accord development deal on the land where he'd grown up. She had no idea why.

"Gabe was on tour in Afghanistan," Nick answered after a long pause.

"Couldn't he have come home for his mom's funeral?"

"I'm guessing yes."

"Why didn't he?"

"Beats me. I don't really know the guy anymore."

"I guess that's my job—to find out who he is. He's going to be a tough nut to crack, Nick."

"You can do it."

"Sure, but it won't be easy. I found out in town he has a lot of people come out for dogsledding, so the business is successful, but he's as closed up as a recluse."

"Maybe we should fix it so his business doesn't make money."

"Whoa. What?" Nick might be crafty, but unethical? "Are you talking about sabotage?" Even Nick couldn't be that driven. She had done a lot for him and she'd convinced all kinds of people to sell their properties to Nick, but he'd never asked her to be this underhanded before.

"No way, Nick," she said. "I won't be part of that."

"It would be a good, quick solution. Get out there and find out whatever you can about his business."

"Nick—"

"Do it. It's your job. Find something I can use. I need him off that land. Convince him to sell however you can."

"Nick, no."

"If you want to keep your job, you'll do it, Callie."

He'd *never* threatened her job before. "Are you serious?"

"Dead serious. I want that land."

Callie held her tongue and thought of her mother. Nick paid her well. Executive assistants didn't come much more efficient than she—qualified, capable and not a complainer. She did anything asked of her, but this was a whole new kettle of fish. She needed the money, though, and so did Mom.

Still, he had threatened to fire her and Callie didn't respond well to threats. Regardless of whatever huge thing was going on with Nick—and she didn't have a clue what it was—her impulse was to tell him where to put this job. Fortunately, sanity prevailed. Quitting would solve nothing and if she could figure out what was bothering him, then maybe she could convince him that underhanded methods were not the way to achieve the desired end.

"Get out on that land first thing tomorrow," Nick ordered, his tone about as hard as cement. "I want shots of that mountain and the land surrounding it from every angle. I need a powerful presentation to lure in these Japanese investors."

This was about more than the investors, but now wasn't the time to probe. "Think you can sell them on the deal?"

Nick didn't deign to answer what had been a stupid question. He could sell ice to the Inuit.

"We need to move forward on this," Nick said. "We've got a narrow window of opportunity before those investors head elsewhere. I won't miss this chance, Callie." He paused then continued in a softer tone. "Don't worry about your mother—I'm taking care of finding her. Take care of Gabe. Study his business. Study him. Find me something I can use against him."

"I'll get the shots, Nick. I'll convince your brother, too, you know that, but I can't be that—"

He hung up.

"Dirty," she finished lamely.

Callie sighed. Wow. When had this job become a trap?

She really needed a day off, but she knew she couldn't take it. What was new? She hadn't taken a vacation in six years. There was always another deal in the works, always another town to convince that a new development would be their salvation. The downside of being employed by a workaholic—he rarely stopped working, so she rarely stopped working. Besides, the money she earned—and the bonus that would be hers once the deal went through—was essential.

Now more than ever, Callie understood it was time to put Mom into a nursing home where she would be constantly supervised. And it couldn't be just any place. Callie wouldn't stuff her away where she would be forgotten or ignored. Callie was determined to find a good place for her mother, no matter the cost.

Man, she was tired. This was her life now, work, work and, oh yeah, more work. When she tried to pull back, to hint at taking a cruise, or at moving on to another job, Nick gave her a raise and worked her harder than ever.

Nick and this job were one big Catch-22 she couldn't seem to break away from—and, with her mother's failing health, the stakes inched higher.

Cut the self-pity and get on with it. Pick yourself up and move on, as you always do.

Right. Move on. She stowed her cell in her bag and got out of the car.

She had parked close to the Accord House bed-and-breakfast where she was staying. A couple of stores down, a gorgeous red winter coat brightened the window display at the Willow Branch. Already imagining how it would look, Callie was tempted to try it on. But Gabe was right. Anything from that boutique would cost a fortune and probably wouldn't meet her needs.

Callie wasn't about to waste money on clothes she would wear while exploring the Jordan land and then never put on again in Seattle. Even more now, she needed to conserve.

She walked past pretty, tasteful shops toward the utilitarian Army Surplus. Callie stepped inside. Foolishly, she hadn't come prepared for the depth of Colorado's cold and snow.

A city girl from Seattle, what did she know about the backwoods and winter?

When she entered the store, an older hippie type stacking merchandise on a shelf, long ponytail tied with a leather thong, turned around. There was an odd scent in the shop—incense mixed with naphthalene. Mothballs.

"Hey," he said. "Haven't seen you in here before."

Up close, the man wasn't old at all, maybe mid-thirties. The long beard aged him and the clothing—psychedelic shirt, corduroy flares and Birkenstocks with thick socks—dated him. Where did he shop? Or was he wearing his father's clothes from the sixties?

His broad smile and welcoming expression made him look even younger.

"You must be new in town," he said. "You moving here?"

"Just visiting."

"We get a lot of tourists these days. I'm Noah Cameron. What can I do for you?"

"I need a warm coat and good boots."

He glanced at her feet and laughed. "Yeah, you sure do. Anything else?"

"A hat and mittens."

He pointed out where to find everything in the store. "I'm stocking today. If I disappear into the back and you need help, ring the bell on the counter."

She quickly perused the merchandise and found a pair of practical, but hardly pretty boots with fleece lining and a camouflage parka at a cut-rate price and brought them to the counter. No more cold toes and chills. She also picked up a red toque and bright blue mittens and carried it all to the front.

Noah was nowhere to be seen, so she tapped the bell.

While she waited she read a notice tucked into a plastic holder sitting beside the old cash register that said Are You Ready for Any Emergency? A line at the bottom noted it was published by the CMOT—Colorado's Ministry of Transportation. It detailed everything she should have in her car for winter driving. That much? The list was extensive.

Noah came out of the stockroom, put down the pile of boxes he carried and approached.

She pointed to the flyer. "Does a person really need that much stuff? Just for winter driving?"

"Yes." Noah didn't crack a smile.

"Seriously?"

"Seriously. What are you driving?"

"A rental. A small sedan."

"You planning to be here a while?"

"Umm, maybe a couple of weeks." Unless something else happened to Mom—like they couldn't find her or she was injured on this foray into Seattle on her own. Then it wouldn't matter what Sophie or Nick thought, she would be on a flight home.

"You need an emergency pack in that vehicle."

"Why?"

"People who live here know enough to have supplies in the trunk in case they get stranded in a storm or whiteout. It's January in Colorado. We get nasty weather here. I advise all tourists who come through to prepare themselves. Three winters ago, we lost a couple who went off the road in a snowstorm. They were found three days later frozen to death."

God. What if something happened to her while she was here? What would become of Mom? Callie had enough in her savings account to cover the cost of her funeral, but what about Mom's care in perpetuity? These days, all questions revolved around Mom, and every worry about worst-case scenarios threatened Callie's composure and her ability to concentrate on the job at hand.

When she got back to the hotel, she intended to order the best insurance policy she could afford. She should have done it two years ago as soon as Mom was diagnosed.

"Okay," Callie said, decision made. If a snowstorm was potentially that dangerous, then she would be prepared. "What do I need?"

Noah grinned, grabbed a shopping basket and took her on

a tour of the store, bobbing up onto the balls of his feet when he walked. He picked up emergency candles with small metal holders and moisture-resistant wooden matches in a tin can.

"The seal on that can's watertight. The candles will burn eight to ten hours. Use only one at a time. Make 'em last. Keep a window cracked so they don't use up all the oxygen in the car."

He picked up a thermal blanket. "Windproof. Waterproof. It will reflect your own body heat back at you."

He tossed a whistle into her basket.

"A whistle?" Skepticism reared its head. "Why?"

"It can be heard farther than a call for help."

Come on, how much of this was really necessary? She put her foot down when he urged her to buy a folding shovel. If the car got stuck in a snowbank, she wasn't about to shovel herself out. She always had her cell phone with her. She would call for a tow.

He tried to sell her neon tape to attach to her radio antenna in case she got stranded in a snowstorm. If the weather got that bad, she wouldn't be driving anywhere.

"Never leave your car," he ordered, pointing a finger at her. "Got it? Wait for help to come to you. You get stranded and step out into a snowstorm? We'll never see you again."

She shivered. "You're scaring me."

"Good."

"What are you?" she asked. "A survivalist fanatic, or something?"

"Yep, and I don't apologize for it." He spun and headed toward another section of the store. "If you won't take the tape or the shovel, how about a Leatherman?"

"What's that?"

"A multi-tool. Everyone should own one. Carry it with you always." He snagged one from the wall behind him, where all kinds of tools that looked vaguely like Swiss Army knives hung from hooks. "This here is the Juice XE6."

Right. Like she was going to lug that around in her purse when she returned to Seattle. Here in Colorado, though, maybe it wasn't such a bad idea.

"How much is it?"

When he named the price, she nearly croaked.

"What about that small Swiss Army knife?" She pointed to a red one.

The cost was considerably lower. "I'll take it."

"The Leatherman's more versatile, but that's okay." He added the Swiss Army knife to her purchases. "This is a heck of a lot better than nothing."

He pointed out health bars and bags of nuts and granola. "Pick up some of those and keep them in the glove compartment."

She did, then paid for everything, barely managing not to cringe at the total. Before leaving she asked the same question she'd posed to everyone she met in town. "How well do you know Gabe Jordan?"

Noah's eyebrows shot up. "Gabe? We grew up together, were in the same grade. Used to hang out together. Used to be good friends. Why do you ask?"

"Just wondering. Do you have any idea what happened to him in Afghanistan?"

Noah's affable expression became serious. "No. Must have been deep, though. He came back a different man."

"Different how?"

"He drank a lot. I mean a *lot.* The bars in town became his second home. He said crazy things, did crazier things. That lasted for about six months. Then he withdrew to his land. Now he hardly ever comes to town, and when he does, he doesn't talk much. Only nods and passes by as though he barely knows anyone."

"How was he before?"

"Friendly. Easygoing. Salt of the earth." He paused, seeming to mull over his words. "He was a great guy until his brother Nick screwed him over. Suddenly, Gabe enlisted and left town. We didn't see him again until he returned from his tours."

Oh, boy. Bad news. She had the sense that this situation between the Jordan brothers was deep and messy. "Nick screwed him over? How?"

"You want to know more about it, talk to Nick," he said with a vehemence she hadn't expected. "Or Laura."

A woman came between them? "Laura who?"

"Cameron."

Cameron. "Your…"

"My sister. She owns the bakery."

What on earth had Nick done to Noah's sister? And to Gabe? She could guess, but before jumping to any conclusions, she should get the full story from the source.

Callie nodded. "Okay, thanks." She exited and carried her purchases to the car.

Who would give up the answers more readily? Nick? Or Laura? No contest. Nick wouldn't spill the beans. She didn't know Laura, but maybe she could talk to her woman to woman.

She tucked the candles, matches and whistle into the glove compartment as Noah had directed and stowed the snacks in the front console. She tossed the thermal blanket into the backseat.

She dropped the multi-tool into her purse then walked to Accord House. It would do the painted ladies in San Francisco proud, might even outshine them, because it was wide and grand, with a porch that wrapped around the entire first floor. Two huge bay windows framed a bright red door. Three stories tall, painted in blues and creams, the entire house framed in tiny white lights, it looked magical and welcoming.

Callie had a beautiful large room on the third floor, with a queen bed and a sitting area beside a large white fireplace.

One good thing she could say about Nick was that he paid for her to travel in style.

She hadn't heard another soul up here since she'd arrived at the beginning of the week. The silence unnerved her so she set a match to the logs waiting in the fireplace behind a black wrought-iron grille.

When it cracked and popped to life, she relaxed.

Picking up her cell phone, she curled into an armchair beside the fire.

The duvet on the bed had a quilted cover in blues and creams, in patches of plaids and stripes, very Ralph Lauren-ish.

Pink cabbage roses dotted the walls. One fresh pink rose sat in a bud vase on the antique bedside table. The room had been designed for love and romance.

And here she was alone.

Story of her life.

She punched in her mom's number. *Please, please, please be there.*

No answer. She called Sophie's cell.

"There's been no change, Callie. I'll call the second there is."

They disconnected quickly. What if the police needed to get in touch with her?

Callie took the Swiss Army knife out of her purse and pulled out every tool—a bottle opener, a small saw, a knife that felt pretty sharp, a corkscrew, something that looked like another opener that she guessed she could use to cut into a tin can if she had to, and last but not least, a small pair of scissors. Interesting.

She snapped everything back into place and tossed it into her purse.

Stopping short of calling Sophie again, through directory assistance, Callie located an insurance company in Seattle with a solid reputation, explained her needs and arranged to have a policy faxed to Accord House for her perusal.

The monthly premium would be expensive.

For the next half hour, she weighed and balanced expenses against income. Nick paid her well, but Mom's care was expensive.

A weight on Callie's chest made breathing hard. Sure, she and her mom had had their differences over the years, but Callie loved her, had expected to celebrate all of the big life changes with her—Callie's marriage some day, the birth of her children.

Her heart hurt. She would never have wished this on her mom, especially not at such an early age.

She rubbed the bridge of her nose where her sinuses hurt.

One of these days, she was going to scream. How long would Mom live? Callie was only thirty-three. She had a lot of years ahead of her of supporting her mother.

Mom's financial well-being depended on her.

Enough already. She couldn't sit here and wallow.

A minute later, Callie stepped into a hot shower to dispel the chill she had picked up out on the Jordan land and then dressed in a warm sweater and pants.

More than ever she understood she had to persuade Gabe to sell his portion of the property to Nick and claim the bonus her boss had promised her.

GABE SLOGGED THROUGH the snow to the veranda of the house he and his two brothers had grown up in. The woman had left his mittens on the step.

He picked them up and put them on, flexing his fingers, imagining that he could feel her warmth inside them.

When Ty drove into the yard and climbed out of his SUV, he didn't look happy to be summoned to the old homestead. There was a time when he'd been perfectly happy to live here and to see his older brother every day.

"Nice, Gabe," Ty said, sarcastic as hell. "You don't call for a couple of weeks and then I get an order to get out here? No *hello*. No *how've you been*. Nice brotherly love."

Gabe stood on the veranda with his feet planted apart. With Ty, he could relax and not worry about saying the wrong thing or making people uncomfortable. When he had first returned from Afghanistan, he'd been grieving and emotional, and had gotten too many odd looks in town to trust his social skills anymore. These days, he kept things to himself.

With that woman, he would have to walk on eggshells. If he said the wrong thing, would it be something Nick could use against him?

He didn't want Callie digging up his past.

In every way, life had been so much easier before his last tour of duty. He should never have gone.

To be honest, it went back further than that. Life had been easier before Laura.

He gathered his thoughts. Ty was easygoing, but like all the Jordan brothers, could be headstrong. If it came to a fight, Gabe wanted to win. "I didn't call you as my brother. I called you as sheriff."

"Oh, well, that's better." Ty strode toward Gabe, but stopped at the bottom of the steps. "Not."

"There's a woman who came out to the house today. A redhead. Who is she?"

"How the heck should I know?"

"You're the sheriff. You should know who's visiting your town."

"Accord is a tourist town now, Gabe. I can't keep track of every person who comes calling."

Yeah, that's true. He had asked a dumb question.

Too bad Accord had grown. There were too many strangers in town these days. Gabe had come home four years ago to a hometown that not only looked different, but also was overrun with people. He had thought his old hometown would be a sanctuary of sorts, but it had been full of strangers. With the people he did know, in his grief he'd misjudged his responses and they had become wary of him. After six months or so, he'd withdrawn to Jordan land and had been here ever since.

"The woman said she works for Nick."

Tyler shrugged. "Beats me."

"Why didn't you tell me what Nick planned to do to this land?"

"Nick is planning something?" Ty looked too confused to be faking it. Nick hadn't told Ty, either.

So, she's here to soften me up first.

Gabe wasn't sure how he felt about that. If Nick had come himself, Gabe would be furious. But this woman had been honest, forthright, had walked right up to his door and had said, "I'm here to talk about your land." Nick would have done it all behind his back until it was a done deal. Nick wasn't above betraying Gabe. Callie worked for Nick. Could he trust her to stay honest? To not hide things from him?

"She's doing Nick's dirty work for him," Gabe said.

Ty placed one foot on the bottom step and leaned his hands on his knee. "What does Nick want with the land?"

"He wants to turn it into a ski resort."

"Yeah?" Ty nodded thoughtfully. "That's not a bad idea."

"I live here. I run a successful business." But he needed the land for so much more. He stared past Ty's SUV at the woods on the other side of the road. Surrounded on all sides by wilderness, Gabe felt safe from society, from people who had the power to hurt him, from those who misunderstood him. On this stunning piece of land, in this familiar old house, he was protected from his own awkwardness in that society, from the mistakes he made too easily with people.

Ty raised a hand. "Okay. I'll talk to her. Find out what's going on." Poor Ty. Always stuck in the middle. Too easygoing, growing up he'd been the peacekeeper between his older and younger brothers. When they were kids, it had worked. Later, when Nick had declared war on Gabe, nothing could have brought them back together. Not even Ty.

Gabe leaned against the veranda post. "I thought you would have already heard about this."

"Why would I? Nick is barely more sociable than you are."

"Talk to her, Ty. Tell her to keep off my land."

"Technically, she isn't trespassing if Nick gave her permission."

Damn that, he thought in frustration. "This place is mine now. Nick abandoned it. So did you. I take care of it."

"I know." Ty's voice rang with sympathy and Gabe appreciated his caring. "That won't mean much in a court of law."

"I don't care. I don't want her here." *Please. Get rid of her.* "Put the fear of God into her."

Ty obviously saw something in Gabe that said more than his words about why he needed the woman off the land. "I'll talk to her," he said quietly. "Do you know where she's staying or what her name is?"

"She said her name is Callie MacKintosh and she wore an expensive jacket and boots." He wasn't so far removed from society that he didn't know certain things. "She looked like she was well off enough to afford the B and B."

"Or Nick is paying for her to stay there."

"True." Gabe studied Ty solemnly. Could he trust his brother? "Don't sell your third to Nick."

"Okay." Ty turned to leave but then came back. "Listen,

Gabe, how about you come over for dinner on the weekend. You can't hole up in this house all the time."

Gabe's kneejerk response was a flat-out no, but Ty watched him earnestly, expectantly.

"C'mon, Gabe. These days I feel like an only child."

Ty had always been the softhearted brother. He also knew which buttons to push in Gabe. Years of taking care of Ty had developed a pattern that Gabe couldn't break. Ty was thirty-four, three years younger than Gabe, but in ways, Gabe still felt responsible for his little brother.

He sighed yes before turning into the house and closing the door behind him, hoping Ty's warning to the woman would work, that the redheaded pixie wouldn't come around to mess with him again.

He heard Tyler drive away.

Of his two brothers, Ty was his favorite. He was a good guy. When they were kids, they ran every inch of this land together then lay in bed at night in the room they shared and whispered about their dreams.

Ty was halfway to achieving his. He had always been crazy about bison and now held a mortgage on a small ranch outside of Accord where he raised them, had a good career with a good reputation and a beautiful girlfriend who loved him without reservation. For the life of him, Gabe didn't know why Ty hadn't yet married the woman.

Ty was so close to those dreams he'd shared with his older brother all of those years ago.

And Gabe? Well, Gabe had only one dream left. Something he had to do that kept him moving forward. Come hell or high water, he was making it come true.

CHAPTER THREE

TY DROVE BACK to town, mulling over this new twist in Accord's life. So…if Nick had his way, he'd put a ski resort nearby. The town would profit hugely.

As sheriff, Ty took great pride in how Accord had picked itself up after losing economic ground over the decades. The townspeople had turned it into a nice place to visit.

A few years ago, town council had decided that their renewal of the town to attract tourists should be a little old-fashioned. A little Victorian. Given the ski resorts Colorado boasted, the state really didn't need more flashy wood-and-glass architecture already out there.

Council members had taken their cue from the sprawling Victorian mansion railroad baron and town father Ian Accord had built in the late 1800s. These days, it served as the B and B where Callie was probably staying.

A lot of the stores were new or revitalized and more upscale than they had ever been, cozy yet on trend, and the town had an air of coming awake after a long slumber.

A ski resort, though? That would make Accord a serious tourist destination. Ty had a good mind to support it, but Gabe would never sell his share of the land.

An old frustration reared. He had always been caught in the middle between the two brothers, had always been able to see both sides. He could see both arguments now. He'd been closer to Gabe than to Nick. After Dad died things only got worse. Mom showered attention and love all over Nick. He was her baby, after all. Gabe and Ty had to depend on each other and their bond had grown.

Ty had lost Gabe recently, though, because of Afghanistan and Billy's death.

If ever there was a man who needed peace and stability in his life it was Gabe.

Ty didn't want to come between his two brothers, but there was no denying he already knew which way he would vote if it came to a head. Gabe needed things to stay the same more than the town needed things to change.

Ty parked then stepped into the small foyer of the Accord House Bed and Breakfast.

Kristi Mortimer came out of the parlor to see who had entered. When she saw Ty, she smiled. "Tyler, what can I do for you?"

He liked Kristi. They had gone to school together and had dated a bit but nothing had come of it. "Hey, Kristi. You got a woman staying here named Callie?"

"Yes, she went up to her room about half an hour ago. Did she do something wrong?"

"No. She went out to talk to Gabe earlier, but he forgot to tell her something. He asked me to stop in for him."

"Go on up. She's staying in the Pink Rose, third floor, first door on the right."

"Thanks, Kristi."

A minute later, he stood in front of a solid oak door with a small brass plate that read The Pink Rose.

Pale light flickered from underneath the door and it felt warm. He smelled smoke from the fireplace.

He knocked.

When Callie answered, he was a little taken aback. Gabe hadn't mentioned how pretty she was. Short red hair made her look a little pixie-ish, not to mention her being height-challenged. Her skin was flawless, her face heart-shaped. The rust turtleneck she wore brought out the green of her eyes.

Ty smiled. Maybe Gabe's resistance to her had as much to do with her being attractive as with her reason for being in town.

She cocked her head to one side and asked, "You're Tyler Jordan, aren't you? I'm Callie MacKintosh. I've wanted to meet you." She stretched out her hand and he took it in his and shook it. Tiny. Petite, like the rest of her. Despite how forward she seemed there was an intrinsic femininity about her.

"Miss MacKintosh…"

"Call me Callie."

"Callie…Gabe asked me to come talk to you, to respectfully ask you to stay off his land."

Callie leaned against the doorjamb and crossed her arms. "He did, did he? That isn't going to happen." She frowned. "Tyler, you seem like a nice guy. Maybe it would be best if you didn't get caught in the middle. I have Nick's permission to photograph the land. My guess is that makes my presence there legal."

She was probably right—he'd make some calls when he returned to the office—but he would push it for Gabe's sake. "I'll check out how legal it is. In the meantime, stay off the land."

He wasn't sure how he knew, but thought he might as well be talking to air. Unless he missed his guess, this redheaded woman had a stubborn streak.

What the hell was Nick up to? Why this sudden interest in the house and the land? He sure wouldn't bring a resort to Accord because it would be good for the town. Everything Nick did was for Nick's own sake. Ty had learned that lesson early on, shortly after Dad's death, when Gabe and Ty had all but ceased to exist for Mom. As soon as she realized there would be no more babies, five-year-old Nick became her favored son.

She'd pampered him. Ty had been only seven at the time. He remembered that awful feeling of loss. First he had lost Dad to death, and then Mom to Nick, and lately Gabe to war. It was immature to remember all of that old stuff from childhood now, but some things stuck with a man over the years.

Nick had ignored the Jordan homestead and land for years. He had always hated the town. So what was up? Why develop the land now? Why develop here at all?

Trying to puzzle it through, Ty asked, "Nick wants to put in a ski resort, right?"

"Yes. He wants to tear down the old house and build a new hotel." Callie leaned a shoulder against the door frame. "It will be gorgeous. He would hire the best architects."

Tear down that old house? Maybe it was time. But Gabe…

Man, oh man, he didn't like feeling so torn.

"Why?"

Callie's expression flattened. "Why what?"

"Why does Nick want to develop that land?"

"I honestly don't know." Callie straightened. "Will Nick have your support in this project?"

He shook his head. "No. Gabe is happy there. Best to let it rest, Callie."

"I can't do that, Tyler. Nick wants that land developed, so it will be."

"You sound pretty sure of that."

"Nick usually gets what he wants."

Ain't that the truth, Ty thought. "Don't expect Gabe to roll over and play dead, Callie. He'll fight you every step of the way." He'd taken off his cowboy hat when he'd entered the hotel. He put it back on firmly. "So will I."

She looked like a woman who was ready to fight and determined to win.

Ty said goodbye. There were bound to be fireworks in and around town in the next few weeks.

CALLIE CLOSED THE door and leaned against it. She'd put on a good front for Ty, but she wished Gabe *would* roll over and play dead. She would feel a whole lot less stress today if he did.

She'd never had trouble separating her business life from her personal, but all she could think about was Mom.

She stepped to the window that overlooked Main Street and watched Tyler Jordan climb into his vehicle and drive away. The Jordan brothers were a good-looking lot. Ty was big like Gabe but clean-shaven. Was Gabe's jaw as square-cut and strong as Ty's?

On the other side of the road, just down the street, sat Sweet Temptations bakery.

Good. Meeting Laura Cameron would take her mind off Mom's disappearance.

No time like the present to find out exactly what Nick did to Gabe. No surprise that it involved a woman. Exactly who was Laura Cameron and did Nick steal her from Gabe? If so, so what? Wasn't adolescent rivalry common among boys? Were these really the kinds of grudges they held on to years later as grown men?

As she always had in life when there had been setbacks, she put one foot forward and took the next step. *Keep moving. Keep working.* Nothing had ever held her back. She put on her jacket, pulled on her dress boots and left the B and B.

Even before she was halfway across the street, she could smell the bakery. Oh, such sweetness. Such yeasty temptation.

She stepped into a stunning little café splashed with color everywhere, the red-and-yellow walls covered with Klimt paintings.

A teenager stood behind the counter.

Callie read the mouthwatering menu on a chalkboard on the wall. Cinnamon buns. Her favorite. Why hadn't she stopped in here the second she'd come to town?

When she ordered a cinnamon bun, the young girl said, "They're all gone for the day. You need to get in here before nine if you want any chance of getting one. They're Laura's specialty."

Tomorrow morning, bright and early, she would be here.

"Is Laura around? I'd like to talk to her."

"She's in the back. I'll get her."

A minute later, the woman who followed the teenager out erased all doubt in Callie's mind about why the boys would have fought over her.

Laura Cameron was a stunner, part earth mother and part seductress.

Thick chestnut hair fell in soft waves around her face and over her shoulders. The streaks of auburn looked natural, not manufactured. Her matching eyebrows arched perfectly, making a statement that was almost arrogant and not quite sardonic.

"Can I help you?"

God, even her voice was sexy. Low and husky, it would stroke a man's erogenous zones with implied intimacy. If she sounded this sexy in her bakery, what the *hell* did she sound like in bed?

"Could I possibly have a few minutes of your time?" Callie asked. "My partner and I are planning a resort outside of town and are talking to local business people about it."

Partner, shmartner. Callie worked *for* Nick, not with him. Sometimes people took her more seriously, though, if they thought she had oodles of money. Which was why she usually spent more on clothes than was wise. In business, impressions really did matter.

If she softened Laura up with the ideas about the business, maybe she could somehow segue into the subject of her and Nick and Gabe.

"Let's take a table by the window." Laura came around the

counter. A gauzy flowered skirt flowed around her ankles. It should have been incongruous with the thick cream Aran knit turtleneck she wore. Somehow, she pulled it off.

"Tilly, bring us a couple of coffees. Thanks, hon."

Hon. Who called people *hon* these days? It should have sounded old-fashioned, but in that beautiful contralto it became a tender endearment.

The way she sashayed her wonderful ass as she strolled to the window was nothing short of awe-inspiring, the effect tempered, though, by Birkenstocks.

Callie followed her.

Why did some women have nice round butts and hips but not a trace of stomach? No matter how hard Callie worked out she couldn't get rid of the puppy fat on her tummy that had plagued her since puberty.

She called it her pudding belly. Mom had come from England just before giving birth to Callie and called all desserts "puddings." Callie had inherited her mother's sweet tooth. Every day was a struggle to stay away from sugar.

Maybe she wouldn't stop in for that cinnamon bun tomorrow.

Laura sat down with a sensual grace she probably took for granted.

Callie sat across from her and explained how a ski resort in the area would do wonders for local business.

Tilly brought their coffees and left.

Laura nodded. "I'll say. It would be wonderful. Where are you putting it?" She stirred cream into her cup.

"On the Jordan property. It's a gorgeous piece of land with a mountain made for skiing."

Laura stopped stirring and carefully put her spoon down on her cloth napkin. This woman with her stunning generous figure and arms that could probably knead yeast breads all day and pound out cinnamon buns by the dozens, looked vulnerable.

"Gabe has agreed to this?"

It wasn't in Callie's nature to lie. Stretch the truth a little? Yes. Lie? "No."

Laura appeared to breathe again, as though she had stopped for a minute. "I'm not surprised."

"My job is to persuade him to. In the interest of making my job easier, you wouldn't care to share what went on between you, Gabe and Nick, would you?"

Suspicion bloomed in Laura's hazel eyes. "Why do you want to know that? Who are you really?"

"I work for Nick. He's building the resort. I need to know whether Gabe is resisting because he truly doesn't want to sell, or because of history between Nick and you."

"Why don't you ask Nick?"

"I will, but…"

"He won't tell you?"

Callie shook her head. "Probably not."

"Bastard," Laura murmured under her breath. A whole cartload of emotion backed up that one word.

What on earth had Nick done?

Laura stood and picked up her still-full coffee cup. "Talk to Gabe. I'm sure he'll relish telling you all about me." The beautiful full lips Callie had been admiring thinned into a flat line.

Laura walked away, taking her coffee with her, and Callie knew she'd learned all she would from her. Great. The only three people who knew the truth about what had happened were possibly the three most stubborn she had ever met.

Callie would ask Gabe, but she wasn't about to hold her breath on his answering her.

Stepping out into the street, she crossed her arms over her midriff against the cold. She waited for traffic to clear, then walked to the other side of Main to head back to the B and B for dinner.

If Laura Cameron were the type of woman Gabe found attractive, he certainly wouldn't fall for Callie. She stumbled. *What?* Why on earth would it matter to Callie whether Gabe found her attractive? The man was nothing more than an obstacle to a business deal.

Besides, she'd only just met him that afternoon. And she knew for a fact that he had been attracted to her.

So what? God, Callie, keep your head on straight.

Back in the B and B, Callie returned to her room to call Nick. This time she planned to get answers.

"Callie, what's up?"

"What happened with Laura Cameron?"

Silence on the other end of the line. It wasn't easy to take Nick Jordan by surprise, but she'd done it. "Why are you bringing up old history?" he finally asked.

"Because it matters."

"No, it doesn't."

"I'll bet it does. If it was something serious enough to cause an estrangement between you and Gabe that has lasted for years, it will affect how I approach him and whether I can convince him to sell. After all, you want him to sell to *you*. He isn't going to do that if he hates you."

"Let it go, Callie." His voice sounded tight.

"No."

"You want to keep your job? Leave it alone."

"Seriously, Nick?" What kind of situation was she involved in? This wasn't one of Nick's regular business deals. He sure as sugar didn't become emotionally involved. He sounded normal, but he'd never threatened to fire her before. He'd never asked her to sabotage a business, especially not his *brother's*.

"It would take you a hell of a long time to replace and train a new executive assistant." She crossed her fingers, hoping that was true. "You need me, Nick." She needed this job.

"Leave Laura alone. Don't go there." Nick sounded far too serious for Callie's comfort. "That issue died a long time ago."

"Too late, Nick. I just came from talking to her."

Again silence. Nick was pulling Gabe's trick. The men were more alike than they thought. She wasn't about to get anything else out of Nick.

"I'll send along photos of the land as I take them," she said with a curtness she wasn't accustomed to using with her boss.

She hung up.

Oh, yeah, this thing with Laura Cameron would be a huge problem. Maybe the only way she was going to find out what happened was to ask Gabe himself.

Yeah, that should be fruitful, Callie.

The man can't talk to you. Or hadn't you noticed?

I noticed, all right.

I noticed a lot *about Gabe Jordan.*

SHORTLY AFTER EIGHT that evening, after she'd eaten next to nothing in the dining room, she returned to her room and dialed her mom's number.

"Hello," Mom answered, her voice querulous.

Callie choked back a sob. They had found her? She was home! Thank God. Why was Mom answering the phone? Sophie was supposed to answer.

"Mom?" she asked, her voice choked up with relief. "It's Callie."

"Who?" Johanna sounded annoyed.

"Callie. Your daughter."

"I don't have a daughter." Callie's heart sank. It was going to be one of those days.

Oh, Mom, where have you gone? Is there even the smallest part of you left inside begging to get out?

Maybe she was just really tired after her adventure.

"Do I have a daughter?" Mom's voice sounded far away, as though she'd leaned away from the phone and was talking to someone else.

Sophie was there with her. Good.

A second later, Sophie's voice came on the line. "Callie, I'm sorry. I was just finishing up with the police. They dropped her off ten minutes ago."

Sophie sounded winded.

"Where did they find her?"

"Downtown."

"What? How did she get so far?"

"I don't know, but it was one of Nick's men who found her and called the police."

"One of Nick's men?"

"He pulled them from the office, but also from one of his construction sites and told them to look outside of the zone the police were already looking in."

"It worked," Callie whispered.

"It worked." She heard a smile in Sophie's voice. "All afternoon, he had hot food delivered for the volunteers and the cops, so they could take breaks to warm up.

"Callie." Sophie's voice cracked. "I didn't want to tell you earlier, but it's been cold and rainy all day."

"Is Mom okay? Did she get a chill? If she gets pneumonia…"

"She was in a coffee shop when Nick's man found her. The owner was feeding her soup and lots of coffee."

Callie choked out a laugh. "Decaf, I hope. Otherwise, you'll be up all night with her."

"*Not* decaf. She's wired." The volume level of her voice rose. "Johanna, close that door. You aren't going out again today." Mom was running circles around Sophie.

"Go take care of her," Callie said. "I'll call back later." She hung up.

Something tickled her cheek and she touched her face. Her hand came away wet. Oh, for God's sake, she wasn't an emotional person.

You thought you were losing your mother.

True.

Before giving in to exhaustion, before she would allow herself to rest for the night, she phoned Nick. What manner of man was he? He threatened to fire her on one hand, but while doing so, fed cops and volunteers and brought her mother home safe and sound.

Callie got Nick's machine and a tremulous breath gusted out of her. She left a message.

"Thank you," she whispered. "I owe you."

CHAPTER FOUR

SHE HAUNTED GABE'S land for three days, messing with his landscape.

He couldn't let it continue.

The footprints Callie had left in the freshly fallen snow led him to the base of Luther. She'd bought good boots with sensible heels, but the impressions they made were still ridiculously small compared to his shoebox feet.

He trailed her until he spotted her with her camera raised to shoot the top of the mountain in the dying rays of the sun, her red toque stunning against the white snow-covered planes of Luther's front face.

She had no right to photograph his land. He asked for precious little from life other than his privacy.

Accord sat fifteen miles east of Pike's Peak, a Colorado state treasure owned by all and sundry. But Luther? That was *his* mountain.

He told Boo to sit and wait while he approached the woman noiselessly in the snow.

"Why are you back?"

She didn't answer and he realized she wore earbuds. He could hear strains of music. Who would want to mess with the simplicity of nature? How could a person not appreciate the magical silence?

He touched her shoulder.

She startled and spun around, eyes huge.

He hadn't meant to frighten her.

She yanked the buds out of her ears. "You scared the ever-living daylights out of me."

Red eyelashes popped in a face nearly as white as the snow. He had forgotten how colorful she was with her red hair and green eyes. Sharp, intelligent green eyes.

The cap pulled low on her forehead covered her red hair today. Her flawless skin glowed in the bright sunlight as though lit from within.

Had he ever been that…new? That clean and carefree? If so, he couldn't remember when. Wait. Yeah, he could. Before Dad died. He'd been only ten and had had to take on the responsibility of his two younger brothers while Mom worked two jobs to support her sons and pay the mortgage.

Callie licked her too-red lips. She'd chafed them raw. Woman didn't know how to live in the cold.

"God, you're the most taciturn man I've ever met," she said. "Say something already."

He was trying to. She rattled him. "Told you not to come back."

"Technically, you didn't. You just told me that I couldn't *be* here. Nick says that I can."

He had noticed the other day how intensely feminine her voice was. He didn't know exactly what he meant by that, just that her voice sounded so different from his own deep underused growl.

She tried a smile, but it was lost on him. Women's wiles weren't worth a handful of snow. They melted away too easily when she didn't get her way. Laura came to mind, but he squelched thoughts of her ruthlessly.

"I need to shoot Luther." Callie showed him her camera.

"No, you don't." He glanced at the mountain and then at her. "You really don't."

"Because Luther will never be a ski resort?"

He nodded. She was quick. Bright.

"Nick will fight you on that, tooth and nail."

"It isn't *his* property."

"It's one third his and I have his permission to be here."

She lifted her narrow chin on that perfect heart-shaped face. *Don't want this woman. Don't desire her.*

I already do.

Remember that she works for Nick.

That cooled his ardor. "What do you do for Nick?"

"Anything he asks me to."

"Really? Anything?" Knowing Nick, yeah, she could be his mistress. Nick took whatever he wanted in life, no matter who it belonged to.

Her expression darkened. "Not *that* kind of anything. Get your mind out of the gutter."

He hadn't meant to insult her. He opened his mouth to apologize but she moved on too quickly.

"Our relationship is professional. I'm his executive secretary. Or his personal assistant, by some people's definition. Sometimes his photographer. Maybe his Girl Friday." Her tone changed throughout her recitation, became light. "A name hasn't been invented for all the things I do." She smiled—a real smile, not something calculating—inviting him to share in her joke. Her eyes, lit from within with humor, enticed him.

He needed to get rid of her.

"Leave." He hovered over her, close enough to see tiny freckles on her nose. She wasn't more than five-four, at the most.

"Oh, back off. That intimidation crap doesn't work with me."

Yeah, he'd figured that out the other day. She'd called him Chewbacca.

He almost smiled. Maybe it was time to cut his hair and shave his beard. He stepped back.

She wrapped a case around her Canon, a professional

model and worth a bit, then ran her mitten across the tip of her red nose, leaving one thin strand of bright blue fluff behind, ruining her hard-assed shell.

She glanced up and something changed in her. She sobered. "Nick won't stop, Gabe," she said quietly. "You know that, don't you? You might as well give in now."

It didn't sound like a threat, but rather that she knew he was bound to get hurt where Nick was concerned.

Gabe refused to admit how strong an adversary the man would be, even though he was five years younger than Gabe. Gabe knew from experience how far Nick would go to get what he wanted.

Acid burned in his gut but he forced his mind away from bitter memories and back to the problem at hand.

"There're a dozen ski resorts in the state," Gabe said. "Colorado doesn't need this." He gestured with his chin toward Luther.

"There can never be too many. Like restaurants. You crowd a bunch of them into the same city block and customers flock to the area."

He glanced at Luther's simple rugged beauty, but all he saw were the scars of bombs that had shredded the mountains of Afghanistan while the Americans had tried to kill Bin Laden. Those mountains had been there for millennia, had weathered so much, but not the bombings.

They want to gouge ski runs into Luther, to scar my mountain.

Desecration.

"Nick will develop this land over my dead body."

"That can be arranged," she murmured under her breath.

Smart-ass. He struggled not to smile. How did she do that? Entice him to share her laughter even while Nick dealt him fatal blows through her.

"It doesn't have to be that way," she said. "This is a deal

that would benefit everyone, you and your brothers and the townspeople."

"How would it benefit me? I have my dogsledding business here." He tilted his head. She was a shrewd woman, probably already knew how successful he was, most likely down to the penny. "You've done your research. You know everything about me."

"You can dogsled anywhere." She didn't deny that she'd researched him.

But leave Luther? Move somewhere else? Generations of Jordans had lived on this land. "I can dogsled here."

"Technically, you own only one third of this."

He didn't want to face some truths. They hurt too much. This woman had no right to come here and throw that in his face. "Leave. Now."

She raised those damned bright blue mittens, as though cajoling a child. "This is getting us nowhere."

She stepped out of his shadow and the sun hit her eyes. He sucked in a breath.

He had liked her green eyes, but the sun shone through them, shocking him with the intensity of their color. Emerald-green. The color of home. The color he'd dreamed about all of those lousy months in the deadening beige of Afghanistan, while the hot sun turned him as brown as a coconut. Then after coming home, trying to claw out of darkness, he'd dreamt about springtime and renewal.

At home, though, the quality of light had changed. The American sun didn't seem to be any different than Afghan light. He'd lost something he couldn't put his finger on, and hadn't known how to get back.

He lived in a black-and-white movie. No, in a beige movie, in sepia tones.

But a pair of vivid green eyes watched him, shone out of long red lashes.

This woman couldn't be on his land dredging up reactions better left buried, and bringing laughter and color back into his life when he was the last person believing he deserved it.

He wasn't a violent man, far from it, but panic was setting in and he needed her gone. "Leave."

"One more question before I go. What happened between you and Nick with Laura Cameron?"

My God, she had nerve. Flashes of that sordid business flooded him, stunning him with how fresh the memories, and worse, the emotions were. He hated his brother. He should hate Laura, too, but all he felt for her was a profound disappointment.

He had known Nick could be ruthless in taking what he wanted, but Laura? He'd thought she was a better person. Someone stronger, with a backbone and solid ethics.

He focused on the woman in front of him. Callie stunned him. A little pipsqueak of a woman, she dared to ask personal questions without a trace of fear.

Under the weight of his grief and anger, at both Nick and Laura, his jaw hardened and he held her gaze. And his silence. That stuff was none of her business.

"Fine," she huffed. "I'll go, but only because I'm cold and tired."

He watched her walk in the direction of the nearest road, doing a funny hop and skip through the deep snow in her heavy boots. Even the way she walked was feminine and light. Fresh and happy. Did the woman never have bad days? Not even in the face of his resistance?

Since returning from the army, he'd felt heavy, leaden. Thank God for dogsledding, for the weightlessness of gliding over snow. For offering a few moments of forgetfulness.

He called to Boo.

Not trusting the woman to leave and stay gone, Gabe followed her to the road. County plows had built towering snowbanks on the sides of the road. She climbed up the side of one.

Just at the top, she turned and studied him as though he were a bug under glass.

Why? What was she looking for, a crack in his armor?

Her eyes reached too far inside him, as though she saw who he really was with her incisive stare, and what he had lived through, but none of it was anyone's business, especially not hers when she worked for his brother. He didn't want that kind of intimacy in his life. He didn't deserve it. No one knew his secrets. No one ever would.

He took off one glove and whipped out his cell phone.

She lifted one eyebrow and called, "A cell phone, Chewbacca? Really?"

A rough laugh chuffed out of him. "Yeah." If he could, he'd live a hermit's life, but he had a business to run. Besides, it was smart to be hooked into technology when you lived in isolation.

When Ty answered, Gabe said, "She's still hanging around. Any ideas how to get rid of her?"

"None, Gabe. Nick says she can be there, so she can."

Damn. He hated feeling powerless. He'd felt that too often in the past few years.

The corner of Callie's mouth lifted in a saucy grin, then she disappeared over the side of the bank.

Gabe climbed to the top to look down on the road. She approached a small red car.

She made him want to laugh again but, today, with her fresh vibrancy spreading hopes and dreams over him like sunbeams, she also made him feel old.

RECLUSIVE.

Obdurate.

Antisocial.

The man was a veritable thesaurus of stubbornness, about as compromising as a glacier, and just as cold. No, that last was grossly unfair. He wasn't cold. He was contained. And he had handled her gently the other day.

And the way he'd looked at her a few times today…with something that resembled wanting or yearning? No, he wasn't the least bit cold.

She could stand here and bandy about adjectives all day, but she had work to do.

Even so, for another moment she stared at the man, compelled by his stillness. There was no hint of tranquility in it, just a deep abiding waiting.

He stood on top of the ten-foot snowbank with the sun and Luther behind him, a massive mountain man. She could almost imagine this as an earlier century and Gabe as a trapper, a fur trader, protecting his land and his family from predators.

Dear God, what a pile of romantic crap. She opened her car door to dismiss him from her thoughts, but halted before getting in and glanced up again, drawn by his unnatural quietude, as though he listened to the air around them and heard something that she didn't.

Not a breath of air moved.

Callie strained but still heard nothing, only that infernal silence that had unnerved her all afternoon. That's why she'd put in her earbuds and had turned up the Black Eyed Peas so loudly.

A storm had chased through last night, dropping fresh snow, but the high wind had eased off this morning and it had been quiet since. She hated the silence. What on earth could Gabe hear?

He watched her with eyes as shadowed as a canyon, with old miseries swirling within their depths. This man didn't trust easily. What had happened to him? What would it take to make him really laugh, to let go, to get him to enjoy life?

That was a job for someone else. She didn't have time for

it. Her life was complicated enough. But what a challenge it would be, to take a man this…injured, and heal him.

His mountain-man beard softened the harsh edges of his face only a little. What had happened to him?

You know everything about me.

Not by a long shot, Gabe, not even close, but by the time she was finished with him, she would. One way or another.

Boo sat beside Gabe on the mini-mountain of snow. Gabe's big hand rested on her head. She licked his fingers.

Callie got into her car and started the engine.

She drove away, but watched Gabe in her rearview mirror, his silhouette against the winter-cool late-afternoon sun as large and unmoving as the mountain he owned. Finally, when she rounded a bend in the road, his image disappeared from view and she could breathe again.

In town, she entered the B and B and found Kristi Mortimer sitting in the parlor.

"Callie, I was hoping you'd make it back for tea." She gestured toward a tray with plates of small sandwiches, cakes and cookies. "Care to join me?"

"I'd love to."

She rested her bag on a small table and sat across from Kristi, who loaded a plate with goodies and handed it to Callie along with a cup of tea, all of it so civilized after her confrontation with the mountain man.

She still had too many questions about him and Kristi had been a font of information about the town, but when Callie opened her mouth to ask about Gabriel Jordan, the front door opened, followed by a lot of boot-stamping. A man appeared in the parlor doorway, mid-sixties or so, nice-looking, with a strong jaw and gray hair cropped close to his head. Salt of the earth, Callie thought.

"The rest of your winter wood is stacked out back and ready to use, Kristi. I'll leave the invoice on the hall table."

"Thank you. Callie, this is Jeff Stone."

Another local. He seemed friendly enough.

"You here visiting?" he asked. "Odd time of year for tourists."

"Actually," Callie responded, "I'm here on business. I work for Nick Jordan."

"Jordan?" The man's expression changed subtly.

"Yes. He wants to build a ski resort on Jordan land. On Luther."

Jeff frowned. "Gabe agreed?"

"Not yet," she said, trying to make a joke of it. "It will be like pulling teeth to get him to okay the project."

"Good luck with that. That man's an animal who doesn't care about others. Only thinks about himself."

The depth of his loathing for Gabe shocked Callie. While she sat back and stared, he stomped out of the house.

"What was that about?" She turned to Kristi. "What just happened?"

"Jeff is my uncle. He doesn't like Gabe."

Understatement. "I gathered that. Why not?"

"It isn't something I share with everyone." Kristi wiped the corners of her mouth with a lace napkin. "I didn't know you were here about building a ski resort."

"Yes, and I'm trying to figure out who Gabe is and how to approach him." She explained Nick's plans for the land and that it was her job to convince Gabe to sell.

"I'd like to see a ski resort in the area," Kristi said. "It would be great for business. Accord House could really benefit."

"Even though the resort would be competition?"

"The area is stunning. A ski resort would be popular and we would take the overflow here at the B and B."

Callie nodded. "I think so, too. There would be enough

business and tourist dollars to go around for everyone. Win-win."

Kristi seemed to come to a decision. "Gabe joined the army with my cousin Billy, Jeff's son."

Small-town relationships. Everyone was related every which way.

"Did he go to Afghanistan, too?"

"Yes. With Gabe. Gabe returned alive. Billy didn't."

Callie choked on a mouthful of tea. Oh. Oh, so sad. "What happened?"

"The truck they were in hit a roadside bomb. All Gabe had to send home were bits and pieces of my cousin. He felt responsible."

"But why?"

"Because Billy was so irresponsible. A charmer. He floated through life. Thought of everything as a joke. He would never have joined the army on his own, but Gabe was his best friend. When Gabe joined, so did Billy. My uncle can't forgive Gabe. He thinks he somehow convinced Billy to join and so should have kept him alive."

"That's absurd."

"I guess so, but I think Gabe agreed with him."

The man carried too much on his shoulders. If this Billy were the same age as Gabe, he was a full-grown man and should have been held responsible for making his own decisions.

She felt only a twinge of guilt when she wondered how she could use this new information to get closer to Gabe.

THE FOLLOWING DAY, Callie strode out onto the land again with her camera, trudging through deep snow in her new boots along a trail that had been carved out of the woods.

She turned in a circle, checking for the slightest breeze, or for any sound to break the maddening silence. Nothing. Out here alone, her skin crawled.

Rummaging in her bag, she found her iPod. A second later, she had her earbuds in listening to Coldplay too loudly, no longer bothered by the infernal vacuum.

She took a shot of the way the trees with their boughs heavily laden with snow hugged the trail protectively.

Thank goodness she had her photography. When she looked through the lens of her camera, everything faded away—troubles, history, stress.

It was the only thing that had kept her sane in her teenage years, in the equally maddening silence of her mother's house. While Mom did her closet thing, hiding in profound darkness and silence to ease her migraines, Callie had wandered Seattle and had shot everything, the best and the worst about city life.

In the past few years, she'd even had a couple of showings around Washington State. Nick had supported her, had brought Emily out with him to see her photographs, had even bought a couple, but he'd also taken advantage of it. Her job description now included *photographer*. So…here she was, out on the land, shooting everything. She probably had enough shots of Luther. She needed to cover more acreage, to showcase the resort potential of this gorgeous land.

Making sure the camera was dry before putting it away, she stored it back in her bag.

She'd love to shoot Gabe, but that wasn't about to happen given how withdrawn and awkward he was with her.

She understood him a bit better since her talk with Kristi yesterday, but even so, she'd—

Something sounded behind her and she whipped the buds out and spun about.

A team of dogs and two people on a dogsled barreled down on her, hard and fast. She cried out and fell. And fell. And landed against a tree. Pain shot through her arm and took her breath away.

"Help!" she cried.

No one answered. Lost. Alone. Silence her only companion. She grasped for her earbuds, but couldn't find them. *Someone...help. Damn.* She would get through this, her worst nightmare come true. She would.

Her fingers worried the snow around her, searching for her iPod.

CHAPTER FIVE

UP ABOVE, ON THE TRAIL, dogs yipped and then a human voice sounded a long, deep "Whooooaaa."

Hallelujah.

"Callie," someone yelled and she looked up.

Mountain man looked down at her from the trail. Gabe. Chewbacca. She couldn't have asked for a more welcome face.

"Gabe, can you help me?"

He cursed and slid down the snow. "Are you okay?"

He took her arm to help her up but she cried out.

"What's wrong?"

"I hurt it when I landed."

"I saw the sled hit you. Is it broken?"

"No. It didn't actually hit me. I jumped out of the way and fell down here. My shoulder hit this tree."

Gingerly, he helped her to her feet.

"Anything else hurt?"

She took a minute to breathe and gather her wits. "Except for a bunch of bruising, nothing serious."

"Why were you on the dogsled trail?"

"I thought it was a walking trail."

"Let's go." Gabe turned to help her up the shallow hill, but she squealed, "My camera."

He picked up the bag, slung it over his shoulder, then guided her up the hill with a hand at her back for support. She swore she could feel the heat of his palm through her coat and sweater. Once up top, he nestled her into a sled under a blanket and a canvas cover.

A boy about eleven years old stood beside the sled.

The six dogs attached to the front barked and yipped. A couple of them strained against the leashes—or were they called reins?—and jumped off the ground, lunging forward as though they could force the sled to move just because they wanted it to.

"Jared, thanks for holding the dogs. Get back on your runner."

Gabe shouted and the dogs took off, fast.

Trees and snow whooshed past and the wind in Callie's face exhilarated her. She laughed. "Woohoo, this is awesome."

Five minutes later, Gabe pulled into the clearing and she was absurdly disappointed that the ride had been so short.

He stopped the sled at the back of a row of them and came around to look down at her. A hint of a smile played around his lips.

"Liked that?"

"I loved it. Holy cow, I had no idea it was so much fun." She grinned up at him. "That was too short. Can we do it again?"

Still with a smile hovering, Gabe said, "Maybe."

Maybe. Callie smiled. Coming from Gabe, that was almost an invitation.

The clearing that had been so quiet and peaceful yesterday teemed with activity.

Four sleds were parked along the side of the clearing ahead of the one Callie sat in, all with six dogs attached to them. Kids, maybe eleven, twelve years old, stood at the backs of them with a few teenagers, waiting for instructions.

"Your arm," Gabe said, but gesturing toward the dogs. "I have to…"

"Go do what you have to do."

The dogs were quiet now. They knew they were home, their running finished for the day. He unhooked the two lead dogs at the front of the sled and led them to the far end of the chain. Jared hovered and learned how to handle the animals.

Three older teenagers helped the kids to unhook each dog from their sleds and walk them over to the long chain linking the trees. Straw lined the snow in front of it.

"Don't ever let a dog off his leash without holding on tightly to his collar," Gabe called to the kids, his voice clear and strong, shocking Callie. He was so shy with her. "These dogs are runners. If you let one go, we might not see him again for days."

The man was downright loquacious with the children.

Her mind began to click, synapses stirring and making connections.

She had just won the lottery. If her injured arm would convince Gabe to let her stay and watch him work with the children, she could learn more about him, about his business, about the business of the dogsledding.

Find out whatever you can about his business. Find something I can use.

She didn't want to hear Nick's voice in her head with his demands. Just the thought of betraying Gabe after the little she'd learned about Laura and Nick left a bad taste in her mouth.

On the other hand, she'd talked to Sophie again this morning. Last night, Mom had been fretful and had talked about moving back to England. She'd come out of her bedroom with a bag packed, wanting Sophie to drive her to the train station, firmly believing that the train could take her across the ocean to England.

Mom's thoughts were no longer connected to reality and the sooner Callie got her into a decent facility, the better. She needed to get this deal moving along.

Her left arm burned. Callie gritted her teeth. She didn't like being idle, but when she tried to rise, she found it difficult to crawl out of the sled without hurting her shoulder.

Gabe saw her and motioned her down.

"Show me what to do," she called. "I can help."

He shook his head. "Wait for me."

She set her jaw against her frustration.

After all of the dogs were unhooked from the sleds and safely attached to the chain where they hunkered down into their nests of straw, Gabe called the children to him.

"First thing you do when you return is take care of your dogs before you do anything for yourself."

"But I'm hungry," one kid whined.

"You're always hungry," another kid joked and everyone laughed. Even Gabe smiled, his manner a heck of a lot easier with the children than with her.

"We need water and wood to feed the dogs first. Then we'll feed ourselves."

Gabe gave an auger and pails to three boys. To two of the older teenagers, he said, "Jack and Robert, take the boys to the lake and drill a couple of holes through the ice. I need enough water to fill those pots." He pointed to two huge pots on the grill sitting on the cold fireplace.

The boys ran off fighting over who got to drill first.

To the three girls, he handed small axes. "Head into the bush and gather dead branches and brush and cut them small enough to fit into the pit. Valerie, teach them how to use the axes. Make sure they handle them safely."

They ran away. "Stay within sight of camp," Gabe hollered to their retreating backs. A minute later, Callie heard those axes being put to use.

"Don't cut down live trees," she heard a voice she assumed was Valerie's from in among the trees. "They'll smoke instead of burning. There's enough dead stuff around. We don't need to kill trees."

Gabe reached into a big cooler and pulled out a freezer pack. Kneeling in front of Callie, he hesitated then asked, "Where does it hurt?"

She tried to show him but her bulky jacket got in the way.

"May I?" He reached for the zipper of her jacket. *May I?* What man said that anymore? Such good manners. Who exactly was he?

She nodded and he unfastened it and eased it over her shoulder. She tried to unbutton the thick sweater she had bought from Noah, but having only one hand to use made her awkward.

He pushed her hand away and did it himself. With movements that were unthreatening and careful, he palpated her shoulder through her turtleneck. She winced.

"It's a bit swollen." He placed a freezer pack against her shoulder and pulled her sweater up over it. Taking her hand, he put it against the lump the pack made and told her to hold it there.

Easing her jacket back up over her shoulders but not being able to zip it up because of her arm holding the pack in place, he arranged the sled blanket up over her chest and tucked it under her chin, all the while handling her with measured care.

He returned to the cooler.

"How long does this stay on?" she asked.

"Ten minutes."

"Only ten?"

"Yes."

There he went with the monosyllabic answers with her again. Because she was a woman? Or because she wasn't a child? Clearly, he was uncomfortable talking to her.

Gabe took slices of something frozen out of big coolers

beside a fire, those same slabs of food he'd fed the dogs her first day here.

"What are those?" she asked.

"Food for the dogs."

"I know, but it looks frozen. Is it?"

He nodded.

"It looks weird. What is it?"

"Ground chicken."

"Why freeze it?"

He looked at her as though she were a riddle he wasn't sure how to solve. "So food is always ready for the dogs. The rest of us will eat later."

As though an afterthought, he asked, "Are you hungry?"

"Not for that."

He pulled up short. Unless she was mistaken, laughter glimmered in his eyes again. Still waters. There was plenty going on underground in Gabe Jordan. Why didn't he just let himself laugh and smile? Why cut himself off every time?

"You sure?" he asked. "Must be tasty. The dogs wolf it down."

A joke! Callie settled into the cocoon of the sled and smiled. They were making progress. "I'm sure. What do they know? They're dogs. They'll eat anything." Eventually, she'd get through to the guy and bring him around to selling. Baby steps.

"Do these kids come from the same school," she asked, "or do their parents send them here?"

"The school organizes it and pays for it. I usually get three or four sets of children here a week, back to back, and then adults on weekends."

"What do you mean back to back?"

"The kids arrive at about eleven in the morning. They get bussed in from Denver." It had taken her about an hour and a half to drive here. "They dogsled in the afternoon, stay the night and leave the following morning. I have about an hour to pull everything together for the next batch of kids arriving at eleven."

"Wow, that's a lot of work."

Gabe nodded, but didn't say anything.

"Do the adults come in groups?"

"Sometimes it's a bunch of friends who've organized a weekend away, or a church group. Other times, it's just people who want to sled. If they arrive on Friday night and stay until Sunday afternoon, they bond over the dogsledding."

The business was a going concern, and Callie had seen nothing so far that she could use against Gabe. The children were well supervised.

"What about the teenagers? Do they work for you? Shouldn't they be in school?"

"They get credits at school for the hours they put in. Next week, it will be a different set. Plus I pay them to work on weekends, if they want to. I've got a good-size pool of trained dogsledders to choose from now."

"Why weren't there kids here when I was wandering around earlier in the week?"

"There was flu rampant in one of the schools, so they cancelled three of the groups."

"That must be hard on your bottom line."

"I budget for cancellations."

He was smart. Callie didn't doubt that he was good with money.

The boys returned with the water. Gabe helped them pour it into the big pots.

The girls returned with the wood and Gabe showed them how to build a fire. Callie noticed that he took care to teach the children how to do things and then only helped when they needed it. Otherwise, they did everything themselves. The man was a good teacher.

One of the boys shoved a girl out of the way so he could help with the fire.

She squealed.

Gabe asked, "Are you okay?"

After she nodded, he placed a hand on the boy's shoulder and pulled him close, then bent his knees to put his face level with the boy's. "Never hit girls. Treat them with respect. If you want to help with the fire, take a turn like everyone else. Understand?"

Subdued, the boy nodded. Gabe let go of his jacket. He hadn't raised his voice, impressing Callie with how he had managed to chasten the boy without undue embarrassment.

Eventually the water boiled and Gabe added a few slices of the frozen meat to the pot while kids hovered around asking questions about every little thing.

They weren't yet so old that they would pretend indifference in their quest to be cool. These preteens showed curiosity about everything, which was great. It meant Callie didn't have to ask Gabe all of the questions she wanted to.

In the middle of the hubbub, he glanced at her. "Off now," he said then answered a boy's question.

She understood and pulled the freezer pack out of her jacket.

"I want you to watch while I feed the first couple of dogs," Gabe told the kids while he walked over to her sled, took the pack from her and tossed it back into the cooler. "Then I'll let each of you feed a dog."

Gabe poured the hot broth into thirty metal bowls.

"Won't it be too hot for them?" a girl asked, echoing Callie's concern of the other day.

"Not by the time we get it to each of the dogs. It's pretty cold out today and the stainless steel is cool."

One boy leaned over the pot. "It smells like chicken soup."

"Probably tastes like a watered-down version. It's the only way I can get water into the dogs."

"Hey," Jared said, "I saw them eating snow."

"Snow is ninety to ninety-five percent air. It might look like the dogs are getting a lot of water, but they're not." He set a bowl down in front of the first dog. "These boys and girls worked really hard for us today. They put their hearts into pulling us. As good mushers we need to take care of them in return."

He put a bowl in front of the second dog, who lapped it up.

Each child took a bowl and set it down in front of a dog. The only one who didn't receive a bowl was the one at the far end. One of the boys grabbed the last bowl to run to her, but she growled and bristled the second he neared her.

"Mike, get away from Daisy!" Gabe took the bowl from the boy. "I told all of you before. Daisy spooks easily. She doesn't like people. Keep away from her."

"What's wrong with her?" Mike stepped far enough away that Daisy stopped growling, but her fur still stood on end.

"I don't know. She was a year old when I got her. Someone must have hurt her when she was small. She's people-shy."

Gabe put the bowl in front of her and smiled. "Watch what she does."

Daisy took the lip of the bowl between her teeth and up-ended it so the broth ran out onto the snow. Then she ate something from the top of the snow.

"Daisy," Gabe admonished, but there was a thread of humor in his tone. "She knows there are tidbits of meat at the bottom of the bowl. She doesn't want the water, only the meat. When she dumps the broth onto the snow, it drains away while the chicken bits sit on top of the snow and she eats them."

The children laughed.

Gabe refilled her bowl and came back to hunker down in front of her.

"How come she lets you get close to her?" Mike asked.

"I'm the only human she trusts. It took a long time to gain her trust so I never abuse it." To Daisy he said, "Drink."

She bent to the bowl and lapped the liquid, all the while peering up at Gabe.

"I'm watching, Daisy," Gabe said, but a trace of affection rode atop his admonishment. "Drink the whole thing."

When she finished, he picked up the bowl. "Gather up the rest of the bowls. They get their food now."

He put slices of frozen chicken into them.

"Why don't they all get the same number of slices?" Callie called, her finely tuned sense of fairness, of equality for all, kicking in.

"Tiger is too thin. He burns calories like there's no tomorrow, so I load him up with food every day." He carried a bowl with only one slice to a heftier dog and said, "Picket, here, is too heavy. She gets winded when she runs and her extra weight is hard on her joints. I give her less food." He scrubbed his hand across her head while she ate.

The children gave the rest of the food to the other dogs, with Gabe feeding Daisy last.

It took all of a minute for the dogs to finish. Callie wasn't sure they ate so much as inhaled the food.

The children gathered up the bowls again and dumped them into another pot on the outdoor stove. Gabe removed it to a makeshift table and dumped in a bunch of snow then tested the temperature. He poured in a scant few drops of soap.

"This is environmentally friendly soap. You might want to ask your parents to switch to something like this at home." He gestured to the woods around them. "We need to protect our land."

Callie glanced up to the tops of the conifers surrounding

them. Green against the azure sky, they whispered secrets among themselves as a breeze moved them about. She recognized something special about this place, as though it deserved a reverence she couldn't give to the brick and concrete and glass of Seattle.

Gabe took a freezer pack out of the cooler and brought it to her. "Put this on again."

"Thanks." She inserted it under her sweater as best she could.

He returned to the pot and handed out cotton towels. He washed the dishes, handing them to the kids to dry. "They go straight into this bag." He pointed to a burlap sack.

The breeze kicked up a notch. Gabe glanced at her then walked over. Without a word, he snugged the blanket up around her chin again, then returned to the children.

She doubted he was even aware of what he'd done.

He's a caretaker. Why? How can a man be that, but also a recluse? He wasn't the least bit antisocial with children, though, was he?

A girl wearing a bright pink hat raised her hand. "I need to go to the bathroom."

"Okay." Gesturing for the entire group to follow, Gabe walked along the side of the big tent and unhooked a bag that hung from a clothesline. He handed it to the girl.

"Always take this bag with you. There's toilet paper and hand sanitizer inside."

He kept walking another dozen feet past the tent until he disappeared around a small hummock. "Here's the washroom. When you're finished, use the gel to sterilize your hands."

"Eeew. We have to go outdoors?"

"Yep. Be glad there's at least a wooden seat for you to sit on. If we were really out in the woods, you'd be squatting in the snow."

"That's gross," another girl said. The boys laughed.

"The rest of us will go back to the dogs," Gabe continued. "We won't see or hear a thing."

"Amy, stay with me," the girl pleaded. "Turn around so you can't see me."

When Gabe came back, most of the kids followed, except for Amy and the girl with the pink hat.

He opened a bag and pulled out a handful of bars. "We won't be eating for another couple of hours. These are energy bars. They taste healthy, but I don't want to hear a single complaint. They're good for you and you need healthy calories out here to keep warm."

He handed them around then walked to Callie and gave her one.

"Thanks. Does that leave one for you?"

He nodded and walked away. He pointed to a big jug. "Fill your water bottles here."

He filled a tin cup with water and brought it back to her.

The man was right. The bar did taste healthy, heavy-duty healthy. He didn't get these in a normal grocery store.

Okay, so far she knew that Gabe kept the children safe, kept them active, engaged and entertained, and taught them about the environment. As far as she could tell, he was doing nothing wrong. Nick wouldn't like that.

When she finished her bar, Callie took the freezer pack from her shoulder and handed it to Gabe then threw off the blanket. "I can't sit here any longer. I need to get up." While she tried to stand, she struggled because she didn't want to put pressure on her sore arm, to undo the good the ice pack had done.

Gabe lunged forward, grasped her around the waist, picked her up then set her on her feet. A small whoop slipped out of her. His strength stunned her. She might as well have weighed as little as a handful of peanuts.

He steadied her then stepped away, but she didn't want

him to. She wanted to lean against him a little longer, to hold on to his heat and his deep, quiet vitality, and that surprised her. She had been independent for so long.

He stared at her with that awareness of her as a woman blooming in his eyes again. Oh, she liked it. Too much. His gaze shifted away. "How's your shoulder?"

"The ice worked. It isn't throbbing as much." Flustered by the attraction humming between them, she wrestled her camera out of her bag with one hand.

While Gabe and the counselors showed the kids how to get the sleds tidied up for the night, Callie took photos of it all, as well as photos of Gabe. Too bad he hid so much of that strong face behind a beard and too-long hair.

She didn't know which photos she'd keep and which she'd send to Nick. He would want to see how the business looked, but the thought of betraying Gabe, of having Nick use her photos to find Gabe's weakness, left her queasy.

"Who wants to sleep outside in one of the sleds tonight?" Gabe asked.

Two boys put up their hands.

"Are you sure? It gets cold out here. You'll be inside a sleeping bag, completely covered, with none of your face showing. There'll be a tiny opening at the top to let in fresh air. Other than that, you'll feel like you're in a cocoon."

Sounded like a nightmare to Callie.

"Sick!" one of the boys said and laughed. "We'll look like mummies."

He and the other boy high-fived.

"Jack will sleep out here, too. If either of you have problems in the middle of the night, if you need to go to the bathroom, wake him. He'll have a flashlight to show you the way."

Callie photographed the dogs, being careful to stay well clear of Daisy.

"Gabe?"

When he turned, she asked, "What breed is a sled dog? They all look a little bit different from each other."

"They are. Many of these are purebred Huskies—Alaskan, Labrador, Siberian. One Mackenzie River. Others are Malamutes. I have one Samoyed. The rest are crossbreeds."

Every one was beautiful, with thick multicolored coats.

"How many are there all together?"

"Thirty."

Wow. Only a going concern could support the feeding of that many working dogs.

Mom had never let her keep a dog when she was growing up, or a cat, or even a bird or fish. Callie's friend Amber owned a tiny poodle she had loved playing with.

When she approached the dogs, most strained against their leashes for attention. She walked down the line petting and talking to them, scrubbing behind their ears until they nearly turned inside out with pleasure.

That pleasure resonated inside of her, too. She'd been so busy running herself ragged for the job she'd been missing warmth and affection in her life. There had been this huge gap she had been hiding from herself.

At the end of the line, Daisy faced away from the other dogs.

"No problem, girl," Callie said. "Message received and understood." She walked back to the center of the clearing where Gabe talked to the students.

She took another shot of them then zoomed in on Gabe's face and shot him again. She had no idea what she was going to do with the photos.

A bunch of girls ran over to her. "Can you take pictures of us with the dogs?"

"Sure."

They laughed and fooled around while she shot them. She'd always loved that teenaged energy.

When she finished, she wrote down their email addresses. "When I get back to my hotel room, I'll download these and email them to you."

"Thanks," the girls chirped then, still laughing, rejoined the group.

The sun had dipped down behind the trees and the ambient light was getting too low for shooting without a flash. Callie preferred natural lighting. Gabe came to stand beside her and she gestured toward the girls with her chin. "A giggle of girls."

He laughed as though he'd forgotten she wasn't a child, but when she smiled at him he pulled away emotionally.

"Why do you do that?" she asked.

"What?"

"Stop yourself from smiling or laughing. With me, at any rate. What's wrong with having fun with me? I work for your brother, but I'm not an ogre."

He shrugged and stepped away from her.

Angered, she grabbed his sleeve.

"Don't turn away. Answer me."

CHAPTER SIX

With one sharp shake of his head, a rebuke when she had done nothing wrong, he walked away. Maddening, stubborn man.

"We need more wood and water," he called across the clearing.

One of the boys groaned. "Already?"

Gabe nodded. "When you live in the bush, all of your energy is spent on survival. No hanging out on computers playing games. No texting friends from iPhones. No TV. You finish cleaning up after one meal, then start preparing for the next."

The kids split off into their former groups and traded chores.

Gabe called back the two boys who wanted to sleep outside. "You see that rake leaning against that tree?"

They nodded.

"Use it to scrape snow from the roof of the tent. Use the flat side and be careful. Don't puncture anything."

Callie stared at the rake. The handle was longer than the boys were tall. She watched them struggle with it, both of them hefting it to the top of the tent and backing away to pull it all the way down the side, taking a good strip of six-inch deep snow with it.

Gabe approached Callie. "How's your shoulder?"

"Sore again."

"Use the ice pack. Get into the sled."

"Do I have to? Can't I sit on a stump somewhere? I like being part of the group."

Gabe disappeared into the tent and came out with a folded chair. He opened it and Callie sat then jumped right back up.

"The metal's cold!" She laughed.

He grabbed the blanket from the sled, folded it and put it on the chair. Callie sat and he handed her the ice pack. For a still man, he did an awful lot for other people. He never stopped.

She stared at the tent.

"Yes," he said.

She whipped around to look at him.

"All the kids will be able to squeeze in to sleep in there."

"Don't do that."

"What?"

"Read my mind."

A tiny smile hovered at the edges of his lips.

When the children returned, he had them carry the wood and water into the tent.

"Open those chairs," Callie heard him say. Dying to know what went on inside the tent, she stood and entered it to check out the interior. A couple of lanterns hung, one at each end.

The kids arranged the chairs in a circle around the inside.

Beside the door, there was a small iron stove.

"This is called a prospector's tent," Gabe said. "It's a replica of what gold prospectors used when panning for gold in the 1800s."

He pointed to two of the kids closest to him.

"Fill this stove with kindling, the way I showed you how to do it outdoors."

They did. "Good job," Gabe said and set a match to it.

To another couple of kids he said, "Okay, now slowly add wood to build a fire."

Before long there was a fire going in the square metal stove. Gabe put a large rectangular pan on top of it and added water from the buckets. From a cooler he produced a bunch of chicken breasts that he added to the water.

"I'm going to poach these, so we'll keep the fire at an even temperature by adding wood only when we have to. We don't want to boil the chicken."

Gabe had everyone wrap clean potatoes in their skins in foil. Then he opened the door of the oven and tossed them in around the edges of the fire.

While the chicken and potatoes cooked, they sat around in a cozy circle and Gabe had them talk about how dogsledding had felt to them. For all of them, today's ride had been their first time.

Almost to a person, they thought it was great exercise, but the best part was the dogs. The impression Callie got was that the animals added another dimension to the sport, a depth of experience that ordinary sports didn't have.

When the chicken was done, Gabe took the boneless breasts from the water and added them to a couple of large zipper-lock plastic bags full of something that looked like cranberry sauce.

Valerie fished the potatoes out of the oven with a pair of large tongs and she and Jack and Robert unwrapped them and dropped them onto plates.

"Who wants butter and who wants sour cream?" Valerie asked.

Gabe added a breast of chicken to each plate and handed them around.

Last, he handed one to Callie. "Are you sure?" she asked. "Do you have enough?"

"I made extra."

He handed around a container of cherry tomatoes and cucumber slices.

The chicken was tender, moist and slightly sweet from the sauce, and the potato piping hot. The meal tasted as good as any she'd ever had in a four-star restaurant. Must be the fresh air that built up such a good appetite.

"Oh wow, that hit the spot," she said, and a couple of the girls laughed. She was the first one who'd finished eating.

The children ate without complaint, all but licking their plates clean.

This outdoor stuff was foreign to her, but so appealing.

When he finished eating, Gabe carried the pan of water in which the chicken had cooked outside to cool in the snow.

"We don't waste anything here. This will be good for the dogs later."

He returned with another pot of water, which he warmed on top of the stove. Before it became too hot, he took it off and added dish detergent.

"These plates are made from bamboo. They're better than plastic because they can be washed and reused, and won't add to our landfills. Manufacturing them doesn't pollute like producing plastic does."

He taught the children valuable lessons, Callie thought, about using everything and about the value of helping our earth to survive.

They dried them as well as the cutlery Gabe had handed around and it all went into a big wooden box just inside the doorway.

"Everyone grab your chair and carry it outside. Set up a circle around that pile of stones behind the brick fire pit."

The children and teenagers did as he asked. So did Callie, curious about what came next. She had been out here for hours. She should leave, but she didn't want to. This was interesting, fun, different, and set up a friskiness in her, almost as though she were one of the preteen girls having so much fun.

She poured too many hours into work and not enough into play.

Yes, she was supposed to be looking for problems with

Gabe's business, but so far she'd seen none, certainly no law-suits waiting to happen. She found it most intriguing that she could forget about work for hours on end here.

When they were finished, Gabe led them back to the tent.

"Rob, Jack and Valerie are going to help you set up the sleeping bags for the night." The kids piled back into the tent. "I'm going to walk Callie to her car."

"No!" Gabe turned to stare at her. She hadn't meant to shout. "I don't want to go." She thought of her empty hotel room. Her hours would be spent worrying about her mother and money. She didn't want the night to end. "I know I should go, but I wish I could stay."

In the overly bright light from the one kerosene lantern hanging outside of the tent, Gabe frowned, turning his face into a maze of shadows and highlights. "Thought you'd want to sleep in a bed tonight."

She shrugged and spread her hands. "I'm enjoying this. I honestly don't know why. It's so foreign to anything I've ever experienced before."

He studied her for a moment then opened the flap. "Valerie, set up an extra sleeping bag beside mine."

A weight in her chest lifted. How many hours of the day since Mom had been diagnosed did she carry around a low-grade anxiety? Gabe was gifting her with a few more hours to forget the big things she couldn't change and enjoy small things that enriched a life so much.

He led her to the pile of stones where he gathered kindling and wood and squatted on his haunches and started a fire.

Callie sat on her chair. The children chattered inside the tent, but out here under the dark sky dotted with stars all was quiet. She sighed. This was lovely, but she was here to work. Tonight had to mean more than just a mini-holiday for her.

"Gabe, can I ask you a question?"

"I guess." He fed a larger log to the fire. Callie felt the heat of it on her cheeks.

"You won't like it." She hated to ask, to disturb the tranquility of this superb night, but she needed to know. "What did Nick do to you and Laura?"

That unnatural deep stillness settled over him again. She thought he wouldn't answer. A full minute passed. Guess he wasn't just being slow this time. He really wasn't going to answer.

And then he did. "He slept with her."

"I figured as much. Was she your girlfriend?"

"Yeah."

"If she decided she cared more for Nick than you, why couldn't you just let them go do their thing? Why hold a grudge so many years later?"

"It was…complicated."

"It usually is between men and women." She took a bunch of long pliable sticks he handed to her.

"Hand these out to the kids when they come out."

"Tell me about what happened. How was it complicated?"

He shook his head. "Not now."

"Does that mean you will some other time?"

After a protracted silence he added one more log to the fire then studied her over his shoulder. With his back to the pit, she couldn't see his face. "Maybe," he said quietly just as the children came out of the tent, officially ending the conversation.

What did that *maybe* hinge on? What did she have to do to make sure it happened? Persist, as she always did, she guessed.

Or, maybe with Gabe the key was to take a page from his book and learn a deep abiding patience. Maybe all she needed to do was wait for him to come to her.

The children sat on their chairs around the fire. The helpers handed out marshmallows, Callie handed out the thin pliant branches and everyone toasted marshmallows.

"Tell us about the big race you said you were going on." Mike ate a gooey marshmallow, leaving a white sugary string hanging down his chin.

Gabe was going on a race?

"The Iditarod?" Gabe asked.

"Yeah."

"It's in March. The dogs and I are in training."

"All of them?"

"Pretty well. I'll need sixteen dogs to run the race. Just before I go, I'll choose the strongest out of my thirty."

"What's the race about?"

"Well, the commonly held myth and the truth are two different things. It's in Alaska and was started by some people to honor a dogsledding companion who had died."

He made himself a s'more then took a big bite.

After he swallowed, he said, "A lot of people think it was designed to mimic an historic relay dogsledders did in 1925 to deliver life-saving serum to Nome for an outbreak of diphtheria that was killing people. That's the myth I prefer. It's more romantic."

Romantic? The man was a romantic? Who knew?

"So tell us about the relay," one of the girls said.

"Nome is way up north on the coast of the Bering Sea. The sea was frozen, so no ships could make it to Nome. Neither the railroads nor roads went that far. So, in the middle of winter, the only way into Nome was by dogsled, so mushers set up a relay to get the serum to Nome. The first musher started in fifty-below-zero weather in Nenana. The Alaska Railroad carried it that far north, but could go no farther."

A pop of resin startled a couple of children, and Callie. She looked around the campfire. The students were riveted by Gabe's story. They had even stopped toasting marshmallows.

"When the last musher took the serum he nearly lost it when a gust of wind overturned his sled. He dug it out with his bare hands, turned his sled over and carried on to Nome. Many lives were saved with that medicine."

"How long did it take?"

"From Nenana to Nome? Five days and seven hours. Non-stop."

"How many dogs were there?"

"There were eighteen teams and their mushers. The lead dog on the last sled was called Balto. There's a statue of him in Central Park in New York City."

"Wow," one of the boys whispered.

"Who's your Balto going to be?" another one asked.

"Who will lead? Daisy. She's the smartest dog I've ever known."

"Are you going from Nenana to Nome?"

"No. The Iditarod runs from Anchorage to Nome, a total of 1,151 miles. During the gold rush days, there used to be a trail used for delivering mail called the Iditarod. The race follows that trail. It takes nine days for the fastest racer to complete."

"Nine days?" Callie blurted. "Are you out of your mind?" She clapped her hand over her mouth.

Gabe smiled, but it looked a tad sardonic. "Not the last time I checked."

"Sorry," she said. "I shouldn't have said that, but you're taking on a monumental task. Why?"

"I need the challenge. I want to challenge my dogs, too." He looked around the campfire. "Do you guys want to see the sled I'll be taking?"

A chorus of *yeahs* broke out.

"Okay, I'll show you in the morning. It's bigger than the ones you were driving today." He stood. "Now it's time for bed. Use the washroom. Make sure to use hand sanitizer when you finish. Find a private spot to brush your teeth then climb into your sleeping bags for the night. While you're doing that, I'll feed the dogs one last time."

The kids dispersed, but then Gabe called, "If anyone needs to go to the bathroom during the night, Valerie and Robert will be sleeping at the back door of the tent. They'll have flashlights. Wake one of them to take you. Don't go out alone in the dark."

They ran off.

"You need a toothbrush?" he asked Callie.

"If you have an extra, that would be great."

"I'll be back." He picked up a flashlight and disappeared down the path toward the house. He returned with a toothbrush in a package.

She filled her tin cup with water.

"Thanks." She found a spot behind a tree and brushed her teeth then lined up behind the kids and waited to use the toilet, not much more than a wooden seat built up over a hole in the ground. Rustic, but it relieved her bladder.

She returned to Gabe.

"You can help get the food ready." He shrugged. "If you want."

That shrug said he didn't care, but his eyes told a different story. He wanted to spend time with her. His desire warmed her. "Show me what to do."

"At night they get a special kibble. It's higher in protein and fat than regular dog kibble." He handed her a plastic cup. "Put this much into each bowl and then cover it with the broth left over from poaching the chicken."

She spooned out kibble into the bowls and poured broth over it. Gabe delivered them to the dogs.

"Can I do a couple?"

"Sure."

She set the bowl down in front of one of the Huskies, who let her pat his head. Then she gave the next dog a bowl of food, but he didn't seem inclined to want her to touch him while he ate.

The simple chore filled her with a sense of rightness. She helped the dogs who had given Gabe and the children, and her, a joy-filled afternoon.

Gabe fed Daisy.

They walked back along the line of dogs together, following the light from the fire back to camp.

This far away from the tent, she dared to ask him another personal question. "Why do you like children so much more than adults?"

Gabe didn't answer right away and she thought she might have offended him, but then he said, "They haven't lost their humanity, their potential to be great people."

That raised so many questions about Gabe's background. Had he been betrayed by someone he had once thought would grow to be great? Nick? Or was he talking about himself, wondering where his potential had gone? Wondering why he felt the need to hide out here on his land?

The man was a recluse only to a point. She'd gotten to know him a little better today and *recluse* was not the right word. To be more accurate, he was merely antisocial. And what did she mean by *merely* anyway? That *merely* made her job tough.

Maybe *antisocial* was as wrong as *recluse* was? Maybe *damaged* would be better. She wanted to know every speck of Gabe's background that caused that damage.

You shouldn't. Only get close enough to find out what you need to know for Nick.

I know.

Inside the tent, many of the children were already inside their sleeping bags, in two rows, with their heads facing the two long walls of the tent and their feet facing each other in the middle. They settled quickly.

"After all of today's exercise and fresh air," Gabe murmured, "they'll be asleep in no time."

Callie shivered. Gabe noticed.

"Are you cold?"

"I have this chill I can't shake off."

"Take this spot." He'd been about to lie down beside the stove, but instead crawled into the next sleeping bag. "I'll have to climb over you a few times during the night to add wood to the fire, but you'll be warm there."

They were lying like fish in a can, side by side, with not much between them but their sleeping bags.

She wasn't used to this. She'd grown up alone in her own bedroom and her own bed.

Even when she'd had boyfriends, she'd made a point of not sleeping with them after they had made love. Not that she could remember much about that. It had been a long, long time since she'd had a man. More than six years. And there had only ever been two.

Strange now to have so many people nearby snuffling and settling into sleep.

An hour later, still awake and lying on her side cradled between the heat from the stove and Gabe's heat behind her, Callie felt him move. Then he was up and stepping over her to add wood to the fire. He glanced over his shoulder to find her watching him.

"Warm enough?" The fire did amazing things to his cheekbones and made his deep-set dark eyes unfathomable. His skin turned to gold. Oh, so dangerous pings of attraction scooted through her heart.

"Yes," she whispered, aware that they were not alone, but strangely wishing that they were. She would ask him about himself, and Afghanistan, and more about Laura, and about his strange relationship with his brother.

He closed the stove door and lay back down behind her. With the fire renewed and warming her, she finally fell asleep.

Gabe stirred beside her and she awoke. At some point, she'd rolled over and lay facing him. He was watching her, not two feet away, close enough for his breath to wash over her face. It smelled sweet, like marshmallows and chocolate.

How long had he been watching her sleep?

Had she been snoring, or worse, drooling? God, she hoped not. Surreptitiously, she touched the corners of her mouth with one finger. Dry, thank goodness.

His hand moved toward her face with the gossamer touch of one finger on her cheek and then it was gone. He seemed to come to a decision and was up and over her and reaching outside the door of the tent for wood.

She was beginning to think of his fast movements as his *lurches*. A pattern emerged, of a shy withdrawn man *wanting* to do something with a woman, with her, and feeling uncomfortable about it, but doing it anyway.

When he finished, he stepped back over her and picked up his big coat and hers from where they had been stored against the side of the tent.

He bent toward her, blocking out everything but the heat of the man. "Come with me," he whispered into her ear.

She followed him outside where she put on her jacket and they both stepped into their boots. He led her away from the students asleep in the tent and the boys sleeping in the sleds to the far end of the line of sleeping dogs.

Moonlight shone on the tent, but this close to the edge of the clearing in the shadow of tall pines where Callie stood facing Gabe, she couldn't see his face.

"You asked about Laura. It's been keeping me awake." His low voice rumbled in his chest. He stepped close so he could speak without waking the kids. "We were engaged."

Engaged. She'd had a feeling the situation with Nick was

worse than it had sounded, that it was more than just a couple of boys wanting to date the same girl.

"Nick had gone off to college in Seattle." He held her hands because they'd both forgotten their gloves in the tent. "Nick dropped out halfway through his first year and it was my job to keep him there."

"Why?"

"What?"

"Why was it your job to keep him in college?"

He didn't answer right away. "It's a long story." He stopped talking and she felt his mood shift.

"I'm sorry I interrupted," Callie said. "Go on."

"Nick had started dating this woman whose father was rich. He'd always wanted stuff, things, and wanted them right away. He had no concept of delayed gratification. He thought that if he married a rich man's daughter, he'd be set for life."

With a jolt, Callie realized that he was talking to her, really *talking,* that these weren't one- or two-word answers. Sometime during this long day and evening, he'd learned to relax with her, or at the very least, had become more comfortable.

As though this were a gift he bestowed on her, her heart warmed.

"He and this girl left school to meet her father. I went there and dragged him back to college."

"Again, why was that your responsibility?"

Gabe sighed. "It became mine after my dad died. In my teenage years and early twenties I worked my butt off to send Ty for police officer training and Nick to business college."

"How old were you when your dad died?"

"Ten. Ty was seven. Nick was five. While my mom worked to support us, I raised the boys."

Ah. Hence his swollen sense of responsibility for those around him.

"I guess I embarrassed Nick in front of his girlfriend when

I forced him back to school, but even worse than that, in his mind, I'd done it in front of the girl's father." He shoved his hands into his pockets. "Nick ran away from college again, but he came home to Accord long enough to seduce Laura and to make sure I caught them in bed together. It was an act of spite. I didn't mind him hurting me, but I hate how he used Laura. Our engagement ended that night."

The words sounded detached, as though he were reciting someone else's story, but his voice rang with deep-seated emotion—anger, regret, sadness.

"The next day, he left Laura and returned to Seattle. Next I heard, his girlfriend was pregnant and they were getting married."

"Emily."

"What?"

"His daughter's name is Emily."

"I've never met her." His frosted breath carried on it a thread of wistfulness.

"She's amazing," Callie said. "She's smart and funny and loves her dad like the sun rises and sets on him."

"Things worked out for him, then."

"I wouldn't say that. He's divorced and spends so much time in the office that Emily is becoming disenchanted. I'm afraid he'll lose her once she reaches adolescence."

"How old is she now?"

"Twelve."

Gabe wrapped his hand around one fist. "I wish I knew my niece."

Nick had a lot to answer for. Callie shivered.

"Still cold?"

She nodded.

Gabe unbuttoned his coat and, taking it slowly, drew her against his chest then closed the flaps of the coat behind her.

She leaned her head against the wonderful warm breadth

of him. "You take care of people a lot, don't you? Because you grew up taking care of your brothers?"

"No." His voice rumbled under her ear.

"Then why?"

"Because I enjoy it."

He tipped her chin up with a finger. She couldn't see his face, but she knew men, could judge his intention and gave in to it.

Oh, yes. She'd wanted this all day, or before, almost since the first moment she'd seen him standing in his front doorway in his big, masculine, virile glory.

He kept the kiss gentle, his lips cool from the night air. He kissed as though his life depended on him getting it right, as though there was nothing on this earth he'd rather be doing at this moment than kissing her, and all of that intensity was a heady thing.

She kissed him back, not with the same intensity, but with the joy she tried to live with every day, with her willingness to go out, to vanquish self-denial, to say "yes, I want this experience in my life." To say yes to life and to step out of the box of her mother's closet—and all of those terrible memories—and live. She forced all thought out of her mind but this glorious kiss.

His tongue swept into her mouth and she'd never felt anything so right as being wrapped in the safety of this man's arms while his body warmed her head to toe and his tongue spoke a carnal language in her mouth.

Without warning, the dogs howled and she jumped away from him.

"What—"

He chuckled, turned her in his arms and pulled her back against his chest, drawing the edges of his coat around her to keep her warm.

She stared at the howling dogs, their throats long as they raised their faces to the distant moon.

"Why are they barking? Why *all* of them?"

"That."

He pointed. In the pale moonlight in the center of the clearing, a white bunny hopped away, more noticeable by his shadow than by his blue-white fur against the blue-white snow.

The dogs howled in unison for a couple of minutes, as though they'd rehearsed this concert all day, and it was haunting and oh, so beautiful.

On a dime, they stopped as one.

Callie stared, stunned. "How do they do that?"

"Stop in unison? I don't know, but they do it every time. Almost always. Occasionally, while I'm lying in bed at night, they'll howl and then will all stop, but then I'll hear a little yip because one of them didn't realize it was time to stop."

When he laughed, his chest moved at her back.

"Nature is amazing."

"Amazing and beautiful," he replied. "And tough, cruel, terrible and stunning."

"You love it, don't you?"

"Yes, and I love this land."

And this land would always keep them apart, because Callie meant to accomplish what she'd come here to do.

And Gabe would resist.

He edged her away from him, took her hand and led her back to the tent.

Without another word between them, they shucked their coats, crawled into their sleeping bags and fell asleep, facing away from each other, because tomorrow they would be enemies again.

CHAPTER SEVEN

IN THE BRIGHT cool morning air, they gathered around a sled that was much larger than the ones they had driven the day before. A canvas sheet had been pushed aside and the sled was surrounded by clothing and food items that would be packed into it for the big race.

"There isn't enough room in here to store everything I'll need for the entire trip. The dogs and I will go through a lot of food. Plus I'll need a ton of juice and Gatorade—at least a few dozen bottles to ward off fatigue, cramps, dehydration. Even if I could store that much, the sled would be too heavy for the dogs to pull."

"Even sixteen of them?" Jared asked.

"Even that many."

"So how are you going to have enough food?" a child asked.

"The race organizers have checkpoints all along the route where mushers will have supplies waiting for them. They'll be flown in by bush plane. I've already arranged with a supplier in Alaska for food to be dropped off at four locations. With the supplies I'll start with in Nenana, that's about eleven or twelve days' worth of food."

Gabe pulled a huge mesh plastic bag out of the big sled. "This is the kind of bag used for the drops. I'll need forty pounds of extra booties for the dogs. Conditions will be harsh, not like the groomed trails I make here. The dogs' feet have to be protected at all times and they'll go through a ton of booties. As well, there'll be batteries for my headlamp, extra snowshoes in case mine malfunction. Ditto for sled harnesses and sled parts. On top of all of that, there'll be a couple of *thousand* pounds of food for the dogs."

"That's a ton of food," Callie blurted.

"Yeah, man, that's a lot," a kid said.

"No, I mean that is literally a ton of food," she explained. "There are two thousand pounds in a ton. That's mind-boggling."

"How will you cook on the trail?" a girl asked.

"See this big stove and water pots? These cookers can bring four gallons of snow to boiling in about thirty minutes. My food will be precooked, packaged and frozen. You know how we boiled the pots of water for the dogs' chicken broth?"

Everyone nodded.

"My food will be frozen in plastic bags in individual portions. I'll throw in a bag while heating the water for the dogs and then I'll set it aside and add lard and supplements to the water. The dogs will need calories from fat as well as their frozen meat. I'll give them probiotics to make sure they digest their food efficiently. After I've fed them, I'll open my plastic pouch and eat my dinner."

"I imagine you must go through a lot of calories," Callie said. "Will your portions be large?"

"You bet. I probably won't stop for lunch. I'll eat energy bars while I'm mushing. By dinnertime, I'll be starving. I won't need as many calories as the dogs, though. They'll need 10-14,000 calories a day. Each."

Callie turned to stare at the dogs and then back at Gabe. What a responsibility he would carry for keeping his dogs healthy.

"That's so cool," one of the boys said. "I wish I could be there."

"You can. Sort of. After I get home, I'll post photos to my

blog, along with the whole story of how things went. Sometimes, I'll wear a camera attached to a helmet and I'll post the videos, too."

"Sick!" another boy said. "I wanna see those."

"Can you take pictures of the food you eat?" a girl asked.

"Sure."

"What are these for?" Callie pointed to a bunch of journals. "Will you have time to write?"

"As in journaling? No. Those are for keeping health notes about the dogs, for recording injuries or illnesses that will have to be checked out at the end of the race."

Gabe walked to one of the big Rubbermaid containers in which he kept dry goods. He returned with business cards that he handed around. "My blog address is on my card. Stow it with your stuff now and don't lose it. I'll start blogging a few days after I return."

They dispersed to put the cards into their knapsacks.

"More technology, Chewbacca? I'm impressed."

He glanced down at her with a peekaboo smile. "It comes in handy. It's a great educational tool."

That fragile bond they had nourished last night was still there. Callie wasn't sure why that made her eyes damp. She turned away and blinked hard.

She worked for Nick and yet she had Gabe's trust. It would devastate her to lose it when she managed to feel so simpatico with him so quickly. When was the last time that had happened? She honestly couldn't remember.

"You like teaching these children, don't you?" she asked.

"Yeah." He loaded goods back into one of his plastic storage tubs.

When he stood to carry it back across the clearing to store it, he studied her head to toe. "How much do you weigh?"

"Ex*cuse* me?"

"Too personal? Sorry." He closed the cover on the sled. A blush burnished his cheeks.

A couple of times this morning, she'd caught him watching her when he thought she wasn't aware.

But she *was*. *So* aware.

"When I don't have dogsledding groups here," he said, "I need to train for the Iditarod and fill the sled with enough weight to mimic what we'll actually be carrying. When you were in the sled yesterday, you felt about the right weight. If you could come out with me tomorrow for a long run, I wouldn't have to load the sled with all of these stores. Only some."

They were playing with fire. Last night's interlude should have ended when their kiss did, but she'd sensed a reluctance in Gabe to let go of feelings she found echoed in herself. "Okay, yeah, I'd like that."

The school bus arrived at noon to take the kids back to school. When all was said and done, even though Callie had to get into town to organize meetings and rally citizens to support the new resort, she didn't want this interlude to end.

The last child got on the bus before it turned out of Gabe's driveway and drove off. Callie missed them already.

"City girl?"

Callie turned to look at Gabe. He wasn't smiling, but there had been humor in his voice.

The kids were gone. They were alone. He looked unsure of himself.

"Come out tomorrow for that ride? In the afternoon?"

"Okay. About one?"

He nodded but didn't move to return to the house. Neither did she move to leave. She just knew she wanted more time with him. Like chocolate, he shot her full of endorphins and helped her to forget the conflict in real life.

At the sound of a car in the driveway they both turned. A

large North American sedan had turned in, with a blonde at the wheel. Callie turned to Gabe with the question "Who?" on her lips, but it died. His face had flattened into neutrality.

Reality had just burst their bubble and Callie wanted the protection of it back. She didn't want another woman invading Gabe's oasis. Only her.

Sentimental crap. She didn't own the man.

She studied the woman who had put that wary paranoia back into Gabe. The tall willowy blonde stepped out of the car and Callie's first impressions of her went into overdrive. Alarms went off.

The woman came from money and the gaze she locked on Gabe was hungry.

So what? What's that to you?

Nothing.

Really?

Really.

"Hello, Gabe." The woman stood on tiptoes and kissed him on the lips.

When he touched her, he was gentle. He kissed her back then stepped away. "Monica, what are you doing here?"

Callie could detect no hint of accusation or displeasure in his voice. Whoever this woman was...well, he might not want to see her here on his land, but he respected her.

"Callie," he said, "this is my...friend, Monica Stone."

"Accord," she said. "I've gone back to my own name."

Callie shook her hand. "Accord as in Ian Accord? Town father?"

"That's the one." Monica smiled but kept her eyes on Gabe. Callie's first impression had been bang on. Monica had a goal whose name was Gabe. Underneath her sweetness was a backbone of steel. She got what she wanted.

Feeling *de trop* all of a sudden, Callie stepped away. "I'll leave you two alone."

"Wait," Gabe said. "I'll walk you to your car."

"That's not necessary. I know the general direction I need to walk to get there."

"Are you sure?"

She nodded, but already he had turned away from her and was staring down at Monica, his hands on her arms. Not that it bothered Callie that he had forgotten about her so quickly. She had no hold on Gabe. Lord, no, she didn't want one.

After all, what was one kiss between consulting adults? Really. These days it signified little.

So why did she feel so lost? He was her adversary, after all.

She had a strange thought as she found her car and drove away. For a man who had a reputation as a recluse, Gabe sure had a lot of visitors to his land.

DISAPPOINTED, GABE WATCHED Callie drive away. Not that he wanted her in his life—or any woman, for that matter—but he liked dealing with her clean, uncomplicated spirit. And he shouldn't.

Monica's appearance brought reality crashing down. What the hell was he doing having fun with a woman when Monica had lost so much?

"Who is she?" Monica asked.

Gabe stared at her. Monica was beautiful in her polished way—tall and tanned, blonde and model-pretty, but too cool, too beige, for Gabe's taste.

"Callie works for Nick," he finally answered.

"Nick? I'm surprised you let her near you."

"He wants to buy the land. She's trying to convince me to sell."

"Is she getting anywhere?"

"No." He waited for Monica to explain why she was here. She didn't. This was her first time on his land. He supposed that meant he should invite her inside, offer her coffee, shoot the breeze, but with Monica it was never that simple. Besides, he honestly didn't know how to be a good host anymore.

He decided on the direct approach. "Why are you here?"

"I haven't seen you in a long time. Have you been avoiding me?"

Maybe. Not consciously. "I've been busy."

"Let's go inside." She threaded her arm through his and all but led him into his own house.

On the threshold, she stopped and looked around, not quite hiding her disappointment.

He saw it from her eyes—the furniture that had seen better days, the old dog asleep beside the hearth, the ordinariness that drew Gabe and kept him here.

He refused to be ashamed.

She said, "I'll make coffee." He didn't know why he was letting her take control in his home. The second she'd driven up paralysis had overcome him. Standing between Monica and Callie, he'd recognized an unavoidable truth. Callie had him dreaming of a future he'd no longer thought possible— of happiness and family, of hearth and home unfettered by loneliness. Monica reminded him of his past and the reasons why that future was impossible.

While he listened to her rummage in his kitchen, he started a fire in the fireplace. The scent of brewing coffee filled the air and he leaned his arms against the mantel, feeling the bite of the stone against his palms like a penance.

Warm arms wrapped around his midriff from behind and locked over his stomach. Gabe tensed then eased into the embrace. Monica laid her head against his back.

"I miss him," she said.

"Me, too." If he sounded resigned, so be it. Grief could be a real bitch. It had been his companion for so long it had become a friend, neurotic maybe but dependable.

"I miss him all the time, Gabe. I want to forget about him. I'm tired of remembering."

"I know," he said. "Then I feel guilty thinking that."

"Sorrow is exhausting."

"Yeah." A lot of Billy's friends had moved away from town to bigger and better things. Jeff Stone, Billy's dad, wouldn't give Gabe the time of day.

Monica, though? She understood Gabe's grief. He could talk to her about Billy. She'd been calling him more often lately, wanting to do more than share memories. He didn't want that. He wanted to talk about Billy. That was it. Nothing else. Yeah, he *had* been avoiding her calls. Shame on him. She was hurting, too.

Gabe turned around and cradled her head against his chest. She raised on her tiptoes to kiss him. He kissed her back, disappointed when all he felt was a mild affection. No easing of grief. No oblivion.

No Callie.

Stop. She's dangerous to your life on this land.

I know, but...she makes me forget.

But you shouldn't.

He eased away from Monica. She'd been pressuring him to take their relationship to the next level. Not that they had a "relationship." Or did they?

God, he didn't know. What did a man become when he tried to take care of his best friend's widow? He hadn't wanted to *become* anything. He'd just wanted to help her.

She'd helped him, too. So why, lately, did their friendship feel like a burden?

He gently pried her away from him and held her at arm's length.

She watched him with such hope.

"Have you gone to any of those therapy sessions the military recommended?" Gabe had given her the address a long time ago.

She nodded, but refused to meet his gaze.

He shook her gently. "The truth, Monica."

"Okay. I only went a couple of times, but they made me cry too hard. Everyone had lost someone, a son or a brother or a husband, and it brought me down. I don't want to feel that sad and cry that much."

"But the point of the sessions is to face your grief and cry if you need to."

"I know, but I'm past that. Really, Gabe."

He suspected she was too strenuous in her assertions because she *wasn't* past it, but what could he do? Nag her some more?

"The only time I truly feel better," she said, "is when I'm with you. I heal when we're together."

Gabe's mood sank into grayness, darkness. Lethargy. He understood Monica, but her need burdened him. Didn't he deserve that, though? If not for Gabe's foolish mistaken belief that he'd known what was best for Billy, Monica wouldn't be alone.

Besides, they shared him. Even close to four years later, it was still hard to let go of Billy.

With a sigh of resignation he tried to swallow, he said, "Coffee's probably ready."

He left her alone to go to the kitchen then returned to find her curled up on the sofa. He handed her a coffee with a little sugar and plenty of cream, just the way she liked it.

"How's work at the Organic Bud going?" She'd gotten a job at the produce market on Main Street just before Christmas.

"I don't work there anymore." When Gabe would have said something, she raised her hand. "I know the smart thing is to keep busy. You've already told me that, a lot, but I hated working evenings and weekends."

Gabe smiled, not unkindly. "That's real life, Monica." Not everyone had a wealthy papa who paid for everything.

"I know, but I got a better job at the Palette."

"Olivia Cameron's shop?"

"Yes. I love dealing with art all day, and with the artists and customers. I think I've found something that really suits me."

Gabe's responding smile was genuine. "I'm glad." Monica had burned her way through too many jobs. She always started with the best of intentions, but then something would change and she would quit. At the beginning her grief for Billy got in the way. There were days when she couldn't get out of bed, let alone go to work.

For him, starting the dogsledding business had been a welcome distraction. Monica found work a distraction, too, but in a negative way. For a long time, he'd thought she wanted to wallow in her grief. Work would get in the way of her wanting to lie in bed all day, drowning in sorrow. Recently, though, she'd been coming along, or so he'd hoped. Maybe the Palette would finally be the right spot for her.

"Why aren't you at work today?"

"I have to work Saturday and Sunday so I have two days off midweek. I don't mind working weekends so much at the art shop. I get to talk to interesting people." She looked a little surprised. "I really like the work."

"Why did you come here on your day off?" She'd never shown an interest in visiting before.

"I've been alone too much. I wanted company."

"Have you been dating?"

She curled her long legs under her. "Yes, and you know what, Gabe? They just don't stand up to Billy. I've never had as much fun with anyone as I had with Bill. I want my husband back."

She sounded angry. Gabe understood. He wanted his friend back, too.

"What do you do with yourself?" he asked. "With your time after work?"

"There's nothing in town I want to do."

There wasn't a huge social life in town, but a lot of women made their own. He'd heard of knitting and reading groups. There was a dance studio where couples learned swing and ballroom dancing. There was cross-country skiing and hiking. He couldn't imagine Monica doing any of that.

Since early high school, Billy had been Monica's sole source of entertainment. Now that he was gone, she had to work on her own. Didn't sound like she was doing a good job of it.

"How about volunteer work?"

"Daddy wouldn't like that."

No. Milton Accord sure wouldn't. Being a descendant of the founding father, he was the closest thing the town had to aristocracy.

"How about starting a charity, or taking over the one your mom ran?"

Monica shrugged. "I've thought of it." Gabe wasn't sure what that meant.

"Remember how Billy used to eat or drink anything put in front of him?" Her smile shimmered like a jewel.

Gabe smiled. She was speaking a language he understood. "I once dared him to drink a bottle of Tabasco sauce. We were at the Golden Leaf with a bunch of friends. Billy was already three sheets to the wind, but he drank the whole bottle and kept it down."

Monica laughed.

"His face turned bright red. He got five dollars from each of us. Twenty-five bucks to drink a bottle of hot sauce."

Monica wiped the corners of her eyes. "He was like that.

Daddy once took us out to an upscale restaurant in Denver. Billy ate escargot and loved them. He didn't know they were snails."

"Wouldn't have mattered. He would have eaten them anyway."

They talked for hours. Billy had been a charmer and a hoot to spend time with. There wasn't a person on earth who hadn't liked Billy Stone.

Abruptly they sobered, staring at each other in heavy silence, with Gabe wondering where to go next. Memories of Billy were stacked one on top of each other like cordwood, but they were finite. There would never be new memories.

Gabe and Monica were destined to continually relive the same memories.

Was this constant rehashing of who Billy was and all of the things he'd done helping them to heal? Or was it keeping them stuck in their grief? Were they rehashing to maintain the status quo so neither one of them had to move on, to move forward? Were they taking the easy road?

That joyful uplifted feeling with Callie last night had shown him something new, had opened his eyes to parts of his life he'd left in shadow.

Maybe because of his responsibility in Billy's death he didn't deserve happiness, but did he deserve this leaden wallowing in grief?

It had been *four* years. Four tough sorrowful years of loneliness and self-imposed penances that were no meek Hail Marys, but gut-wrenching isolation.

Abruptly, Gabe stood. "I have to feed the dogs."

Monica popped up beside him. "I can help."

"Sure."

Once outside, she did little. She looked lost. Out of her element. He couldn't help but compare her to Callie who found pleasure in everything.

Stop. Callie hasn't lived with the loss Monica has.

"Why do you do this, Gabe?"

He shot her a look. She didn't get it? Callie did without being told. "I enjoy it. I love the dogs. I always wanted a dog when I was little and couldn't have one. Now I own as many as I want."

When that didn't seem to be enough for her, he added, "I love working outdoors. There's no nine-to-five time clock."

"Yes, but you can't make a lot of money doing it. This seems like a hobby. Why don't you get a real job?"

Gabe had to bite his tongue so he wouldn't blow his stack.

Monica didn't have a mean bone in her body, but she sure could be clueless sometimes.

"To me," he said, "this *is* a real job. It's the only one I want. I make enough to support myself and my dogs with extra set aside for emergencies. What else would I need?"

"A nicer house. A better car."

"I don't crave those things."

Monica followed behind him while he worked. He missed the sense of sharing the work that he had with Callie, of her getting why he did this.

Stop thinking of Callie!

"I know you don't crave things, Gabe, but I don't understand why."

He shrugged. "They just don't mean much to me."

"But what if you get married? How are you going to give your wife the things she wants?"

Married? Was that why she was here? She thought he would *marry* her? He'd never said as much. He'd never even hinted it. They had never slept together. He'd never promised her anything other than a shoulder to cry on.

A shot of pure panic-laced anger rattled his nerves as though it were caffeine. "Don't look to me for marriage, Monica. I'm nobody's hero." His hard-edged voice cut through the peace of the woods. "I can't be your savior. I can barely deal with my own problems."

She didn't respond.

"Get it?"

"Yes, Gabe, I get it."

Her look of reproach when she turned away undid him, deflated his anger.

She wanted her husband back, couldn't have him, felt herself heal when she was with Gabe, and so wanted to marry Gabe. He could see how that would make sense to her. He couldn't fault her for thinking she would be moving forward.

He took her arms and made sure she was looking at him.

"I'm never going to get married. Is that clear?"

"Why not?"

He didn't want to be cruel, but... "Because there's no one I love enough to marry."

"Oh." Her voice sounded small.

"Maybe you should go now."

"No, Gabe. Don't send me away. Let me stay for a little while. I won't bother you. I promise." Her neediness disturbed him, dragged him down. He'd always thought she was a strong person. Maybe he'd misjudged her.

Against his better judgment, he nodded. Man, he was a pushover.

He made dinner for the two of them and washed their dishes afterward.

She sat curled into an armchair he'd moved in front of the fire. She'd draped an afghan across her lap and sipped a glass of wine. She didn't look like she was going anywhere tonight.

When did she plan to leave? And if she was staying, where did she think she would sleep?

He went out to make sure everything was set up for the adult group coming in on the weekend. When he returned a half hour later, he found Monica snoozing, her breath whooshing in and out of her softly. Although he was only a year or two older than her, she looked young and fragile and so pretty it hurt to look at her. It seemed cruel to send her away tonight.

He could put her in Nick's old room.

Touching her shoulder gently, he woke her.

She smiled sleepily and looked up at him as though they had already shared intimacies.

He recoiled. *Don't look at me like that.*

"Hey," she said, her voice sleep-husky, staring up at him as though he was capable of rescuing her from her demons.

God, no. How could he when he couldn't save himself from his own?

She stood too quickly, surprising him, brushing against him before he had a chance to step away. She stood on tiptoe and brushed her mouth across his.

He hadn't slept with a woman in a long, long time, another one of his cockamamie punishments he'd thought would absolve him of guilt. Nothing ever did. Like grief, it was a constant.

Monica was soft and warm enough to melt his resistance. "Please," she whispered, enticing him with her sweet voice.

She needed. He needed. Who would it hurt? As she kissed him, encouraged him with her lips and body, he couldn't remember why he was holding back when he had so much need inside of him, so much craving for love, for touch, for happiness.

Happiness. A needle scratching across an old record, that one word brought a halt to his desire. He knew he didn't deserve it.

I'm sorry, Bill. I'm so damn sorry.

I should have taken better care of you.

Gabe didn't know when he would ever deserve again. He just wanted life to be good like it used to be, but he knew in his soul it never would be.

When he stood here with Monica's arms like a vise around his neck, he felt trapped by her need.

Last night, though? During the kiss he'd shared with Callie? He'd soared. For a few brief moments, he'd been free, as though he were flying above responsibility and guilt and numbing grief. Then Monica had shown up, bringing his elation crashing to the ground, reminding him of how deep his responsibility to her went. Did he feel guilty enough to sleep with her?

No.

He set her away from him.

"It's late. I'll put fresh sheets on Nick's bed. You can sleep in his room."

Beneath Monica's disappointment, there flashed anger. He knew in her mind, a pairing of the two of them made perfect sense. Gabe didn't feel that way. He couldn't help that.

After he got Nick's room ready, he handed Monica an old T-shirt to sleep in and left the room to walk down the hall to his own bedroom.

Once inside, he closed the door. He debated shoving a chair under the door handle so Monica wouldn't come in during the night, or maybe hauling his old dresser up against the door. That was overkill, though. She'd gotten the message loud and clear.

He crawled into bed and fell asleep as soon as his head hit the pillow.

Sometime during the night, he woke up to a warm body beside his and a woman nibbling on his lip.

"Monica!" He leaped out of bed. "Damn, you're persistent."

Taking one of her hands in his, he dragged her out from under the blankets to steer her back to Nick's room, but she'd taken off the T-shirt.

In the faint moonlight shining through the window, her

body glowed, beautifully. Long and tanned, her legs went on forever.

"Gabe, please make love to me."

A puddle of white on the floor snagged his eye and he picked up the T-shirt and shoved it back over Monica's head. This was too much. He had to get her out of here.

"What part of *no* don't you understand?" He was tired and confused and too close to giving in out of pure utter guilt, and unbridled lust—God, he needed a woman—but he had enough sense to know how wrong it would be. "I can't be your whole life."

If he gave in tonight, he'd never get rid of Monica. That thought set off another wave of guilt. He shouldn't *want* to get rid of her. Billy would want him to take care of his wife. But did that include sleeping with her? How far should his sense of responsibility take him?

She tried to get close to him again. He held her at arm's length while he steered her down the hall back to Nick's room.

"Monica, we aren't making love tonight." In case she took that to mean it would happen eventually, he added, "Or ever." He sat her on the bed and closed the door behind him, but not before catching a glimpse of her devastated expression. In the past Gabe hadn't really understood. He did now. Monica was every bit as weak as her husband had been.

He'd done his best to help Billy over the years.

After everything he'd seen in Afghanistan, after his own grief over Billy's loss, how could he help Monica? He'd tried. He really had.

He doubted he had the strength to help her anymore. Because of Billy, he doubted he could turn her away altogether.

So how many more nights would he have to fight this battle?

Bill, what am I supposed to do?

This time when he closed the door of his bedroom, he

wedged a chair under his doorknob, and wasn't that ridiculous? An Afghan vet—a former soldier, for God's sake—protecting himself from a woman?

CHAPTER EIGHT

ON THURSDAY AFTERNOON, Callie went over the numbers umpteen times and came to the only conclusion that made sense. She'd have to sell her condo.

She'd bought it as an investment, one she'd meant to cash in on in the future—the *future,* meaning twenty or thirty years from now—not five years after she'd bought it. Even so, she should have made a profit.

Then she would move into Mom's house. She'd keep Sophie on until she could find a suitable long-care facility for her mother. Then she'd sell Mom's little bungalow, too, and put the profit from both sales into Mom's care. It was the only solution she'd been able to come up with.

Resting her forehead on her hand, she remembered the pride she'd felt after purchasing the condo. She'd put herself through college then had paid off all of her student loans early so she could save a down payment. She'd lived paycheck to paycheck to get ahead.

Now, a dozen years later, it would start again, living paycheck to paycheck with nothing to show for all of the hours she'd put in for Nick.

Sure, Mom was worth it, but that didn't mitigate her disappointment, her sense of futility, of never getting ahead.

She would barely be able to cover her life insurance premiums, which meant she couldn't buy medical or accident insurance. What if she got really sick? What if she was so laid up she couldn't take care of Mom or pay for the facility Callie would put her in?

Oh, lord, all of this set off a panic in her unlike any she had ever felt before. She looked down at her hands. They were shaking.

It isn't that bad, Callie. Buck up.

But it could change in the blink of an eye. Anything could go wrong in life.

Don't go borrowing trouble. Protect Mom as best you can and get on with life.

Underneath all of her fear was something she didn't want to feel. Anger. How petty was that? Mom couldn't help what was happening to her.

She called Sophie.

"How's Mom?" she asked without preamble, a sure sign of how rapidly Callie's spirits were plummeting. She used to have a good chat with Sophie before asking about Mom.

"She hasn't run away again, thank goodness." Sophie sounded like she was trying to put on a good face, but she also sounded tired. "I've been sleeping on the sofa in the living room so Johanna can't sneak out at night."

"That must be hard on your back. Mom hasn't bought a new sofa in twenty years."

"It isn't great, but at least it's keeping your mother safe."

"I owe you danger pay."

Sophie's answering chuckle sounded sad.

"You were right about it being time to get Mom into a good home."

"Callie, I'm sorry it has to end this way, but it was inevitable."

"Don't be sorry. You're right. I'm going to sell my condo and Mom's house. I'll contact a real estate agent, so one might be dropping in this afternoon or tomorrow morning. Okay?"

"That's fine. Johanna and I had a long walk this morning, so we aren't going out again."

Otherwise, Sophie had nothing new to report. Same old, same old. What had Callie expected? That there had been a miracle? That Mother had made a spontaneous recovery from an incurable disease?

Still, at least she wasn't worse. That "same old, same old" represented stability.

Best to just get on with it. No sense wasting time. She contacted a real estate agent in Seattle about selling the condo and Mom's house.

"Will that be possible?" the agent asked.

"Yes. I have power of attorney over my mother."

"How about if I head over to both properties now?"

"That would be wonderful."

Callie felt better. She had come up with a plan and had set it into motion.

Next she called the concierge of her building and gave him permission to let the agent into her unit to assess it.

A knock on the door drew her attention. Kristi delivered the fax of the insurance documents to her. She scanned, signed and delivered them to Kristi's office along with a cancelled check so they could start automatic deductions from her account right away. Kristi faxed it all back to the company.

Callie breathed a huge sigh. That was done. Things weren't going the way she'd thought they would at this stage of her life, but they were moving forward. She was taking steps toward handling it all. There was nothing else she could do.

After a superb dinner served in the B and B's dining room, Callie returned to her room and looked up the Iditarod on Google. She watched a few videos about it. So cool. So perfect for mountain-man Gabe. She noticed several short bits about concerns whether the dogs were treated well. Gabe would treat his like gold. He would take care of them better than he'd take care of himself.

Her phone rang—the real estate agent. Wonderful. Good service. Things were moving along.

"I'm afraid I don't have good news for you."

Callie's heart sank. "What is it?"

"With the unemployment rate hovering at eight percent, there are too many houses and condos on the market and not enough people to buy them. If you sell now you'll realize a loss."

Damn. Damn, damn, damn.

She'd been doing all the right things—had gotten herself a good education and spent her twenties saving money. She had a job that paid well at which she worked damn hard and had bought a condo as an investment. None of this freaking stuff had done her a bit of good. She was at the mercy of market forces. Her life was spinning out of her control.

Helplessness threatened to clog her throat.

"I guess it's the same with Mom's house?"

The agent quoted an asking price. It was low. At least Mom's mortgage was paid. There would be some money there.

"It can't be helped," she said. "I need to sell."

She'd put herself into the cheapest apartment she could find.

"Pull the papers together and fax them to me." Callie rattled off the number at the B and B.

After she disconnected, she leaned forward and hugged her knees to her chest, so damned disappointed.

She was stuck.

She went to bed and lay awake for hours. When she did sleep, she dreamed about Gabe, about being in his arms in the moonlight in the woods, about feeling his strength and warmth at her back, about leaning against him for just a few moments to feel supported for once in her life. To not feel so alone and so burdened and so overwhelmed. She awakened feeling warm and optimistic. At least she was moving toward getting her mom a safer environment. The optimism followed her into the shower and through breakfast and while she dressed for a day of dogsledding with Gabe. There had been promise in her dreams. Oh lord, she was falling for the man. This couldn't possibly be good.

MONICA HAD STAYED the night.

Callie pulled into the driveway and parked beside Monica's car.

Rather than skulking around on back roads as she usually did to photograph behind Gabe's back, today Callie had driven around to the front of the property. She'd been invited, after all, for a sled ride. She wasn't sneaking around on the land today.

She had emailed photos of the land to Nick. So far, she'd held on to the photos of Gabe and the children. What if Nick found something in them he could use against Gabe? Some way he could sabotage the business?

Wuss. You have to give Nick something at some point. It is your job.

Callie still needed to get into Gabe's house and get hold of his business records. How was she going to make that happen without getting caught?

Damn you, Nick. I hate my job.

That brought her up short, shocked her. When had her dissatisfaction with the job started? Slowly, insidiously, getting so much worse with this current problem with Gabe. She didn't want to spy on the man. How ruthless was Nick? If she didn't give him what he wanted, *would* he fire her?

He'd saved Mom, though.

What a mess.

She'd never held out on Nick before. Nothing seemed

simple these days. This whole business seemed fraught with issues.

Speaking of issues…it bothered her that Monica was still here. It shouldn't. She had no hold on Gabe.

She shook off the disappointment that he'd been enjoying another woman's company while she'd been dreaming about him.

So much for the promise of those dreams.

She gave herself a good talking-to and shook off her bad mood. Gabe's romantic liaisons had nothing to do with her.

She supposed she could get some info about Gabe from Monica, but she really didn't feel like talking to the woman. Call it jealousy, call it whatever, but she just wasn't up to tackling her today.

Maybe tomorrow if she felt better.

The front door opened and Gabe stepped out. Monica followed. Gabe enfolded her in an embrace that, even from her car, Callie could tell was warm.

It hurt to watch. Was Gabe Monica's? So what? She didn't want him that way, anyway.

Liar. Yes, you do.

Monica nodded at Callie before getting into her car. She drove off, leaving Callie standing in the driveway staring at Gabe. He sneezed, blew his nose then stood on the veranda with his hands in his pockets and his shoulders hunched.

"Well," Callie said and then ran out of steam. Well, what? She wasn't sure why she found this so awkward. Maybe because Gabe so obviously did?

She offered him a lifeline. "Should we get out on the land?"

"Yeah," he said and a breath whooshed out of him. "I'll be out in a minute."

"I'll meet you out back. I want to see the dogs."

Gabe entered the house without another word.

Callie walked through the woods to the clearing.

As soon as the dogs saw her, the barking started, and her discomfort about Monica took a back burner to her joy. She laughed. They were happy to see her. Okay, so maybe they would be happy to see anyone, but she chose to believe they were happy to see *her*.

Their barking turned to howling and they did their wolf impersonation for close to a full two minutes then stopped as one.

"You guys are amazing." She shook her head. How did they do that? What kind of communication that she couldn't hear or sense existed between these dogs?

Gabe showed up five minutes later, coming down the trail from the back door.

He stopped and stared off into the distance, avoiding her gaze. "I need to explain…about Monica."

"No, you don't. Hey, we're virtual strangers. Your women are none of my business. It's perfectly fine." She was talking too quickly, her voice too bright. Why did this embarrass her so much? It wasn't like *she* wanted to sleep with him. She barely knew the man. Besides, getting involved with a Jordan man was a bad, bad idea. She knew that from experience.

"Yeah," Gabe said, his voice low and insistent. "I do."

She gave in and waited for him to continue.

When he seemed satisfied that she was really listening, he said, "Her husband, my best friend Billy, died in Afghanistan and it was my fault. I owe it to him to take care of his wife."

So Monica had been his friend's wife. "'Take care'? Does that include sleeping with her?" She clapped a hand over her mouth. "I'm sorry. I am *so* sorry. That was uncalled for. What you do with her, with any woman, is none of my business."

He'd gone stony. "Right."

He stomped away, his strides long and angry, took one of

the dogs from the chain and hooked him up to the big sled he planned to use for the Iditarod. Callie caught up to him.

She realized she'd missed what was really important in what Gabe had said. His friend's death was *his* fault?

"What happened to your friend?"

He wouldn't stop walking. He hooked another dog up to the sled.

"Will you stand still for a minute?"

"No."

He continued to hook dogs up to the sled.

She grasped his arm and spun him around. *"What happened?"*

Gabe's eyes blazed. "I killed him. Okay?"

He jerked his arm out of her grasp and walked away, his body all but trembling with anger.

She'd seen him with the children and had felt his gentle touch too often in the past week. There was no way he killed a man. Absurd.

Watching Gabe's stiff, lurching movements, she wanted to be here for him. He might not know it, but he needed her.

"Gabe," she said quietly. "Explain it to me."

He tried to step around her.

"Please."

He stopped.

"I want to know what happened." She placed one hand on his chest. He made to remove it, but stopped. His face changed, became softer, losing the harshness of his resistance. He covered her hand with his.

"Billy said he wasn't feeling well, wanted to stay in bed. I egged him into getting out of bed and coming on the mission. Bill could be…lazy. It was part of his character. I took it as my duty to cure him of it."

Oh lord, Callie could see the way his mind would work. He'd taken on the responsibility of caring for Billy, of making him a "better" man, and Gabe's arrogance had been his undoing.

He could see in her eyes that she understood. He stepped away from her. "I should have left him alone. We drove over a roadside bomb that day. If I hadn't convinced him to come on the mission, he would still be alive and Monica would still have a husband."

"You can't know that. He might have been killed at another time."

"Or he could have survived and come home."

"Yes, but—"

"Are you coming sledding or not?" he called, anger back in his tone, but self-directed. He most definitely was not angry with her.

A breath of frustration hissed out of her, but she followed him to the sled. The man had made a mistake that had cost a friend his life, but maybe not. How was Gabe to know they would drive over a bomb? So, was this part of why Gabe had stopped socializing, why he'd pulled inside of himself? Why he stayed out of people's lives? So he wouldn't be tempted to help them fix what was wrong and somehow make a colossal mistake again?

There was no fighting a belief that deeply ingrained in a man.

She let go of her frustration and turned her attention to the dogs, to their joyful noise. They yipped and barked and jumped forward, straining against the brake to start running, to *go,* the second Gabe hooked the first one of them to the sled and they understood there was to be a run today.

She felt a bit like them. Hadn't she always wanted to break out of the confines of her mother's restrictions? She'd gotten away for a while, but these days they flooded back in, restrictions that took the form of her mother's illness and Nick's demands.

"Do they do this every time?" she asked.

He nodded. "Get into the sled." He tucked supplies around her then wrapped her in a blanket, with that gentle touch that belied his peevish tone.

There were sixteen dogs on the sled today instead of the six on the smaller one she'd ridden before.

Gabe strapped Daisy in at the front beside Bopper, ran to the back, released the brake and yelled "Hike!" and the dogs took off.

Again today, the exhilaration Callie had felt on that too-brief ride the other day took over.

She laughed, exulting in the wind in her face. The dogs ran and ran, never seeming to tire.

She turned back to glance at Gabe. He grinned down at her, anger gone. Callie smiled and faced front. The wind roared as it rushed past her ears.

She could do this for hours.

Could she convince him to let her try controlling a sled? He let teenagers do it.

They took a turn too widely and the sled threatened to slam into a tree, but Gabe physically manhandled it back onto the trail, amazing her yet again with his strength.

Her confidence in his strength to keep her safe, to make sure that the sled didn't roll over and toss her out, deepened. He would take care of her. How long had it been since anyone had?

Mom's migraines had made her childhood a time of dichotomies, when Mom would love and hold her in the good times, followed by long stretches of Callie having to take care of both of them.

She'd started taking care of Mom too long ago to recall the luxury of having someone else tend to her. It felt strange. Foreign. Wonderful.

Gabe took her farther than she'd ever been on his land,

turning in a huge wide arc partway around Luther's base, then driving the dogs toward a wide open field.

She hadn't photographed this.

"Is this Jordan land, too?" she yelled.

"No. My neighbor's."

If Nick could buy up this land, too, he'd have an amazing resort that would include downhill skiing on Luther, cross-country skiing across these fields and hiking and snowshoeing in Gabe's forest.

Gabe's forest. Careful, Callie. It belongs to all three men. Don't lose your focus.

No, she wouldn't, but it felt good to set worries aside for the length of this ride and to just enjoy the day.

Gabe pulled up beside a wooden fence, set the brake and opened a gate.

"What's happening?" Callie asked.

"I'm going to take the dogs off the leash and let them run."

"I thought you said they would run away off-leash."

"I'm putting them inside this run I built."

She crawled out from under the blankets and watched while Gabe took the dogs off one at a time and put them through the gate. The second he let go of them, they took off across the pen.

Gabe's run was an enormous square fenced off from the rest of the farmer's field.

"Do you rent this land?"

"Yes." When he put the last dog into the run, he closed the gate and came to stand beside her with his arms folded on top of the fence. "The rent is reasonable and I let Ron come over and try his hand at dogsledding when he feels like it."

"So how do you remain solvent? With school kids?"

"Mostly. I charge the adults more on the weekends. I do all right." He watched the dogs yip and run and roll in the snow.

Their enthusiasm was contagious. No wonder Gabe spent so much time with them.

There had been a frown creasing his brow since she'd arrived and she wondered about it now. His skin looked pale beneath his tan but his cheeks were red.

"Are you okay?"

"I've got a headache that won't quit."

She rummaged in her bag. "Sorry. I don't have any painkillers with me."

"Not a problem." His voice sounded huskier than usual.

They watched the dogs for twenty minutes. Their energy never flagged.

"I have a group of adults coming up tomorrow morning," Gabe said. "That will be lucrative because they'll stay for two days of dogsledding."

"In the tent?"

Gabe looked down at her and smiled. "Yep. In the tent."

He rubbed his knee. "I have my doubts they'll actually make it here, though. There's a storm coming in."

Callie glanced at the cloudless sky and sunshine sparkling diamonds off the snow. "Really?"

"Yep. I can feel it in my knee."

"What's wrong with your knee?"

"It took shrapnel in Afghanistan." Gabe clammed up, as though he'd said too much.

He called the dogs and hitched them back up to the sled.

Without a word, Callie settled into her warm nest.

They slipped quietly across the fields and circled back around to the forest, without ever meeting another soul. Gabe lived on a slice of heaven and Nick wanted to boot him off of this.

What a damn shame.

Too soon, they returned to the clearing. The sky had darkened and wind whistled through the trees.

Gabe was right. There was a storm coming in. Fast.

He hovered over the sled. "Sorry, that should have been a longer ride, but I'm tired today."

"What's wrong with your voice?"

"Throat's a bit sore."

"Maybe you should rest."

"Can't. The dogs."

"I can help. I've watched you feed them twice."

A brisk breeze blustered in a circle around them.

"What's happening with the wind?"

"It's bringing in the storm quickly now."

He stared at tree branches roiling like waves on the sea.

"You need to leave now." It sounded like an order.

"Always trying to boot me off the land, aren't you?" Her remark didn't elicit the smile she'd hoped for. He looked bad.

"I'm staying to help with the dogs. Half an hour won't make that much difference."

Gabe glanced at the sky. "With a snowstorm in January? In Colorado? Yeah, it will." He coughed. The deep chocolate of his eyes looked watery.

"Be quiet," she said. "I'm staying to help. What can I do?"

"Gather wood. I'll get water."

"You got it." She grabbed one of the axes out of a plastic tub and ran into the woods, remembering that she should cut only dead wood. She hauled out a huge tree branch and started to chop it.

Gabe carried pails of water from the lake. She was glad she hadn't taken that job. She could carry only a fraction of the water he could in one trip. She would have run back and forth too many times to fill one pot. On the other hand, the man was moving awfully slowly.

"I'll sleep here tonight," she said.

"No." He sounded winded. "Leave soon. Weather's getting bad."

He was right about that. The wind was bringing with it the scent of snow. "You start a fire and get more water," she ordered. "Worry about your dogs. I'll take care of myself."

He obviously didn't have the strength to argue and barely mustered a shrug.

The dogs were still attached to the sled. So unlike Gabe to do this stuff out of order.

"Can you unhook Daisy and I'll unhook the rest?"

"Can't. Have to change the straw."

"Can't it be done tomorrow?"

"No. Snow won't make it possible."

"You think it's going to be that bad?"

"Damn straight."

"Then leave the straw until after the storm."

"Nope. It's stale."

Callie stifled her exasperation. They were running out of time, but Gabe was doing what was best for his dogs. "You finish with the fire. I'll rake straw."

Gabe added wood to the kindling and filled the pots with water.

While Callie raked straw to the edge of the clearing, she kept an eye on Gabe. He was deteriorating rapidly.

She glanced at the sky. It looked as dark as twilight. She raked faster.

"Okay, move Daisy."

"Not...yet."

Gabe laid fresh straw along the chain then moved the dozen dogs who hadn't run today to the clean spots.

Callie raked their used straw to the edge of the clearing. Her biceps burned. The wind picked up and she ran to one of the bales for straw and finished spreading it. She filled Daisy's spot, then Gabe unhooked her and put her to bed. He shuffled back to the pots of water to get chicken into them.

Callie unhooked the other dogs, straining against the wind

that threatened to knock her over. Snowflakes whipped into her face.

"Show me where the chicken is," she shouted over the howling of the gale through the treetops.

He pointed to a container. She grabbed a bunch and followed behind him with the food.

"Too soon," he shouted.

"We need to get this done and get you inside." He looked ready to collapse.

"I feel as weak as a day-old kitten."

She believed it. His hands were shaking.

She gathered the bowls, ran back to the pot of clean boiling water and tossed them in. Already, she was having trouble seeing past the line of trees into the woods.

Gabe was right. Once one of these storms moved in, it roared across the landscape like a demon.

She spun around to determine what needed to be done next and her heart stopped. Gabe lay in a heap on the ground beside Daisy.

CHAPTER NINE

TYLER KNEW COPS weren't supposed to play favorites.

Where Tammy Trudeau was concerned, though, he had trouble holding back, had for a couple of years now. The way she dressed—demure white lace blouses and conservative skirts—was a direct contrast to her bright, sexy personality and drove him mad. He knew what she hid under those modest clothes. Tammy had a beautiful body and the greatest gams.

A schoolteacher in Accord, Tammy was a woman of contrasts and he liked that.

He sat in the cruiser on the edge of town on Friday evening waiting for her. Tucked into the shadowy edge of the Rocky Mountains, the small town looked like a life-size version of those miniature villages people put out at Christmas. Warm yellow lights shone from the shops, most closing up for the day. Tall black lamps with glass globes glowed out of baskets of winter greenery hung high on each post.

A light snowfall overnight had drifted from a smattering of clouds, covering the old snow with a virginal duvet.

Accord settled into its Friday night routine. People headed home to family dinners or to the two restaurants the town boasted, and Sheriff Jordan waited for Tammy Trudeau.

Any minute now.

Sure enough, dead on time, she sped through the last intersection on Main Street in her white, spit-shined Neon. She was driving the girls home.

Putting the cruiser into gear, Tyler pulled out onto the small highway out of town.

The town had mounted American flags on every second hydro pole in every direction for half a mile out of town. Flag after flag flapped hard in the rising wind—the sight of which never tired him. It raised a lump in his throat.

He knew the exact moment Tammy realized he was following her. She accelerated.

He grinned and turned his flashers on.

The Neon's brake lights came on and it drifted onto the shoulder. Tyler stepped out of the cruiser into the crisp Colorado air and approached Tammy's car, the cold so dry his boots crunched on the snow-covered road.

When Tammy rolled down her window, Tyler leaned his arm on the car door. Melanie Tormé, Tammy's best friend, sat in the passenger seat. Suzie and Cheryl Vinnie, sisters he called the twin twitterers, sat in the back.

"Is there a problem, Officer?" Tammy's voice, still high and breathy at thirty, sent shivers along his skin. A person might be excused for thinking Tammy a sweet little pushover, but she had a spine most men would envy. She straightened it now, pushing her breasts forward. "Did I do something wrong?"

She never wore a coat while she drove and, in the chilly air, he saw the barest hint of her nipples peak behind her beige cardigan.

Tyler, in the middle of enjoying the view from above, almost missed the question.

"Ma'am, you have any idea how fast you were driving?"

"I wasn't that bad, was I?" Her smile lit the interior of the vehicle. The sisters in the backseat whispered and giggled.

"I've got a mind to teach you a lesson." He pulled his ticket book and a pen out of his pocket.

Tammy put her small bare hand on the worn leather of his

glove, stalling him from writing. "Officer, please don't. I'll slow down. Honest. I'll do anything you want."

Her smile spoke of sweetness and light. Goodness. Innocence. Her eyes told a different story.

"Why, Miz Trudeau," Tyler drawled as he stared into her glass-blue eyes. "Are you in the habit of propositioning members of the law?"

"Only you, Officer." She smiled her adorable smile.

Melanie leaned across Tammy. "Will you forget about the speeding if we promise to buy tickets to the next Policeman's Ball?"

Tyler stopped writing, looked at Melanie and said, "Mel, here in Accord, policemen don't have Balls."

Even as the words tumbled out of his mouth, he wanted to bite them back.

The stunned silence following that idiotic statement thundered in the dark frozen landscape.

Lord, if only the road would split open and swallow him whole. The next moment, the ladies broke into peals of laughter.

Tyler's face heated so hard and fast it was a wonder his ears didn't steam. He folded his ticket book carefully, stuck it into his pocket and trudged back to his cruiser. He smacked his hand against his forehead. Damn, when his partner heard about this, he'd never let Tyler live it down. And his partner *would* hear about it. The whole town would, thanks to the Vinnie sisters.

It was an old joke he'd heard years ago. True to her trouble-rousing character, Melanie had set him up and, like the naive fool that he was, he'd walked right in. Stupid.

He heard footsteps running behind him a split second before Tammy grabbed his arm and spun him around.

In the headlights of his cruiser, her white teeth flashed in a grin.

She took fistfuls of his sheepskin jacket and hauled him down to lock lips with him. Her tongue entered his mouth, bringing with it boldness and visions of more where that came from. She tasted like hints of black tea with orange zest, her favorite.

He tried to resist, just wanted to get into his cruiser and race away from his own stupidity, but Tammy Trudeau knew her way around a French kiss.

He pulled her off her feet, hard against him, and savored every drop of heat and passion her mouth offered. By the time he finished with her, they were breathing hard. The steam of their breath mingled, as reluctant to end the intimacy as they were.

"Policemen don't have balls?" Tammy murmured. "I beg to differ."

Ty rested his forehead on top of hers then set her away. "Get on home now. Safely. There's a storm brewing."

She sprinted back to the car, but turned with her hand on the door.

"Ty?"

"Yeah, honey?"

"Don't forget to pick up a quart of milk on your way home."

"You got it." Ty drove back to town to fill out his reports for the day.

An hour later, he pulled into his driveway. The house sat dark in the snowy landscape save for one light that glowed in the kitchen window.

A small figure leaned on the fence of the bison pasture. Tammy. Tyler high-stepped through the snow toward her.

Just shy of reaching her, he stopped and waited. The wind ruffled her hair. The moon, not yet completely risen, lit a softly waving halo around her blond curls. She should have worn a hat if she was going to stand out here in the cold.

Clouds on the horizon foretold of the storm barreling down

on them, but they had a few moments yet before they obliterated the moon and sent every sensible person indoors.

In the unearthly blue glow of the moon, Hirsute wandered over to the fence, enormous and shaggy, blowing woofs of vapor as he trudged through the snow. He went to Tammy first. She was his favorite, after all.

She reached out her mittened hands and the bison sniffed for treats. She didn't have any, opting instead to give him soft pats on his muzzle and forehead. He lapped up the attention.

Hirsute shuffled, his leathery legs rubbing against each other, his big body radiating heat. Weighing in at two thousand pounds, Hirsute was the largest bison in the herd, and hairy in his raggedy winter coat. He stood with his big head in Tammy's small hands, like an overgrown baby nuzzling its mother, and Tammy looked delicate beside him. Tyler liked that delicacy that lurked beneath the sass.

"He could stand there all night letting you pet him." His voice jumped out of the hallowed stillness of the evening.

So could Tyler. There was something about Tammy's touch....

She studied him over her shoulder.

"Hey, honey," she said softly.

He stepped closer. Hirsute raised his head and stared at Tyler with eyes too small for his oversize skull with what Tyler could swear was reproach.

"Hey," he told the big animal, "it's my turn with her."

Hirsute snorted and shuffled in the snow. He didn't want to leave Tammy. Who said bison were dumb beasts?

The wind picked up. "We're getting weather. Storm should be here soon."

A chill rippled up his back—one of his witchy feelings that he got before something went wrong. Like when he'd sensed as a kid that Dad wasn't coming back home. Like when he'd known that Gabe had been injured in Afghanistan.

Standing here with Tammy, he shoved that chill away. No. Nothing was wrong here.

He placed his hands on her shoulders. "Let's go inside."

Her pale skin shone in the moonlight. She sighed and her breath frosted on the air.

Tyler might have moved first, or maybe Tammy. A split second later, she was hard against his chest with his arms wrapped around her.

God, he loved this woman.

He gave Hirsute a slap on the shoulder to send him back out to pasture, then grabbed his girlfriend's hand, small and trusting in his. That trust intimidated him. He heard her teeth chatter and swung her up into his arms.

"Your boots are soaked. Why didn't you wait inside?"

"I knew you'd be home soon."

He carried her across the snow and into the house. He toed off his boots and walked straight into the kitchen.

"What smells so good in here?"

"Lasagna. I made a pan of it at home last night. It's reheating."

As always, Tyler wondered whether he should ask Tammy to move out of her apartment above the shop in town and into the house with him. Also as always, something held him back. Same with asking her to marry him.

Another chill rattled him. *Stop already.*

He put her down on a chair and knelt in front of her to take off her boots. His hands slid up under her skirt, over her shapely calves and great thighs.

She moaned but stopped him.

"The lasagna's ready."

Tyler turned off the oven. He had a different kind of appetite right now. He was starving for Tammy. Crazy for her. That chill had spooked him.

He squeezed her thigh and said, "Later, babe."

He carried her upstairs.

"I can walk, you know," she said, humming low in her throat.

He nuzzled her neck. He wanted her close. If he could lock her into a vault to keep her safe, he would. "Yeah, I know." He carried her into his bedroom.

The duvet and the rest of his bedding were dark chocolate, like the walls. He dropped Tammy onto the bed. Running his hands up her legs and under her skirt, he hauled off her panties and pantyhose.

He reached into the bedside table for a condom and wrapped himself.

Five minutes later, seated deeply inside of her, Tyler groaned and Tammy answered in kind.

CALLIE RAN ACROSS the clearing to Gabe, but stopped at Daisy's growl. Gabe lay on his back, his eyes closed. Snow coated his eyelashes and beard already. It was falling that fast now.

"Daisy." She forced her panic down and managed to sound soothing. "Let me help him."

She took a step closer. The hair on Daisy's back stood on end. Callie stopped.

If she didn't get Gabe on his feet soon, she wouldn't be able to find the house.

"Shhh," she crooned as she stepped closer. She squatted on her knees beside Gabe, pulled off her mitten and touched his forehead. She bit off a curse. He was burning up.

"Gabe," she whispered while a low growl emanated from Daisy's throat. Callie noted that the dog didn't stop her from helping Gabe, almost as though she understood that Callie needed to get close to help Daisy's owner.

"Wake up." She touched his cheek and he stirred.

Daisy's growl morphed into a whimper. She licked his

cheek. Gabe opened his eyes and blinked against the falling snow. "What—"

"You passed out." Callie slipped her hands under his armpits. "Stand. We have to get to the house now."

With Callie's help, Gabe staggered to his feet. "I'm weak. Sorry."

She wrapped his arm across her shoulders and together they stumbled to the back of the house, leaning into driving snow. Callie was breathing hard by the time they set foot inside and closed the door behind them.

"Where's your bedroom?"

"On the right." Gabe put one hand on the wall and his other on her shoulder and they made it to the bedroom together.

Beside the bed, she helped him take off his clothes. Oh goodness. Oh great balls of lust. He was gorgeous with a capital *G*.

Stop it. He's sick.

I know, but I'm not.

His body long, toned and muscular, his outdoor physical activity kept him as fit as any million-dollar athlete.

And she couldn't do a thing about it. He was sick and, worse, he was Nick's brother.

She stripped him to his drawers and he crawled under an old quilt.

"What's your doctor's phone number?"

He didn't respond. Out like a light.

Callie hurried to the front of the house where she guessed the living room would be. She turned on a floor lamp. An old flowered sofa and a couple of armchairs bracketed a fireplace. Boo got up from the hearth and ambled over. She sniffed Callie's boots. She'd forgotten to take them off.

She slipped out of them and carried them to the back door. Boo whined.

She let her outside. "Don't go far." Snow flew into the

house and she had to put her shoulder against the door to close it. Just as she arrived back in the living room, she heard Boo scratching to come back in.

Callie raced to let her back in then returned to the living room. She spotted the phone on a small end table with a drawer. Inside the drawer she found an ancient phone book. She thumbed through it until she found a name that started with *Dr.* and dialed the number.

After the third ring, someone finally answered and she said, "Dr. Travis? My name's Callie MacKintosh. I'm out at the Jordan house. Gabe is sick and I don't know what to do for him."

"How did you get my number?"

"I found it in an old address book. Gabe's unconscious. Are you his doctor?"

"I was, years ago. I'm retired now."

"Oh. Sorry I bothered you." A low sound of exasperation issued from her. "I don't know who to call."

"Tell me his symptoms."

"He's unconscious. Before he fell asleep, he complained of a headache and a sore throat. His eyes were watery. His knee was aching. He said it was the storm coming in and the shrapnel in his leg, but I saw him rubbing his shoulders, too."

"What else?"

"He was coughing a bit. His voice sounded rough. He's burning up, but I noticed his hands and feet were cold when I undressed him."

Travis seemed to be waiting for more.

"That's all I've got," Callie said. "Oh, wait, his skin is really pale, but his cheeks are red."

"Sounds like the flu."

"What should I do about it?"

"Ideally you'd get him into a clinic or doctor's office, but that's out of the question with the storm. It's going to be a bad one."

"That's what Gabe's knee said, too." She didn't ponder how ridiculous that sounded.

"Keep his extremities warm," Doc said. "Keep him warm until he complains and then cool him down with damp cloths as often as you have to."

Damp cloths. On his skin.

"If he wakes up, get fluids into him. Gallons of it. You got any chicken soup?"

"I don't know. I don't live here. I was just dogsledding with him."

"You're stuck there now."

"How long does the flu last?"

"Usually a week."

A week!

"You won't have to stay with him once the weather and roads clear, but you should be there a good couple of days. I'll give you his brother's number. Tyler should know where everything is in the house."

She wrote the number down.

"Spoon as much soup into him as you can. Science thinks it's an old wives' tale and does nothing, but I've known too many people who swear by it. It can't hurt."

"Anything else?"

"He can have painkillers for the headache. That's all for now. Call me when he wakes up and gives you more info."

"Will do. Thank you."

Callie glanced out the window, half hoping Gabe had been wrong about the storm, but heavy snow lashed the windows. It was here for a while.

She'd had plenty of experience with her mother's migraines, and with nursing herself through colds, but that was the extent of her skills.

In the bathroom cabinet, she found painkillers and carried them to the bedroom with a glass of water. She managed to wake Gabe up long enough to get a couple into him.

She called Ty. When he answered, she explained her problem.

"Gabe keeps a well-stocked freezer. It's in a room beside the back door. Check the fridge for vegetables." Ty cursed. "I wish I could get out there, but it wouldn't be smart to navigate those back roads. Call me if you need to know where anything is, day or night, especially if you lose power."

"Lose power! Oh dear lord, what should I do then?"

"You should get ready now. Put the receiver down for a minute. Don't hang up! Go to the back room where the freezer is. Gabe keeps kerosene lamps and a camp stove back there. You should see other stuff there, too, that you can use if you have to. There should be matches."

She heard Ty talk to someone then come back. "If the power goes out you'll lose heat. Is there wood inside the house beside the fireplace?"

"Yes. A lot of it. I've never started a fire before."

Ty gave her instructions. They sounded thorough.

"If anything goes wrong, call me back. Y'hear?"

"Don't worry. I will."

She hung up and took a deep breath. She was going to be busy. She called Nick and told him what was going on.

"Good. If he's feverish, maybe he'll tell you about the business. Let something slip that we can use against him."

"I didn't call to get instructions on how to sabotage the man," she admonished, her voice sharp. "I just wanted to let you know I'll be out of touch for a few days taking care of Gabe. Besides, there's a terrible storm here. I'm stuck at the old homestead."

"Fine. Use the situation however you can." Just as she was

about to hang up he said, "Your photos were beautiful, Callie. I met with the investors this morning. They loved them."

She glowed under Nick's praise. He gave it out so rarely.

In the back room, she found the freezer and opened it. Gabe had plenty of frozen food, including a couple of roasts and a whole chicken.

She brought the chicken out to the kitchen and went back for a camp stove and lanterns in case she needed them. She found a crank radio and matches. She also found a large flashlight.

After filling a pot with water to heat up for soup broth, on impulse, she called Information and was put through to Noah Cameron's Army Surplus store. When she explained what was happening, Noah gave her clear instructions on how to use the camping gear.

"Gabe will probably have the crank radio set to a local news station so you can get updates on the weather."

He asked what she'd done so far. She told him.

"Fill every pot and kettle with water. If you lose power, the pump will quit."

He gave her his personal home number in case she needed more advice if the power went out. "I'm just closing up shop."

She thanked him profusely.

"Not a problem. If you had to be stuck somewhere, it might as well be with Gabe. He's the most prepared guy I know besides me."

After she hung up, she calmed down. She had good resources at her fingertips. She could do this.

This town—the people here—were amazing.

Before starting on the soup, she looked in on Gabe. He'd thrown his sheet and quilt off. She put the back of her hand to his forehead. Still burning up.

She hurried to the kitchen and put the chicken into the simmering water with onions, carrots and celery that she found in the fridge. In a cupboard, she found thyme and bay leaves and peppercorns. It was the best she could do.

While the chicken simmered, she filled every container she could find with water then carried a full basin to the bedroom, along with a facecloth.

She dunked the cloth in the water, then dabbed it across Gabe's face. He seemed to follow the motion. She dipped the cloth again and dribbled water into Gabe's mouth. He swallowed and opened his mouth again, like a baby bird waiting for food.

She smoothed the damp towel over his shoulders, arms and chest, soaked it and wrung it out and continued down his legs. She did that over and over again, cooling Gabe as best she could.

"Gabe," she whispered close to his ear. Despite the fever, his hair smelled like shampoo and his skin like soap. "Can you roll over?"

He opened his eyes and stared at her, not quite comprehending where he was or what she asked of him. With one hand under his shoulder, she lifted and he got the idea. When he lay flat on his stomach, she cooled his back and legs with the dampened cloth top to bottom and then again.

When she stopped, Gabe moaned.

"I'll be back," she said. "I need to check the broth."

She turned the chicken in the big pot and returned to Gabe. He'd seemed stiff and sore on their dogsledding ride. He still lay on his stomach. Sitting on the side of the bed, she rubbed his shoulders. He moaned, but it was a good one that said he appreciated what she was doing.

Twisting her spine hurt, so she straddled him to massage his back. Oh, it was so close to a terrible mistake. Gabe was a fine-looking man with beautiful skin. It felt like sleek satin under her hands. She worked until her arms ached then left the room, afraid to touch him any longer, afraid of the tenderness that flooded her when near him.

When she was halfway to the kitchen, the lights went out.

Profound darkness.

Here we go.

CHAPTER TEN

TAMMY HUMMED WHILE she made a pot of coffee. Tyler was still upstairs, taking a shower. He wouldn't be long, though. When she'd come downstairs after their lovemaking, Tammy had turned the oven back on. The lasagna should be warm enough by now.

She glanced through the kitchen window to the backyard. Swirling snow obliterated the three outbuildings she knew by heart—a barn that housed Tyler's horse and food for the bison, the garage with his riding lawn mower, two snowmobiles and a dirt bike, and the original owner's old outhouse, with the crescent moon cutout in the door, that Tyler kept around as a joke.

She loved this property, loved that she stayed here every weekend with Ty.

During the week, she lived in her apartment above the gift shop she'd inherited from her aunt. A couple of women ran the shop for her while she pursued her teaching career. Looking out on Main Street wasn't so bad, but at the back, where her bedroom window was, she sat over the laneway and garages of the houses on Nelson Street, behind Main.

Here, though? This land? Beautiful.

Ty had never asked Tammy to marry him. She had yet to figure out what was holding him back. She loved him. She thought he loved her. So what was the problem?

She planned to find out tonight. All sorts of women around her were having babies and it was her turn. She needed to talk to Ty, to ask *him* what the problem was instead of trying to figure it out on her own.

And if he said he didn't want to marry her because he didn't love her? What would she do then? Walk away?

Maybe all he needed was a nudge in the right direction. If it turned out that he'd been stringing her along, that he'd never intended to marry her, she'd have to make a decision then. And she'd better be certain ahead of time that she could live with whatever she decided.

Would Ty do that to her, though? He wasn't a dishonest man. He cared for her. His every touch said as much. When he made love to her, he did it with his whole being. Could a man have sex with a woman with such intensity if he didn't feel something for her?

She threw a salad together too roughly. It had to be tonight. She couldn't wait any longer. It had already been four years. What on earth was she waiting for?

She'd expected a ring at Christmas. Before that at Thanksgiving. Before then on Valentine's Day.

It was a new year. She couldn't continue to mark them off by holidays that didn't deliver what she wanted.

Just as she set the lasagna on a trivet on the table, someone knocked at the front door. In this weather? An emergency? She didn't want Tyler out in this storm. She turned off the oven and walked down the hallway. She heard Tyler on the move upstairs, talking on the phone. Good, he'd finished his shower. She thought she heard him say his brother Gabe's name. What was up with Gabe? They rarely spoke.

Tammy opened the front door and stared at the young teenager waiting on the veranda, covered head to toe with snow, her arms crossed over her body.

"You're frozen," Tammy blurted. "Get inside."

Snow blew in.

The girl stepped into the house and Tammy closed the door. She didn't recognize her. "Can I help you?"

A little younger than the girls in Tammy's grade eight class, she bit her lip and nodded. "I want to see Tyler Jordan."

Despite not recognizing her from town, Tammy did think she looked familiar, but she couldn't place where she'd seen her before.

"Sure." She called up the stairs. "Tyler, there's someone here to see you."

"Be right down."

She turned back to the girl who'd taken off her toque. Blond hair stuck out in all directions with static electricity. Coffee-brown eyes watched her steadily, staring as though Tammy were an oddity.

"Are you his wife?"

"No." Confused by those flashes of dim recognition, Tammy asked, "Have we met before?"

The girl shook her head. Her square jaw moved, as though she were chewing on something. Or nervous.

"Are you sure?" Tammy asked.

Maybe thirteen years old or so, the girl dropped her knapsack on the floor. She peered around, cataloging everything about the house.

Spotting Tyler's big shearling ranch coat, she touched it, almost reverently.

The hair on Tammy's arms stood up. There was something going on here that had a chill running through her blood, a fear that life was about to change in a big way, that the talk Tammy wanted to have with Ty was about to become moot.

She sensed, no, *knew,* that it was already too late. She had let too much time slide and this girl was about to blow their complacent world apart.

While Tyler ran downstairs tucking his shirt into his pants, Tammy continued to stare at the girl, unable to look away, as if an accident were about to happen in front of her and she was helpless to stop it. "You have a visitor." Her voice sounded like someone else's, toneless, empty.

Tyler smiled at the girl. "How can I help you?"

He obviously didn't know her.

Tammy looked from one to the other, once and then again, and she knew. A surge of nausea rose from the pit of her stomach. The young woman was the spitting image of Tyler.

There was more, though. She had soft golden curls and looked an awful lot like Tammy had at that age. What was going on?

"Hi," the girl said shyly. "My name's Ruby."

Tyler continued to stare, but his look became wary, as if he too were apprehended by a terrible suspicion.

Before he could open his mouth, Ruby said, "I'm your daughter."

IN DARKNESS MORE profound than she'd ever known, darker even than the one in Mom's closet in which Callie had spent so much time rocking herself to sleep, she felt her way to the kitchen with a hand on the wall, each step feeling as though she were stepping into an abyss, and grappled for the kerosene lamps and candles. She found the matches, but her hands shook.

Calm down.

This isn't Mom's closet. Mom isn't sick. You aren't a child.

Finally, she managed to get everything lit—two kerosene lamps and six emergency candles. She should conserve, use only half of everything—who knew how long this would last?—but that darkness darker than death spooked her.

She turned on the burners of the camp stove.

With the strange hiss of the kerosene lamps and the wind howling around the house creating an otherworldly soundtrack, her strength returned.

Get busy.

She took the chicken out of the pot and cut it into portions then put it back in to finish cooking through.

She chopped vegetables, all the while thinking *I am a pioneer in this dark formless wilderness, and I am coping.*

TY SAT AT THE KITCHEN TABLE with Tammy and the young girl who had just blown his world apart.

He was a father.

Ruby chattered away about the storm.

"Is it always like this? I've only been in snow once before when Mom took me skiing. This is awesome. It was really hard to see. I could barely find the house."

She was lucky she'd made it here safely, crazy girl.

He was a father.

He couldn't take it in. His mind couldn't compute.

All he could do was stare at the little piece of himself sitting across the table. With those eyes, that jaw, yeah, she was his. He and Winona had made this pretty young thing with the gangly limbs?

There was no need to ask Ruby who her mother was. She was exactly the right age to be his and Winona's. The tiny divot in her chin matched his. She was his daughter, all right. The sense of wonder flooding him warred with anger.

Why the hell hadn't Winona told him he had a child? He would have manned up and raised her, supported her, loved her. Above all else, he would have loved the daylights out of her. He didn't much go in for violence, but the urge to punch a hole in the wall rattled him. God, all of those years lost. Thirteen of them.

And Winona's pregnancy. She would have been beautiful carrying his babe. He wished he'd seen her body ripen and change with Ruby in her womb.

Ruby. Pretty name. Pretty girl.

Wow, this was surreal. Underneath his shock, he was overwhelmed. If he'd been there years ago through Winona's pregnancy, he would have had time to settle into the idea of parenthood, but here it was staring him in the face without a trace of warning, without an anchor to ground him or a compass to orient him. Just poof! *I'm your daughter.*

A small part of his heart took flight. He wasn't getting any younger and here was a tiny piece of himself already born and grown.

He let out a long sigh and Tammy's gaze shot to his. He'd been avoiding her eyes since the girl arrived. Tammy didn't yet know it, but trouble was heading to town, and her name was Winona.

Buckets of fire, the shit was going to hit the fan. He should have told Tammy about Winona. How? I started dating you because you were the spitting image of my first love? How weird was that? Tammy was going to be devastated.

Ty hadn't been a virgin when he'd met Winona, but he sure as hell had never loved before her.

Ruby finally stopped talking.

"How did you know about me?" Ty asked, unable to keep the wonder out of his voice.

"I found my birth certificate."

Winona had put his name on it? That surprised him. He'd learned to his detriment that Winona was not always a truthful woman.

"How did you find me?"

"On the internet. You can find out anything on the web."

"How did you get here?"

She didn't answer right away, just stared at the table, the sink, the walls, anything but him.

"Ruby, how did you get here?" Tammy asked, her teacher tone in place and apparently effective, because Ruby answered Tammy right away.

"I took an airplane then a bus."

"You were able to buy a ticket on your own? You're only thirteen."

"I used my mom's credit card."

"Hmm," Tammy said. "I guess we'd better call your mother to tell her where you are."

That rattled Ty. Yeah, he'd have to talk to Winona.

"Not yet," Ruby cried. "I want to get to know my dad." She stood up. "Where's the washroom?"

Tammy told her and she left the room.

When Winona showed up...Tyler could envision the pain it would cause Tammy. The hurt...the anger...

Tammy didn't deserve the shit that was about to rain down on her, and all of it Ty's fault. He slammed his coffee mug onto the table, stood and hauled Tammy against his chest. That love he'd been thinking about earlier in the evening backed up in his throat with a desperation that robbed him of breath.

Why hadn't he ever told her he loved her before? He should now. The words wouldn't come, though. In the years since Winona had booted his tail from here to kingdom come, he hadn't grown a backbone, still didn't have the courage to commit to another woman without the fear that Tammy would rip out his heart like Winona had.

If that bed of indecision hadn't been plowed with the seeds of his own parents' problems, he might have survived Winona better. He might be a better man for Tammy.

The fight he'd overheard the night before Dad left on his last trip had terrorized Ty. The screaming had been intense, coupled with the dread that life was about to change too quickly for a seven-year-old boy. His mom yelled, "If you leave this time, don't bother coming back. I mean it."

Ty had run to his room and had covered his head with his blankets, trying to hide from the words. He hadn't even had his big brother there to comfort him. Gabe had ridden his bike into town to pick up a last-minute item for Dad.

Despite Mom's objections, the following morning, Dad left anyway.

He never returned from that trip.

"I can't breathe," Tammy mumbled and Ty eased his grip.

Taking her small chin in his big fingers, he kissed her, but not with this evening's horny desperate lust. Now he was gentle, tender, so afraid these kisses might be his last with her.

When she saw Winona they would be.

Ruby returned to the kitchen and Tyler stepped away from Tammy.

"I need to call your mother," he said. "What's her number?"

Ruby looked like she would protest, but Ty raised a staying hand. "She needs to know where you are. She'll be worried."

Ruby rattled off a number that Ty wrote down. "Where is this?"

"Mendocino."

So Winona had stayed in California. Ty had studied law enforcement there, had wanted to get away from small-town life for a while, and had met Winona in a bar one night.

The sex had started their first night and had been meteoric. To that point in his life, he'd never experienced anything so hot or so brilliant. For him, every time was better than the last. It mustn't have been the same for Winona. Apparently, she'd soared with him, but crashed and burned. An on/off woman, somehow she'd turned a corner too quickly and had found someone else.

After she'd ripped his heart out of his body, he'd returned to Accord.

He'd heard she'd gotten married soon after he left. Too soon after. There had been more than one man in her life. Ty had never known a more profound betrayal. Now he had to talk to the woman again and conflicting emotions buzzed through him—anger that she'd hidden his daughter and hope that she still cared a little for him. How pathetic was that?

He picked up his cell and walked to the living room, away from Tammy and Ruby. After he punched in her number he wiped his sweaty hands on his jeans. A man shouldn't feel this nervous calling an old flame, especially not when he felt so much for his current girlfriend.

He let it ring for a long time before ending the call, let down but also strangely relieved that he hadn't had to talk to her. Not yet. Not until he got used to the idea.

Tammy and he put Ruby to bed in the spare bedroom. Together, they got the house ready in case of a blackout. A blizzard in January in Colorado. A power failure was inevitable.

He hoped Callie was coping. She'd seemed a capable woman.

Ty strung sturdy ropes between the house and the barn and the bison pen so he wouldn't get disoriented and lose his way if the storm still raged in the morning.

When he stepped back into the house, Tammy was waiting for him.

"Who was she?" she asked.

"Just a girlfriend in college. Nothing serious." Major understatement. He pulled her into his arms. "I never knew we'd made a baby. This will all work out."

"Are you sure, Ty?"

He didn't know. Not for certain. This clusterfart of a situation could turn out so many different ways.

He should have told Tammy a long time ago that he loved her, but now Winona rose between them like a ghostly specter.

Ty might have started dating Tammy because she looked like his old girlfriend, but he'd fallen for her. For *her*. She was humble where Winona was vain, compassionate where Winona was selfish.

Winona had that passion, though, that could set the night on fire. Ty didn't know whether he was the same man he'd been back then, when he wanted fireworks so hot they scorched.

Why was he comparing? Tammy and he burned up the sheets pretty damn good. But what if he saw Winona and fell for her again? Where would that leave him and Tammy?

Over the years, he'd wondered. What if Winona wanted him back? How much did he still care for her? *Did* he still carry a torch?

Just after the power went out, he kissed Tammy good-night then went downstairs to call Winona again.

Still no answer. Still that mixture of disappointment and relief.

He called her repeatedly through the night but never got a response. There didn't seem to be a way to leave a message, either. He called the cops in Mendocino, but no missing person report had been issued for Ruby. He told them where she was in case Winona contacted them.

Why wouldn't Winona be worried about her missing daughter?

At two in the morning, he gave up and went to bed. He wanted to roll toward Tammy and take her in his arms, but somehow, for no good reason that he could pinpoint, it felt all wrong.

A DEEP MOAN from the bedroom snagged Callie's attention.

Grabbing a lantern, she rushed to Gabe's room and found him thrashing on the bed, the bedsheet tangled around his legs.

His forehead was even hotter than it had been. There had been a couple of bags of ice in Gabe's deep freezer. She retrieved a bowl from the kitchen then turned off the burner under the soup. Gabe wouldn't need it for a while. As well, she grabbed the second lantern and blew out the candles.

She made her way to the back room where she filled the bowl with ice.

Back in Gabe's bedroom, she ran ice cubes over his body, working quickly to cool him. Her heart pounded. Did fevers kill people? She knew a child could die from one, or so she thought, but big, strapping, healthy men like Gabe? She prayed not.

After what seemed an eternity, he cooled down.

Afraid to trust that she was doing all that she could, she stumbled to the phone in the living room. God, she was tired. She called Doc Travis.

When he answered, he sounded groggy. Good lord, she hadn't even noticed the time.

"I'm so sorry. It's Callie. What time is it?"

She heard rustling, then, "It's twenty after three in the morning. What's going on?"

"Gabe's so hot, Doctor. I wiped him down a million times with a damp cloth and he was okay for a while." Her voice cracked. She was scared. Terrified. She'd never had a person's life in her hands before. "Then he got really hot. He was burning. I've been rubbing ice all over him and he seems better, but he isn't going to die, is he?"

"As long as what you're doing makes him feel better, keep doing it."

"But then he gets really hot again and I get worried."

"That's part of the illness. Rub him down with cool water as much as you need to. Maybe go a little easy on the ice if his skin starts to feel too cold."

"Okay." She breathed out heavily. "Okay. Thanks. Sorry about waking you up. I panicked."

"That's okay. Took me back to old times when I was still on the job."

Callie went back to the kitchen. She took one of the bowls she'd filled with water earlier in case of a power failure and carried it to Gabe's room where she added ice. Picking up the cloth, she dunked it into the cool water and started in again cooling his body.

An hour later, her arms were ready to fall out of their sockets. She needed to lie down. She'd planned to sleep on the sofa tonight, but "tonight" must be close to being over. Not that she could tell by looking out the window.

A wall of white, accompanied by the howl of the wind that had become white noise to her, blocked any inkling of how late it was. Or how early in the morning.

Afraid to leave the room in case she wouldn't hear him call when she fell asleep in the living room, she lay down beside him.

She didn't think she'd ever been so tired in her life. She needed to close her eyes, just for a few moments. For half an hour.

Send For
2 FREE BOOKS
Today!

I accept your offer!

Please send me two free Harlequin® Superromance® novels and two mystery gifts (gifts worth about $10). I understand that these books are completely free—even the shipping and handling will be paid—and I am under no obligation to purchase anything, ever, as explained on the back of this card.

❏ I prefer the regular-print edition
135/336 HDL FNM5

❏ I prefer the larger-print edition
139/339 HDL FNM5

Please Print

FIRST NAME

LAST NAME

ADDRESS

APT.#   CITY

STATE/PROV.   ZIP/POSTAL CODE

Visit us online at
www.ReaderService.com

H-SR-S13

CHAPTER ELEVEN

TY RETURNED TO the kitchen where Ruby and Tammy sat. He'd just called Winona and still no answer.

Ruby must have left home early on Friday to reach Accord by Friday evening. Now it was Saturday morning. Didn't Winona wonder where she was? Wasn't she worried?

They wore multiple sweaters to keep warm in the cold house.

"Let's move to the living room," he said. "I built a fire."

They carried their coffee, and hot chocolate for Ruby, to the other room.

"Is there any reason why your mom isn't answering her phone? Why isn't she worried about you and trying to find you?"

Ruby slumped in her seat. "She thinks I'm staying with a friend for the weekend. She's at a spa. She always turns off her phone when she goes. She calls it her 'me' time."

"So there's no point in me continuing to call her. She thinks you're safe."

"Yeah."

"You should have told me."

"Mom isn't always predictable. Sometimes she changes her plans and does different things."

Yeah, he remembered how mercurial Winona could be.

No sense trying to contact her today. He'd try again tomorrow.

GABE ROLLED OVER and wrapped his arms around the woman
lying beside him.

Then his eyes flew open.

Callie MacKintosh! What? How?

Just as quickly as he'd opened his eyes, he slammed them
shut. They burned, felt gritty as sand on a hot August day.

His whole body ached, as though he'd thrown himself
headlong into an empty pool. He had the flu or something
that made him feel like death half-baked.

Callie stirred and his arms locked around her reflexively.
He didn't want her to go anywhere. She felt right in his bed.

He peeked under the bedsheet. She was wearing clothes.
He had on his underwear. Nothing had happened.

Too bad.

He ran a finger down her soft cheek. She looked tired.

Tiny red freckles ran across her nose. Otherwise, her skin
was unblemished. Pure. She smelled sweet, like flowers. He
leaned forward and sniffed. It was her hair.

It was a mess. He ran his fingers through it to straighten
it out. It was barely a couple of inches long, pixie-ish and
chili-red.

A chill had settled in the room. The power was off. Before
long, it would be freezing in here.

He needed to wake her. If they were in a blackout, stuff
needed to be done.

Rolling over, he took a look around the room. A kerosene
lantern burned on the bedside table. So, she'd managed to
find one. Good.

He rolled back onto his side to face Callie. Her eyes were
wide open and watching him. He'd awakened her. This close
he could drown in how green they were, like a meadow after
a spring rain, fresh and bright and alive. She had shadows
under her eyes, though.

He had a vague fevered memory of her small hands on

his hot body, of her easing his fever with cold cloths. Those hands had also massaged his aching muscles. She'd been taking care of him.

"Hey," she said. "How do you feel?"

"Better. Because of you, I'm guessing."

"No fever?"

"Seems to be gone."

She shrugged. "Are you hungry?"

"Starving."

He moved to get up, but she held him still with a small hand against the hair on his chest, each nail painted perfectly with pink polish.

"I'll get you some soup." She pushed until he lay back down. Good thing. He felt like crap.

"I might have a can in the cupboard."

"I made fresh."

Homemade?

She left the room before he could ask her anything. He checked his watch. Nine in the morning. At a guess, he'd say he'd slept through since early yesterday evening.

The last thing he remembered was feeding the dogs. Had he finished? Were any left hungry?

He rolled up to sit on the side of the bed, but the room spun. When he tried to stand, his knees gave out.

He swore. A hard wind buffeted the old house, but all Gabe could see through the window was a white sheet of snow.

Callie entered the room with a large mug in one hand, a spoon and serviette in the other.

"Sit back against the headboard." She set the soup on the bedside table and fluffed his pillow behind him. "I didn't make it too hot, so you should be able to drink it right away."

He took a sip and his gaze shot to hers. "This is good. Really good."

"Thanks. I like to cook." She pulled a rocking chair close

to the bed. "I've never had to cook on a camp stove before, though."

"You found the stove. Good."

"I called Tyler. He told me where you store stuff. Later, when I was afraid I wouldn't be able to figure everything out, I called Noah and he walked me through it all."

She shook her head a little. "They were so nice, and so worried about me being here alone with you sick."

He heard the wonder in her voice. Yeah, the people of Accord were that good. He'd forgotten what a small community could be like when you needed them.

She laughed. "I called Dr. Travis."

"Travis! He's been retired for ten years or more."

"I didn't know that. I found his name in an old address book. He told me what to do. Said I should feed you chicken soup, so—" she swept her hand toward him "—you have homemade chicken soup."

A slow smile spread across his face. She was proud of herself. *He* was proud of her. He finished the soup.

"More?" she asked. "I used a whole chicken so there's lots."

"Later. I need to sleep again."

He slid over to leave room for her, but she shook her head. "I'm going to lie on the sofa. Where can I get a blanket?"

"It will get real cold in the house soon."

She rubbed her arms. "It already is."

"In the hall closet, there are a bunch of quilts. Lay them out on the floor in the living room. Build a fire. I'll be out in a minute to help you."

"No you won't. You'll rest. Ty told me how to make a good fire."

She was gone before he could protest.

He heard her build a fire then get bedding from the closet. A while later, she came in and said, "I've made a bed for you."

He shuffled out to the living room and lay on the floor in front of the fire. She followed with the quilt from his bed.

She didn't lie with him, though, and that disappointed him more than it should have.

She curled up in a sleeping bag on the sofa, facing him. They stared at each other and, as her eyes drifted shut and her red eyelashes fanned her cheeks, a peace settled over him that he hadn't felt in a long, long time.

Soon, the only sound in the room was of her breathing and the pop of resin on a log in the fire.

CALLIE AWOKE TO a sound she didn't recognize. Where was she?

She saw Gabe on the floor and remembered. He was shivering. The sound she'd heard was of him groaning. She jumped up and stirred the ashes. How long had she slept? Wind still rolled around the house but with less ferocity. Maybe the storm was wearing itself out.

When she had the fire going full tilt, she ran to Gabe's room and flung open dresser drawers until she found a warm long-sleeved undershirt. She found a heavy flannel shirt in his closet.

She carried them back to the living room and managed to rouse him enough to get him into them. Still his teeth chattered. She hauled the sleeping bag from the sofa and spread it over the quilts that covered him then climbed in beside him. He dragged her into his arms flush against his chest, as though he'd crawl inside of her if he could.

She didn't mind. She wrapped her arms across his strong back and held him while he slept.

SOMETHING WARM AND WET touched Gabe's hand and he heard whimpering. He came awake instantly and tried to orient himself.

Boo nudged his hand.

Callie lay in his arms. He didn't remember her climbing under the blankets with him.

The fire had gone out and a profound darkness enveloped the room.

Gabe heard whimpering again and realized it wasn't the dog. It was Callie.

He touched her shoulder. "What's wrong?"

She startled then said, "Too dark. Too quiet." Her voice sounded strange, shaky—too unlike the woman he thought of as spirit and backbone personified.

He stood to build up the fire. She stopped him with a hand flung out that connected with his knee in the blackness.

"Don't leave!" Her voice rang with panic.

He didn't reach out, afraid that he might startle her in the darkness. "I'm just going to make a fire."

"Okay." He barely heard her childlike whisper.

He waited until his dizziness passed, then hunkered down in front of the fireplace and stirred up the ash until he found red coal. He added kindling, waited for it to catch and then added a log.

She watched him with wide eyes, a mist of terror still shrouding the green.

The fire spat and crackled and she seemed to settle a little. He added another log and stepped aside so the fire would warm her, would bring her relief from the icy fear gripping her.

"Can you turn on the lights?" Her fist wrinkled a handful of the top quilt. He tried a floor lamp. Nothing happened.

"We still don't have electricity. Looks like the kerosene lamp ran through all its fuel. Want me to get another one?"

"No, that's okay." She seemed to be trying to pull herself together. "Why is it so quiet?"

He cocked his head and listened. "Storm's died out. There's no wind anymore."

"I took your bed," she said. "You were shivering. Your teeth were chattering so I crawled in with you."

She was babbling. Gabe settled on his haunches in front of her, ignoring the weakness in his knees. "What's wrong, Callie?"

"Lie down with me. Please. I—I can't be alone right now."

Gabe lay down beside her. She turned onto her back so her side touched his.

"You're the one shivering now," he said. "Boo, come here." He reached across Callie and patted the quilt on her far side.

Boo walked over, licked Callie's face then lay down flush beside her.

When her shivering abated, Gabe whispered, "What is this all about?"

She didn't speak for a minute, just stared at the ceiling and slowly eased into a semblance of relaxation.

"You'll think I'm nuts." Her voice sounded less shaky. Thank God.

"Probably."

She looked at him with a hint of defiance before she understood that he was joking. Her answering smile looked forlorn.

"It was my mom. When I was growing up, she used to have really bad migraines."

"So she kept the house quiet? And dark?"

"Worse. She used to close heavy curtains over her bedroom window and go into her closet, close the door and not come out for a day or two." She lifted one arm out from under the quilts and rubbed her eyes. "Mom came from England only a few months before I was born so she didn't know anyone here. The first time she had a migraine, when I was too young to understand what was going on, she took me into the closet with her. It was so dark. So quiet. I should have been okay because I was close to my mom, but she was like a block of ice. I mean, in the way she felt, unmoving, unresponsive. It happened so many times when I was a baby and a toddler. We'd sit in the closet for hours. She didn't talk. She would have a stash of diapers for me and a bottle."

"Why didn't she breastfeed you? That might have helped you feel less alone."

"I asked her that years later. She said her migraines made her so weak she couldn't hold me. I would lie in a cocoon of blankets and she would hold the bottle to my mouth."

"Did it happen often?"

"I'm guessing about once a month. We would stay in the darkness, in silence, for as long as it took for Mom's headache to go away. After I stopped wearing diapers, she would take me to the bathroom, get me a snack and then bring me right back to the closet. Her face looked bad. She didn't even look like my young, pretty mom."

Gabe touched her hand. He'd never heard anything like what Callie was describing. He shook his head, ruefully remembering how he'd thought she'd never known hardship. Her mother, through no fault of her own, had screwed Callie. But then he thought of his own parents and their faults, his mom's need of his dad and his dad's need to get away, regularly, to climb whatever mountain needed climbing, no matter that he had a wife and children to support. Didn't all parents screw their kids up one way or another? All they ever really did was their best and hope that it was good enough.

Callie rubbed her forehead, as though one of her mother's headaches had invaded her own mind.

"Eventually, when I got a little older, she let me stay in my own room, but I still couldn't make a sound. I got used to taking care of myself, and of her when she needed it."

"Where was your dad?"

"I don't know. I never met him. Mom would never tell me

about him." She stared at the ceiling. "He lived in England. She never married him. She was pregnant when she left and came here to the States to live alone."

Gabe could imagine the terror of the woman alone and pregnant in a strange land, with no support nearby.

"She would never tell me why she did that. I've never met my grandparents. She never wanted me to, so I guessed maybe they wanted her to abort and she wouldn't. Either that, or they might have kicked her out."

An overreaction in this day and age. "So she ended up here alone."

"Yes, and I understand why she did what she did. I was a baby. She couldn't crawl into her dark quiet closet and leave me untended so she took me in with her. Unfortunately, in order to deal with her migraine, she had to crawl inside of herself to kill the pain."

"So while you were in the quiet darkness, you thought your mom had abandoned you."

"Yes. And when she felt better, we left the closet. Then she was herself again."

"So, darkness and silence make you feel abandoned."

"Over and over again. I understand where my fear stems from, but I haven't figured out how to get rid of it. My brain understands that it's an irrational fear, but my heart succumbs every time."

It was going to take a superhuman feat of self-discipline for Callie to get over it. "I wish I could help in some way."

She shrugged.

He couldn't lie beside Callie much longer. He wanted to soothe away her fears, her vulnerabilities, but the only way he could think to do it was to love the daylights out of her, and that would be for *his* sake, not hers.

Her eyes haunted him, bottle-green to match the sweater she wore. They had been brilliant in the sun the other day, like spring grass, but up close with firelight flickering in them, they were dark and deep like precious gems.

Again he thought of those dark times in Afghanistan when he'd dreamed of the green grass of home. He'd had enough darkness to last a lifetime.

"Callie," he breathed. The woman was color and sass and trouble.

He'd worked hard to shape a predictable life.

Now here was this woman turning it upside down merely by being here.

His body wanted to know hers intimately.

He wanted her.

"You're okay now?"

She nodded and crawled out of the makeshift bed, almost as though she'd read his mind.

"I'll go make dinner. You rest."

She turned on every kerosene lamp in the kitchen and lit all of the candles. They had big bowls of chicken soup and bread from the fridge.

After cleaning up, all while Gabe rested to recoup his strength, she curled into the sleeping bag on the sofa and rested her cheek on her hand. "What about the dogs? They haven't eaten today."

Gabe crawled into the quilts, cold without Callie beside him. "They'll be hunkered in against the storm. We'll feed them in the morning."

"*I'll* feed them. You'll get better."

He nodded.

She blinked, slowly, and said, "Thank you."

After her eyes closed and Gabe was certain she slept, he turned off the lamps and blew out the candles in the kitchen. He built up the fire in case she awakened during the night.

CHAPTER TWELVE

On Saturday evening, Ty and Ruby sat at the kitchen table playing cards by the light of a kerosene lamp.

Tammy cleaned up after dinner. She'd been listening to them talk all day.

Forcing herself to be objective, Tammy had to admit this teenager that Ty had created with another woman was a sweetheart. Her manners were good, her mind inquisitive and active, and her curiosity about her father boundless.

Ruby had even asked Tammy about herself, about where she was originally from. Tammy taught kids at school. She knew what teenagers *could* be like—self-indulgent navelgazers who cared only about their own needs.

Ruby was refreshingly down-to-earth and considerate of others. Whoever her mother was, she'd done a good job.

She wrestled with scrubbing the frying pan in the too-small pail of water sitting in the sink. Ty stood up. "Let me do that, honey. Sit with Ruby and play cards."

While Ty finished the pots and pans they had used to cook dinner on Ty's camp stove, Ruby and Tammy taught each other card games and tricks that were more hilarious than good, until they were laughing so hard tears streamed down their cheeks.

Tammy caught Ty watching them, his eyes suspiciously moist. To lighten his mood, so none of them would slip too far into sentimentality, she asked, "Can you make popcorn on that little stove?"

"I can make anything on it. Ruby, you want popcorn, too?"

"Yeah! I love popcorn." She shuffled the deck and accidentally spilled the whole thing onto the floor. She and Tammy started laughing again and they ended up sitting on the kitchen floor picking up cards.

When he finished making popcorn, Ty sat down and plopped the bowl in the middle of the three of them. He tossed a roll of paper towels beside it.

They leaned against the cupboards and ate buttery popcorn with greasy hands.

Tammy had often imagined this kind of heartwarming scenario, with Ty and her and their children, but Ty had never let her finish conversations about getting serious in their relationship.

He'd even said he didn't want children. And yet, here he was, falling in love with a pretty young girl who was his. Two days into the relationship, he was putty in her hands.

And yet, he'd never wanted children with Tammy. Should she be hurt?

Why hadn't he wanted children with her? Did it have anything to do with this girl's mother? Who exactly was that woman who had kept Tyler's daughter a secret from him for thirteen years? Tammy knew in her heart, *knew,* that he would be a great father to a baby. Tammy had wanted that with him from the start of their relationship. She'd always thought that if she was patient enough, she could bring him up to scratch, and that eventually they would marry and have a family.

As far as she was concerned, there was no other man for her than Tyler Jordan.

But Tyler already had a family. He had a daughter. Did that mean she would never be able to convince him to make babies with her?

"You guys are a lot more fun than my mom and dad," Ruby

said, then covered her face with her hands. "I mean, my *other* dad. I mean, my *pretend* dad."

Her shoulders started to shake. She was crying. Tammy took her hands away from her face. "Hey, hey. It's okay."

"No, it isn't. When the storm's over, Mom will come to take me back home and I don't want to go." She swiped her hands across her cheeks, leaving a trail of butter that Tammy wiped away with a paper towel. "I hate my new school. I hate our new house. I hate that I didn't know my real dad all along."

Ty opened his arms and she climbed into them. He held her while she cried and his eyes misted over again.

In all the time Tammy had known Ty, she'd never seen him emotional. An even-tempered, easygoing guy, he'd never come close to shedding a tear, but since Ruby's arrival, he'd been an emotional basket case.

And no wonder.

"Slow down," he said. "Tell us everything. Who's your stepfather?"

"His name's Kevin. He's a good guy, but Mom let me believe all those years that he was my real father."

"How did you find out he wasn't?"

"He and Mom are getting divorced. She left a whole bunch of papers on the kitchen table and my birth certificate was there. I saw your name and looked you up on Google."

Ruby's mother was getting a divorce. Tammy didn't like that. Would she be coming here to get her daughter or would Ty go to her? Either way, he would have access to a brand-new divorcée he'd once made a baby with.

"What's this about a new school and a new house?"

"They sold the old one and we moved to a smaller one so Mom could send me to private school, but the kids there are snobs. I don't like them."

What if this girl didn't want to go back to her mother, but

wanted to stay with Ty? What if her mother agreed? Could this be the start of a family for Ty and Tammy? What if he liked having a child so much he wanted more? Would he then agree to have children with her?

"Tell me about you guys," Ruby said. "Do you live here, Tammy?"

"No. I live in an apartment above a shop that my aunt gave me. I'm a teacher in town."

"A teacher! What grade?"

"Eight."

"Wow, that's awesome." Ruby snuggled against her father's chest.

Ty was a father. The shock of it left Tammy speechless. How long would it take her to get used to it?

"Ruby," Tammy started, unsure how to phrase questions that Ty probably didn't know needed to be asked. "Why did you come? What do you expect from Ty? From your…father?"

Ruby looked up at Ty shyly and then back at Tammy. "I want to get to know my real dad." She looked down at her hands folded in her lap. "I want to maybe, you know, if it's okay, live here for a while."

There it was—the elephant in the room. Life was about to change big-time.

At Ruby's statement, Ty looked shell-shocked.

"I think we're all too tired to talk anymore tonight. How about it we head to bed and talk again in the morning?"

Tammy climbed into bed with Ty.

They lay on their backs, staring at a ceiling they could barely see by the faintest of illuminations of a weak moon.

"Who was she? Really?" When Tammy spoke, Ty startled. She might as well have shouted, but she hadn't. "Tell me about her."

"There isn't much to tell. Her name was Winona. I met her in California just before I finished school. We hit it off."

When he didn't say any more, she asked, "That's it? How long were you together?"

"About four months."

"And?"

"*Aaaand,* she dumped me for another guy. Until today I didn't know his name was Kevin."

She wanted to ask if he'd loved her, but was afraid of the answer.

Instead, she came at it sideways. "How broken up were you?"

"Some."

Some. What the hell did that mean? How much was *some?* A little? A lot?

"Tammy, I really…" Ty pounded a fist against the mattress. "You know how I feel about you. Right?"

She turned her head on the pillow and studied his profile, but he avoided making eye contact. "No, Ty, I don't."

Finally, he looked at her. "Tammy, baby." His voice was rough, broken. A sigh gusted out of him and then he was on top of her, inside of her, and they were making love frantically, muffling their cries with kisses, with their mouths and tongues and hands when necessary, so the girl down the hall wouldn't hear them.

This swollen, emotion-laden, mixed-up situation was more than either of them had bargained for.

Ty came, shuddered and pulled out of her. He turned her until her back was against his chest and she felt him limp and damp behind her.

He'd forgotten, she thought with wonder. He'd never done that before. She put a hand on her tummy.

Please.

He'd forgotten to use a condom.

She squeezed her legs together to hold in Ty's semen.

Please form. Become. Be there, little one.

GABE AWOKE TO find Callie sitting on the sofa with the quilt wrapped around her and a coffee in her hand. He assumed it was morning.

"Hi," he said quietly.

"Hi," she replied, but didn't smile. He guessed what was wrong. She'd shown him her vulnerability last night.

A fire burned in the grate.

"How are you feeling?" she asked.

"Better."

"Already?"

"Yeah. I tend to bounce back from things. What time is it?"

"Nine."

"What day?"

"Sunday morning."

"You did a lot of work taking care of me. Rest while I feed the dogs."

"I'm coming with you."

She studied him for a while then said, "I'm really sorry about last night."

"I'm not." Gabe shrugged and looked away. "We all have problems. No one's perfect."

He hoped to hell she never discovered his problems or she wouldn't be looking at him like he hung the moon.

"There's coffee," she said. "I made it half an hour ago."

"I'll grab a cup and then head outside. Okay with you if we hold off on breakfast until after the dogs are fed?"

She stood and picked up a bundle of clothing from an armchair. She'd slept last night in one of his T-shirts. It looked a hell of a lot better on her than on him. He was never going to wash the thing again. He might bronze it, though. Her legs were superb.

After washing up using buckets of water in the bathroom and getting dressed they left the house to feed the dogs.

Not a breath of wind stirred the winter wonderland they

stepped out into. Snow had been swept into large graceful arcs against the house and the trees. Puffs of snow clung to tree branches like meringue.

Gabe watched Callie's face, noticed the awe that caught her in its grip. Yeah, given her terror of darkness, the white icy splendor around her would appeal.

He smiled, as though he were personally presenting this gift to her. He took her hand in his and led her through the woods, high-stepping through two-foot-deep drifts to the clearing.

The dogs stirred, shook snow from their coats and went wild when they saw Gabe and Callie. Callie laughed. Gabe wanted to drink that joyful sound from her lips.

"Let's get started," he said.

They worked in harmony, with the dogs getting huge portions and, when they were finished, returned to the house hand in hand. What was happening between them? Gabe didn't know, but given this respite from real life, he planned to see it through.

To his surprise, Callie took over in the kitchen, saying, "You still look tired."

He nodded. She was right. He didn't have his normal energy. Just feeding the dogs, even with Callie's help, had wiped him out.

Breakfast was a bunch of scrambled eggs, to use up the carton from the fridge, and bacon she must have taken out of the freezer yesterday or last night.

They ate breakfast beside the fire in the living room.

"I guess there's no chance of having a shower." The longing in Callie's voice was unmistakable.

"Nope. I have more jugs of water I filled before we lost power, if there's none left in the bathroom. You can give yourself a sponge bath if you want. That's what I usually do."

After Callie finished cleaning up, Gabe used the washroom. When he returned to the living room, she sat curled up on the sofa again, holding a second cup of coffee.

He liked her here in his house. Where Monica had felt like an intruder, Callie felt right here.

He sat on the hearth and asked a question that had been bothering him since she'd first knocked on his door.

"Why do you work for Nick?"

"He pays me well."

"And that's all that's important to you in a job? Money?"

"No." She worried a loose thread on the hem of her sweater. Something was bothering her. "But it's what I need right now."

"Why?"

"It's my mom. She has Alzheimer's. I pay a caregiver to live with her. As soon as possible when I get home, I'll need to find a good long-term care facility for her. That will cost."

"How bad is she?"

"Bad enough. She can't live alone anymore. Many days she doesn't know who I am."

"Do you have siblings?"

She shook her head.

So, she had no one else to help her take care of a mother who didn't always recognize her. And Gabe had thought she had fewer worries than Monica had. That she didn't know loss like Monica did. But wasn't Alzheimer's a type of death?

She hunched forward as though the load she carried weighed too heavily on her shoulders. He didn't know what to do for her, this bright unconquerable woman who carried a bigger burden than he could have guessed by her sunny nature. Years ago, he would have wrapped his arms around a woman who felt as bad as she did, but he no longer trusted his responses to the signals women gave out.

She'd let him kiss her the other night, but that could just have been the moonlight or the novelty of camping or an odd idea of romance.

He wanted to touch her, though. He really wanted to.

"The first day I came here," Callie said. "I didn't know that she'd run away sometime the night before. I found out when I returned to town. It terrified me." She brushed an imaginary speck of lint from her pants. "Nick came through for me. He sent out a posse of his employees onto the streets of Seattle until he found her. He ordered food for the cops and volunteers out searching for her."

Nick? Really? Gabe had spent too many years remembering him as a spoiled brat who thought only of himself. Who was his brother now? The hero of the hour? Or the businessman who wanted to cut Gabe off at the knees?

And why was this man giving so much of himself to other people, but not to his family? It was too much like Dad, who'd cared more for others than for his wife and three sons.

Gabe had worked so hard to raise his two younger brothers after Dad died, and all he'd gotten back from Nick was a kick in the teeth. A pretty awful one. Now Nick wanted to knock the land out from under Gabe's feet and carve it up. What had he done to Nick that was so bad that he deserved this?

"I don't get him," he murmured.

"Nick?"

"Yeah."

"I've worked for him for six years. Every time I think I have him figured out, he surprises me, not always in a good way."

"Why did he send you?"

Callie's brows rose. "I'm his assistant. I'm good. I get the job done."

"No, I mean, knowing that Nick wants to knock down this

house and develop the land, why didn't he come to face me down himself? Why did he send you to do the dirty work?"

Callie shrugged. "I honestly don't know. He's never struck me as a coward. He's been up against stiff competition in the past and never backed down."

Which meant that Nick was afraid to face *Gabe*. Why? Guilt over what he'd done with Laura? Not likely.

Resorts could be built all over the U.S., but Nick had chosen *here* to build. If that wasn't a personal attack against Gabe, he didn't know what was. He did know that he'd have to come up with ways to fight the man. And Callie. He didn't want to fight her, though. He wanted to...

Pulling himself away from thoughts of what he wanted to do with the woman who worked for his brother—after all, the last time they'd had trouble was over a woman—he said, "There's something else I don't get."

Callie waited.

"Why, if you have such a heavy burden, are you always upbeat? Always sassy and in a good mood?"

"It's something I trained myself to do when I was young. To get up and dust myself off and keep moving forward."

He had to admire her strength, but wondered at how her perkiness might put a distance between herself and those around her as much as Gabe's neuroses did around him. Yeah, he knew how neurotic he was. His just showed more on the surface. Callie's neurosis looked better than his, but was there nonetheless. If not for her breakdown last night, he would have never known anything worse than a broken nail had ever happened to her. He knew he shouldn't, knew how dangerous it was when she worked for Nick, but he wanted to get to know her better.

She had depth Monica didn't stand a snowball's chance in hell of ever matching. It took balls to pretend that everything was fine when it wasn't and this colorful dynamo had strength in spades.

Funny, though, what appealed to him was her softer side, the truth beneath the sass.

THE MAN WAS an enigma. A puzzle. The more she got to know him, the more that puzzle deepened rather than clearing up. She wanted to know so much about him, and not just for Nick's sake so he could use it against Gabe.

Callie wanted to know for her own sake. "Why do you like taking care of everyone around you?"

"I grew up doing it. My dad died when I was ten. Tyler was seven and Nick was five. My mom went to work at two jobs and I took care of my brothers. I guess it's a habit now."

Callie studied him shrewdly. "It's a lot more than that. You said you enjoy it."

"Yeah, I do."

"You need to have a bunch of your own kids," Callie joked.

On the flip of a coin, Gabe's face transformed from an easygoing bonhomie to stoniness. She could feel him draw away from her and close off his emotions. One moment, the sun was shining and the next it was the middle of the night and Callie was alone. Gabe had gone somewhere dark.

"What's wrong?" She stood and touched his arm but he refused to look at her. "Tell me why that bothers you."

"Never mind." He stepped away from her. "It's time to wash the dishes."

"The dishes can wait five minutes."

"Callie," Gabe said, his expression sober. "It would take a hell of a lot longer than five minutes to tell you what's wrong with me." He left the room.

Anger simmered in her chest. Damned if she'd let him walk away just because it hurt to talk about his problems. She'd bared herself to him, had told him her weaknesses.

Had made herself vulnerable to him. He could bloody well do the same for her.

She turned to march into the kitchen, but a photograph on the mantel caught her eye. She'd been meaning to ask Gabe about it but had forgotten.

A man crouched in the sun on the top of a mountain, his face mostly hidden by a big hat and goggles.

They couldn't hide his big smile, though. She imagined it was as beautiful as Gabe's would look if he ever really let go.

Callie knew he was on top of a mountain, because a mountain range stretched out behind him in the distance. He was on the tallest of them.

Where had this been shot? Somewhere in the Rockies? Or on Mount McKinley? Or on Mount Rainier?

She carried the photo into the kitchen.

"Tell me about this."

When Gabe turned and saw what she was holding, she knew she'd hit pay dirt. He seemed to stop breathing and that stillness that had slowly been loosening with her returned full force.

CHAPTER THIRTEEN

GABE'S HEART STOPPED beating, no longer sent oxygen to his brain, to his vital organs. Fingers, toes, lips—everything went numb, as though a mini-death spread through his body.

Don't. Don't ask me about him. How could she not? She'd shared all of herself with him. She would expect the same in return.

Maybe he wasn't as brave as she, though.

"Your father was a mountain climber?" she asked. She had no idea the damage she was doing to him. "Where was this shot taken? It's stunning. It looks like it's at the top of a mountain. Which mountain?"

"Everest."

Callie's mouth dropped open. "Your dad climbed Mount Everest? He made it to the top? Wow." It came out on a shallow gust of air. "What an accomplishment. You must have been so proud of him."

"Yeah." He barely choked out the word.

"Okay, I'm sensing that you weren't. Why not?"

"He didn't return from that trip."

"What do you mean?"

"He died on the mountain that day."

Callie stared at the photo and then at Gabe. "Then who took this photo?"

"Dad handed his camera to another climber who took the shot."

Callie shivered as though someone had stepped on her grave. "I don't get it. What's the full story?"

He didn't want to tell her. If he did, she would pick up on his feelings and wonder why he was still so angry, so petty and small-minded despite what a great guy Dad had been. What a *hero* he'd been. Still feeling so abandoned all of these years later, his anger made him feel small, but damned if he could stop it.

She'd been honest with him, and Gabe had held in too much of himself for too long. Maybe he was nothing more than one of his dogs lapping up attention, but Callie did something to him. *Meant* something to him.

"I don't want to share with a woman who works for my brother."

She nodded. "I understand." She picked at the hook in her sweater again without meeting his eyes. She was as shy, as confounded by this situation, this, this...*something* growing between them as he was.

After a while, she looked up. "I don't want to know for Nick. I want to know for me."

Well.

Well. That was good. It had been a long time since a woman had *really* looked at him. Callie was *really* looking at him, and it felt good and right.

He sat on the hearth beside Boo and rested his hand on her side, taking comfort from her warmth and the steady rise and fall of her breathing.

"Dad died on his way down from the top of Everest. The area above 26,000 feet is called the Death Zone, for good reason." God, it hurt to talk about Dad. *Make it general.* "Of the thousand or so climbers who attempt the summit each year, fifteen to twenty die."

Callie shook her head. "I had no idea."

"Many of those bodies are still up there. It's too hard to

retrieve them and bring them down." A sigh chock-full of disgust burst out of him. "Dad is still up there."

He heard Callie gasp, but wouldn't look at her. She would see the rage that still blackened his heart. Dad should have never gone up there.

"Mount Everest's South Col is known as the world's highest rubbish heap. Climbers have left behind empty oxygen bottles, old ropes, tents. Food." Gabe laughed roughly. "The highest mountain in the world is a trash can. Aren't we a great species?"

"Tell me how it happened."

"No!" The word exploded out of him. He settled his elbows onto his knees and squeezed his temples with his thumbs. Christ, this hurt to talk about. He'd buried it for too many years, had taken on the responsibility of raising his brothers. They had been so young. He hadn't been able to talk to them about it.

After Dad died, Mom had taken on a second job. She'd had no time for him.

The only woman who should have been his support, the woman he'd planned to marry, had betrayed him with his brother. Billy had been a charming ne'er-do-well. How on earth would he discuss this kind of thing with a boy like that? Maybe that's why Gabe had chosen him for a best friend. So he wouldn't have to face all the shit that Callie wanted to drag out of him.

Maybe it was time to face it down. Keeping it in couldn't be healthy, but man oh man, it killed him to talk about it.

"Sorry." A heavy breath whooshed out of him. "I've seen photographs of the top of Everest. Of bodies frozen in grotesque shapes littering the snow. They've been there for years and every year more are added. Dad would hate knowing that his body is no more than a sack of pollution at the top of Everest."

He surreptitiously swiped his thumbs under his eyes.

"Have you ever talked about this before?"

"No," he admitted, his equilibrium worn raw. "I've never wanted to."

"You carry a lot of emotion around it." Callie leaned forward. "Talk to me."

He shot her a look—of exasperation and fear and anger. "You're brave," he said, and meant it. This tiny female pixie had no trouble standing up to him. He felt like a big hulking caveman next to her. "If only I had your backbone."

"We both know you do."

Her faith in him humbled him. He scrubbed his hands over his face, then jumped up from the hearth, suffocated by his emotions, by having been trapped indoors by illness and the weather.

"I need to get out of here."

"How?" she asked quietly. "Will the roads be cleared yet?"

"No. I'm going to get out the old tractor and blaze a trail for the dogs. Do you want to come out in the big sled again? The dogs that didn't get out the other day need to be trained."

He held his hand out to her. She watched him steadily and then took it, as though understanding that this wasn't the end of the conversation, only a break.

Her hand felt small, fragile, but also surprisingly strong in his big hand. He rubbed his thumb across her palm.

"Did you see what I loaded the sled with the other day?" She nodded.

"Gather all of that around the sled for me while I make the trail."

They dressed and left the house.

When Gabe finished with the trail, he put booties on the dogs and attached them to the big sled.

He settled the supplies around Callie under the blankets and canvas, then drove them through the forest and around

Luther and as far as the dog run, pulling up just shy of the gate. All the while, the beauty of the land and the gentle whoosh of the sled on the snow eased his pain, calmed his emotions. *Let it go.*

He took his time unleashing the dogs and putting them into the run, allowing their enthusiasm to lift his spirits, to give him strength to face what he had to tell Callie.

Because he did have to tell her. For some reason, he felt compelled.

Finally, he had nothing left to do but to let it all out. He leaned his crossed forearms on the top of the fence. He meant to make it more than just a story. He meant for Callie to see him for who he truly was, to see his anger and resentment against his father, to wipe that look of admiration of Gabe from Callie's eyes.

"Between the cost of outfitting an expedition," he began, "plus the $25,000 the Nepalese charge for a license, climbing Everest is almost a rich man's sport these days. Mom and Dad used to fight about how much Dad's hobby was costing them. While he was climbing, he also wasn't working, so there was little money coming in.

"Dad wasn't a rich thrill seeker. He was just a guy who loved to climb. He started as a child here on Luther, climbing with his father." Gabe stared at the mountain for a long moment, remembering those times his dad had climbed with him. They had been magical. Dad had taught him how to use his body to the fullest, to push it to the max. "He moved on to McKinley, Rainier, K2. He enjoyed the challenge. Dad was always pushing himself.

"He had the ultimate respect for nature and the mountains he climbed. He was aware of the risks, but wasn't a hotdogger.

"I know he was careful, always cognizant of the danger—he used to talk to me about it, to teach me to have respect for the danger and to take it seriously—but I still can't forgive him for leaving us. Abandoning us. Why have children if you plan to do something so dangerous you might never return to them?"

"On the other hand," Callie said. "Your mother knew she was marrying a mountain climber."

Gabe glanced down at her. "You're the voice of reason."

"It's easy for me to be. I didn't lose my father the way you did."

"I'm guessing that Mom thought she could reform Dad. That once they started a family, he would be happy to take a job in Accord and stay here the rest of his life. She was so naive," he finished bitterly.

Callie's touch on his sleeve through his heavy coat felt as ephemeral as the brush of a butterfly wing, but he took comfort from it and went on with the story. No, not a story. Not fiction. Dad's history.

"At the top of Everest, there's only a third of the oxygen as at sea level. Trying to do anything at all, walking, talking, just *breathing,* let alone scaling a mountain, can make you desperately sick. It can kill you.

"Dad had climbed before, on other mountains, without oxygen, but he chose to use oxygen to ascend Everest to be smart and safe.

"I found out later that he was on his descent from his successful summit when he stopped to help a man, a purist who'd attempted the climb without oxygen. Others passed by, told him the man was dying and that Dad should worry about himself, but it wasn't in Dad's nature to abandon someone who needed help. Dad persisted in trying to rescue him. They died together. Someone brought back Dad's camera with that photo on it. He's still up there somewhere in that litter heap at the top of the world."

"Have you considered going to retrieve his body?"

"My interest in climbing ended the day Dad died. He used

to take me up on Luther and teach me climbing. I loved those times with him."

He pierced Callie with a look that let her know exactly how he felt. "This is how petty I am. I resent that some stranger refused to use oxygen and now my dad is dead. I resent that Dad tried to save this stranger when he had three boys and a wife at home who loved him. I resent that the world thought he was a hero while I hated him for not coming home."

He could tell he'd stunned her.

"I'm sorry," he said.

"Shut up."

"What?"

"Don't ever apologize for honesty. I imagine I would have felt the same way."

She surprised him, this woman who refused to flinch when faced with his ugliness.

She leaned on the fence and watched the dogs. "Is that why you want to run the Iditarod?"

Her perception surprised him. "Yeah. I can get my fix for adventure by pushing myself, by testing my limits, but the race won't kill me. I'll always come back home. If I ever had kids, I'd come home to them after every race."

"And yet you enlisted. You could have been killed. What if you'd had children?"

"But I didn't. And I don't now."

"Is the Iditarod your first race?"

"Yes."

"What about the dogs? Will they all come back?"

"Why do you ask?"

"I researched the race on Thursday night and it seems that every year dogs die."

"I know. Mine won't. I'm not racing to win. I'm racing to test myself. If any of my dogs get hurt, I'll carry them across the finish line. They won't die on my account."

She smiled. "Exactly what I wanted to hear. I should have known that about you. I've seen you with your dogs. I know you love them. I wanted to be certain. I read some horror stories."

"I know. My dogs won't be any of those." He tapped the fence with the side of his fist. "We need to get back on the trail."

Gabe called the dogs to him to finish the ride. Before he opened the gate, Callie stopped him with a hand on his arm again.

"Know what?" she asked.

"What?"

"You're more like your dad than you think."

White fury shot through him. How could she say that after what he'd just revealed about Dad? After he'd bared his soul to her.

Undeterred by what must be showing on his face, she said, "I think you'll stop to help anyone in that race who needs your help, despite any danger to yourself."

He opened his mouth to speak, to deny it, but nothing came out. She was right. How could Gabe not stop to help a fellow human being? She knew him too well.

The problem with emotions that clung to you long after you'd grown up was that they were still a child's emotions, swollen, unreasonable and panic-filled.

He turned away from her because he had a lot of thinking to do. One thing he did know, though, was that he felt better than he had in years. Telling Callie about his dad, about his feelings, had been the right thing to do. He couldn't have chosen a less judgmental person to help him heal.

He hooked the dogs back up to the sled and finished the ride. Exhaustion rode with him for a while. Maybe that's what sharing anger and grief did to a man. After a while, though, the wind rushing by while he glided over pure fresh snow cleansed him.

The dogs, as always, healed him. Callie, he thought, looking down at her bundled up on the sled, with only her head showing, had done her part. Had done more than any woman ever had.

He wanted to make love to her.

Back in the clearing, she helped him rake out the old straw and scatter new. Together, they fed the dogs then returned to the house.

The lamp in the living room was on.

"We have power," Gabe said.

Callie's expression brightened. "Does that mean I can have a shower and wash my hair?"

"Yeah."

Her laugh was so genuine and infectious that Gabe laughed, too.

She threw her arms around his waist. "I wish you'd do that more often."

He stared down at her, stunned by her affection and her genuine joy. This had nothing to do with neuroses and keeping her distance, and everything to do with enjoying life.

She stared at him for a long time, for so long that he wondered if she was waiting for him to say something else. He didn't know what, though.

She pulled away from him slowly. "I get first dibs on the shower." She turned away from him, entered the bathroom and had her shower.

He napped before having his.

AFTER DINNER, CALLIE helped him feed the dogs their bedtime kibble. When they finished they returned to the house. While she used the washroom to get ready for the night, he spread the quilts on the floor. He'd already built up a big fire and had turned off the lights.

When she returned to the living room, she carried her clothes in her arms. She wore only his T-shirt and her legs were so perfectly shaped his body wanted to perform backflips.

"You're so pretty." God, she was beautiful, but he didn't usually say things like that out loud. She made him behave differently, unlike himself, and he was beginning to see that wasn't a bad thing.

Uncharacteristically, she looked shy. She bit her bottom lip.

"I want you to sleep here." He rubbed his hand across the worn cotton. "With me."

"You mean…"

"I mean, Callie, that I want to sleep with you." He stood and approached her, taking his time as though she were a wild animal who might spook and run.

When she didn't, he drew her clothes out of her arms, dropped them onto a chair and pulled her to him. He kissed her, gently at first, because she tasted good and clean and perfect, and then with mounting heat, because she became womanly and passionate in his arms.

Afraid that they might not make it into bed, he bent down and turned down a corner of the top quilt. She crawled underneath. Then she patted the spot beside her, giving him permission, and turned back the other corner of the quilt for him.

He lay down beside her and eased her into his arms.

"Callie," he whispered, because it felt funny to speak aloud in their tiny oasis of light cast by the fire. The rest of the room in darkness, they lay in a cotton-shrouded bubble of warm isolation.

He hadn't held a woman in so long.…

She had a healthy, soft and supple body, and felt right in his arms.

Her clear, uncomplicated eyes watched him without guile. There was honesty here.

He stared at the skin exposed by his old shirt falling from one of her shoulders, the neckline worn and gone baggy long ago. He put a finger into it and pulled it down farther, baring more of her arm and the skin above her breast. Small, pale freckles dotted alabaster skin and he wondered how far south those freckles went.

With one insignificant flick of his finger on the neckline of his shirt, her breast popped out. Round, slightly heavier on the bottom than the top and dotted with more pale freckles, it filled the palm of his hand. Warm. Weighty. Feminine.

She closed her eyes and stretched her head back, exposing her neck. He kissed it.

He touched her breast again and she leaned into his hand.

They had shared so much of themselves—their secrets and vulnerabilities. It was only right that they share their bodies.

He rolled her onto her back and sucked her nipple into his mouth. Her breath hitched. Her skin came alive against his tongue. Her nipple, her breast, her legs intertwined with his— all of her, every inch of her—was alive and real and responding to him. Like the green of her eyes, this woman awakened in him a part of his soul he'd thought dead.

He'd been living in black and white, half-dead. She painted the room verdant, as though Irish moss were growing inside his home, turning a dead landscape into something breathing and vibrant.

His hand moved to her stomach, climbed up under the T-shirt and tossed it over her head. He leaned back to look at her. She was small and formed to perfection, her hips and breasts full for her height, with a little layer of fat on her belly. A triangle of dark red curls beckoned.

He moved his mouth down her body, touched, kissed, licked everything. Pulling tummy skin between his lips, he sucked on it. It was softer than anything he'd ever felt in his life. He rolled her over. By the glow of the firelight, he licked a path up her spine.

Turning her around again, he feasted on her breasts.

"Want to see you," she whispered and those small perfect hands pushed the blankets aside and found their way to him. A moment later, she wrapped her cool fingers around him and they both groaned.

"I want you."

He snagged a condom he'd put beside the quilts earlier and rolled it on. Raising up over her, he took his time entering her, going slowly because she was small and he wasn't.

She opened like a flower for him. Her body accepted him by degrees and when he was fully sheathed, they moaned. He'd never felt anything more silken or perfect than the moist, warm acceptance of him into her body.

He looked down at her, at the brilliance of her gaze, at the frank desire he saw there. She raised a hand and brushed the hair back from his forehead, the gesture strangely comforting.

There was something going on here that he didn't get, as though this carnal acceptance of him were an act of selfless generosity, but he didn't want that. He wanted heat and flaming desire. And that was all.

He began to move, touching her with his fingers while he eased in and out of her, to stoke the flames, to make her forget pity, or compassion, or whatever it was that he'd glimpsed in her eyes.

He drove her wild, drove her to passion, to lust until she cried out and he came inside of her then lay on top of her floating in a strange exotic blend of exhausted satisfaction and benediction.

She laid her hand on his hair and whispered something he didn't catch. He had the unmistakable impression that she'd bestowed a blessing on him.

He pulled out of her and got up to take care of the condom.

When he came back with a towel to clean her, he stared down at her, knowing that he should run for the Rockies as fast as he could away from this woman. Somehow, in a way that he couldn't name, she was dangerous to him, to his peace of mind, and it had nothing to do with her working for his brother or trying to take over his land.

Without a word he cleaned her and himself. Words escaped him. She'd given him a gift of such rare proportions she left him speechless and humbled. He didn't know what she thought, merely watched her eyes drift closed until she slept. Gabe loaded up the fireplace and then lay down with her again, despite his misgivings.

He spooned with her, tucking her against his chest, holding on to that feeling of benediction, even though he knew he deserved neither it nor this bright, fiery-haired gem of a woman.

CHAPTER FOURTEEN

SOMETHING HAD CHANGED.

Pulling out of sleep slowly, Gabe raised up on an elbow and stared around the room and then down at the woman beside him.

The room was the same.

The woman in his arms was new. He'd never made love to a woman here before. He'd never wanted that kind of intimacy to invade his personal sanctuary.

He'd invited Callie in, though, with open arms.

Something inside of him had changed. The hollow ache he hadn't even been consciously aware of yesterday had been filled with a fledgling sense of peace.

And how was that possible when he really didn't believe that he deserved peace?

Gabe arose and started up the fire again, but it was only for the scent and for show. When the power returned, the furnace had kicked in. The room was cool, but not icy cold.

Not cold like the fist squeezing his heart. What to do about Nick? About how the man compromised both Callie and Gabe and any relationship they might forge?

Gabe would hold out. All he had to do was to be strong. Nick couldn't force him to sell.

What would happen if Nick won? If Nick somehow managed to wrest the land away from Gabe? He didn't know where the man would hit, but Gabe knew from experience that it would be below the belt. What could Nick possibly find to use against Gabe? Where would Gabe go? Outside of his time in the army, he'd only ever known this land. He'd loved Luther since he was old enough to toddle beside his father.

Dad was part of the problem. Where else on earth could Gabe feel close to his father? When he looked at Luther, he felt a connection.

What did his future hold? Yes, he loved his land, he loved his dogs, he loved the business that allowed him to live off the land. What about when he turned forty? Or fifty? Or sixty?

Did he still want to be alone? After his dreams of a family with Laura had been shattered, he might have gotten over it in time. He might have been able to see life with another woman and children. But Billy's death had sent him spiraling so far down that Gabe had locked himself on this land.

Had he made a prison of it? No! He loved living on the land. *But you have no mate.*

He'd been drifting. So? What about now? Did he continue to drift? Or did he make decisions for his future that involved more than hiding out and wallowing in his grief over Billy? And what about his guilt? Where did he stand with that? He didn't know, but something inside of him had changed.

He looked at Callie, ran a finger along her pale shoulder. She had brought color into his life. Could she also have brought a future? What of her job? Her boss?

"Damn you, Nick," he whispered.

He crossed to the front window and stared outside. The sun rising on the horizon sparkled pink off snow on trees, and glistened orange-red on power lines and telephone poles. There wasn't a speck of breeze to disturb the tranquility and beauty of the storm's aftermath.

He looked around the room. Callie's hair was brilliant red against the faded quilts. Everything in the room was faded, the rug, the worn sofa, the old afghan lying on old armchair.

But not Callie. She was new and fresh and strong and vibrant. He'd never met a woman like her, someone who could rise above her worries so well.

Except for those years in Afghanistan, he'd lived the same life for too long, had changed nothing in here. Afghanistan had been shades of brown and beige. He'd come home to his mountain and his land, had hoped to come back alive. Hadn't really. Had coasted.

Who was this woman who awakened long-dead hopes and dreams?

She roused by bits until she looked across the room at him with clear eyes.

"How do you feel?" he asked.

"Fabulous," she answered.

He walked over to her and didn't miss the way she drank in the sight of his naked body.

"What's it like outside?"

"Quiet. Peaceful." He held out his hand to her. "Come on."

"Where to?"

"Outside. This is the prettiest time of day. I want to show you something."

She threw back the covers and stood. He touched her belly with his finger. "I left a mark. Sorry."

She looked down at her stomach and yelped, then glanced up at him. "You gave me a hickey." She laughed. "You're not the least bit sorry."

"You're right. I'm not. Get dressed."

He pulled on his pants and a sweater in his room while he heard her dressing in the living room.

They both suited up for the cold then slipped outside through the back door with Boo on their heels. Boo went to the bathroom against a tree then followed them down to the small lake where Gabe got his water for the dogs.

Not a breath of wind stirred.

Sheltered by trees on all sides, the lake hadn't yet been touched by the sun. It still held the chilly gray hush of predawn.

"I haven't been down here before. It's beautiful." Callie wrapped her arms across her chest. "There's a bite in the air today."

"I'll keep you warm."

Gabe nestled her back against him and wrapped his arms across the front of her waist. "We're going to do something, an experiment," he whispered in her ear. "We have a nice quiet morning for it. Lean back against me and close your eyes."

She did.

"We're going to stay completely silent for a few minutes. Don't say a word. Okay?"

She nodded against his chest.

"Now, listen. Don't talk. Don't move. Just listen."

They stood silently for minutes on end.

He felt Callie start to stiffen and knew it was too quiet for her.

"Shh," he whispered. "You aren't alone. I'm here."

She settled.

Minutes later, Gabe broke the silence.

"What did you hear?"

"Nothing but my own heartbeat."

"That's my point." He turned her around in his arms.

"What do you mean?"

"That there is never, ever, complete silence. Even if you think the rest of the world has abandoned you, there is still your own heartbeat. This—" he laid a hand over her left breast "—keeps you connected to the rest of the world. It's part of the healing heart of life beating all around you. Even if the rest of the world is asleep, your heartbeat lets you know that you are never alone."

"That's beautiful."

"Let's go back inside."

Boo followed them when they entered the house and lay down by the fireplace with a contented snuffle.

They took off their outer clothes. When Callie started to follow the dog to the living room, Gabe waylaid her, gently propelling her into the bathroom and closing the door.

"What are you doing?" Callie asked.

"I'm having a shower. With you."

"Oh." She smiled and the corners of her eyes crinkled upwards. She wrapped her arms around his neck and kissed him long and deeply. "Okay."

Gabe turned the water on and adjusted the temperature. When he turned around, Callie stood naked before him.

His mouth went dry. "My God, you're pretty."

He scrambled out of his own clothes, picked her up and stepped into the shower.

They washed each other and rinsed, then Gabe took both of her arms and held them above her head.

"What are you doing?" she gasped.

"Loving you." He licked her arms from her wrists to her breasts, first one and then the other, sucking on her nipples to make her whimper.

She tried to pull her hands out of his grasp, but couldn't.

"I want to touch you," she cried.

"No."

"I want to," she panted.

"Later. Right now I have dibs on doing all the touching." It came out muffled because he couldn't stop stroking her nipple with his tongue.

He brought her hands down behind her back and held them there easily with one hand.

He got down on his knees in front of her and licked her belly. While she writhed, he left another mark on her stomach then whispered his breath along her skin until he reached the

V of red curls between her legs, all while hot water poured down his back.

His tongue entered her. She gasped. He stroked her, sucked with his lips and she squirmed.

Breathy gasps slipped from her. Gabe laughed low in his chest. She was exquisite and, for this too-brief time, his.

It would end. Of course. For now, though, he wanted her. He would take her.

She fell apart in his arms. He stood and held her until her orgasm faded.

He turned off the water and dried her with his towel, then dried himself. They returned to the living room and settled before the fire.

Something on her face stopped him. "What is it?"

"This is just an interlude. Reality will intrude at some point."

"I don't want to talk about that."

"I have to leave soon and everything will change. The real world is still out there, Gabe."

Here it comes, Gabe thought, his aching loneliness threatening to seep back in. She was going to dump him before whatever it was they'd shared last night had a chance to catch between them. So, it wouldn't even survive twenty-four hours. They wouldn't have even that long.

He lunged up and wrapped his arms around her.

She gasped.

He stilled. "Okay?" he asked.

"Mmm. Yes." She rested her forehead on his shoulder.

"Can't we change the real world to reflect our reality?" he asked. "Just for a few days? Why can't we stay here and make love on the quilt until we're sick of each other?"

"There's still Nick and the ski resort and my mom." She sounded sleepy, drugged, as reluctant to talk "reality" as he was, but they had to.

"You could always stop working for Nick," he said.

"No. I need the paycheck. It would take me too long to find another job that paid as well."

She tried to move away but he wrapped his fingers around her tiny waist and held her still.

"Nick has you trapped."

"I owe Nick a lot, though. He's been a good friend." She tried to move again. He held her still. "As much as Nick can be friends with anyone."

Gabe slashed a hand through the air. "I don't want to talk about Nick. I want to talk about *us*."

"We *are* talking about us. We can't do that without discussing Nick."

"The hell with that." He stormed away. "I'm going to feed the dogs."

"I have to—"

"Don't go yet. Be here when I get back."

Gabe stared around the clearing. He was out here to feed the dogs, but nothing looked the same. Over the course of the weekend, his life had become new, had filled with possibilities.

Engulfed by a feeling he barely recognized—hope—he spun about.

His dogs barked for his attention while he dreamed of the future.

Was it possible for him to have a future? Dared he dream about things he'd thought would never be his? Family? Love? He wrestled with a decision that had been rolling around in his brain since yesterday, and that filled his mind the second he opened his eyes this morning.

She'd disrupted his life, had turned him inside out. She'd encouraged him to dream.

What if he could convince her to move here, to bring her mother and her mother's caregiver and live with him on his land, to quit her job with his brother and work with Gabe? To love him.

While he fed the dogs, his hands shook.

JUST AFTER CALLIE checked in with Sophie, her phone rang. She checked the number. Nick. Damn. Reality was definitely raising its godawful ugly head.

"Where are you?"

"Still at Gabe's."

"Why?"

"I've been trapped here by the storm. Apparently, the roads have been cleared so I can drive back to the inn now."

"Where's Gabe?"

"Outside feeding the dogs."

"Does he have an office in the house?"

"I don't know. I haven't looked for one."

"Look now."

She didn't want to. She knew what would come next. The spying.

She checked the door on the other side of the washroom. It had been closed all weekend.

It was a small office.

"I found it."

"Check it out."

"Nick, don't ask me to do this. *Please*."

"Callie, watch where your loyalty lies. I deserve yours. I've given you a good paycheck. I've made sure your mother was safe. Do. Your. Job."

He hung up.

With a sense of inevitability, with all of the lovely senses Gabe had awakened in her shutting down, with her heart going numb, she stepped into the office.

She opened Gabe's desk drawers. Nothing. Next, she went

to his filing cabinet and opened drawers, not even truly worried that he would catch her.

She'd warned Gabe that reality would intrude. Hadn't she also been warning herself? This was her life these days, working for Nick and supporting her mother and her mother's caregiver.

She had no right to dream about love or family or…Gabe. This had been a beautiful interlude, something she'd taken for herself when she'd had no right to. She should have been stronger. Should have resisted Gabe and the beautiful urges he'd created in her, and oh, those gorgeous possibilities that were too unrealistic to survive the light of day.

Her fingers were clumsy because her hands shook.

Damn you, Nick.

Whatever Nick wanted, she couldn't find it. As far as she could tell, Gabe was a smart, honest businessman. She doubted that he evaded paying his taxes. Everything here seemed ethical and aboveboard. The business was solvent.

Just as she closed the last cabinet drawer, she heard, "What are you doing?"

She straightened and turned slowly. Gabe stood in the doorway of the small room and his face might as well have been carved from a chunk of Luther. She was lower than a snake. She couldn't lie to him.

"Spying. Nick called. He wants dirt on your business."

He didn't say anything.

"I told you we can't separate Nick out of our lives. I have a job to do."

"It includes spying?"

She shook her head, jerkily, like a puppet whose strings were too tight. "It never has before."

"This is no way for you to make a living."

"That's easy for you to say, Gabe. You don't have dependents. I do. I have my mother to support. I have Sophie's paycheck to meet every week. As soon as possible, I have to get my mother into a home." She had to make him understand what drove her to do things she wouldn't normally do. "I want her in a good home with staff I can trust to take care of her. To do that, I need money."

The backs of her eyes stung because the look in Gabe's was tearing her to shreds. He had high standards. She used to. Times had changed. Events in her life had changed her. She was doing what she had to do.

"For what it's worth," she said, "I *hated* doing this to you."

She tried to brush past him, but his hand on her wrist stopped her, bruising her.

"Quit the job. I'll give you money."

"Oh, Gabe." She tried to touch his cheek, but he pulled away from her. "You are one in a million. The best. These days, I'm not anywhere close to good enough for you."

He let her go and she collected her hat and gloves and coat and slipped her boots on and left the house. She would never be welcome here again and that started an ache inside of her she found hard to name. Definitely loss, but so much more. Something profound had broken inside of her. She managed to drive back to the B and B and get up to her room and out of her clothes and into the bed, to pull the covers over her head and burrow into a fetal ball before she fell apart.

CHAPTER FIFTEEN

TY FINALLY GOT through to Winona on Monday morning.

A woman's voice, deep and sultry, and more mature than he'd remembered, answered. "Who is it?"

"Winona?"

The woman was silent for a moment and then asked, "Tyler?" and it sounded like she smiled. So did Ty. She hadn't forgotten the sound of his voice.

"Ruby's here. Thought you might be worried about her."

"There?" He heard the shock in her voice. "Where?"

"In Accord. In Colorado. At my ranch."

"But— What's she doing there?"

"She came to find me. To get to know me. Why didn't you tell me about her?"

"When did she get there?" How like Winona to ignore a tough question.

"She came on Friday night in the middle of a snowstorm. She was lucky she didn't get lost and freeze to death. The power's been out all weekend until this morning."

"I'll come get her." He thought he detected anger in her voice. "I need directions."

He gave her the ranch's address.

"I'll book a flight. I should be there late today or early tomorrow."

"Good. I didn't want to send her home alone."

"It will be good to see you, Ty. It's been a long time. I've missed you."

The last statement took Ty by surprise and it warmed him. He laughed, then sobered.

"We need to talk. I mean to get answers about why you kept my child from me." He hung up. His blood thrummed through his veins like electricity.

The woman baffled him, left him feeling good and bad and angry and not quite steady on his feet. Winona had always kept him off-balance.

He hung up and the breath he'd been holding throughout the conversation whistled out of him.

Winona was coming here. To his ranch. What would she think of it? Would she recognize how well Ty had done in his life?

TAMMY WASN'T ANGRY. She had no right to be. She hadn't been living here fourteen years ago, so would have had no claim to Tyler then. She'd inherited Aunt Edna's gift shop only six years ago and had relocated here from Boston. A teacher by trade, she hadn't wanted to give up her career, or the shop she liked to buy for, so she'd hired women in the community who ran the shop while she taught.

In busy seasons, she worked there, too, and loved it.

Many times over the past six years, she'd thanked Aunt Edna in her prayers for leaving it to her. Tammy had made a great life for herself in this town, had made a good circle of friends and…she'd met Ty.

On day one, she'd noticed the big, handsome sheriff. It had taken him a couple of years to finally ask her out.

For the past four years, she and Tyler had been close, had spent every weekend together and attended every town event together. Everyone expected a wedding soon. So did she. Apparently, Tyler didn't agree.

She wanted a family. She wanted children, soon. Teaching them wasn't enough. She wanted her own and she wanted them with Ty. Whenever she brought up the subject, though, Tyler cut her off. How ironic to find out he didn't seem to want children and yet had one while she wanted one, yet wasn't a parent.

Tammy was left to wonder at what point a girl should cut her losses and look elsewhere.

But she didn't want to. She wanted Tyler. She loved him. Dearly. She could swear he loved her. So what held him back? She wished the stubborn man would talk about his background. What drove Ty to be who he was?

An entire weekend had passed since they had learned that Ty had a daughter and nothing had been resolved, as though whatever happened between Ty and Tammy depended on whatever happened with the girl's mother.

She wandered to the dining room and put away a serving bowl she'd used for last night's dinner. Ruby was standing in the hallway just outside of the living room doorway.

Tammy crept over. "What's up?"

Ruby put her finger to her lips. "He's talking to my mom," she whispered.

Tammy eavesdropped, unashamedly curious about Ty's old girlfriend. She couldn't hear specific words, but when he laughed, it sounded husky and intimate, and the sound cut through Tammy like broken glass.

Ruby turned to look at her, her gaze solemn while she studied Tammy's face. "You look like her," she said, quietly.

What?

Ruby motioned for Tammy to follow her. She pulled a small wallet out of her knapsack and took out a photo of Ruby standing beside a woman who could have been Tammy.

She couldn't look more like Tammy had she been her twin. Tammy's hair was curly and Ruby's mother's straight, but the blond was the same, the blue eyes the same, the heart-shaped face the same.

Tammy's world shattered. Ty had used her as a substitute for a girlfriend he couldn't have? Had their relationship been built on a lie? No! She refused to believe that. She knew Tyler. He was good, honorable. He loved her.

She stared at Ruby. Why had the girl shown her this? Worry? Concern for Tammy? Spite?

Tammy walked away. She needed to get out of here.

AS MUCH AS it would hurt Ty to let Ruby go, he had to get her back to her mother. With a little luck, Winona could be in and out of Accord in one day. Tammy would never meet Winona and their lives could go back to normal.

And his bison would sprout wings and fly. There was no more "normal" for Ty and Tammy anymore. Everything had changed and he didn't have a clue where they went from here.

The front door slammed.

He saw Tammy stomp to her car and start to clean it off with a vengeance. What was going on?

He passed Ruby in the hallway. "What's up?"

"I showed her a picture of me and Mom."

Shit.

Aw, Tammy. Honey.

He put on his coat and stepped out into the dry cold.

He approached Tammy cautiously.

"I'm sorry, Tammy. So goddamned sorry."

She didn't say a word, just kept cleaning that car with stiff harsh motions, her jaw tight enough to crack.

"Say something." She didn't. "Please."

Still nothing.

She got into her car and reversed out of the driveway he'd cleared first thing.

He watched her drive away.

Acid ate his stomach lining. Tammy was driving away for good.

Ruby waited for him inside. "Can we have a snowball fight today?"

"Sure," Ty said. Would he ever get used to having a child?

Even while Ty lobbed the first snowball at his daughter, he worried about Tammy. She would be hurting. He was a chickenshit, a snake. Lower than low. He should have told her from the start about Winona, but he'd learned as a child to bottle things up. He'd never changed that over the years.

God, he felt hollow, as though a cave had opened up inside of him. Continents had shifted and ground apart to create a cavern named Tammy.

You don't know what you've got 'til it's gone.

He had a lot to work out with Winona. Winona had a lot to answer for. She'd given Ty's baby to another man. She'd be lucky if he didn't strip the hide right off her.

After the anger, though, what then? He couldn't deny what he'd refused to admit to Tammy. He wanted to see Winona, wanted to know if he still had feelings for her. He'd been crazy for her, and her betrayal had been profound, but just the sound of her name set his heart to *boom, booming*. Why would a man do that for a woman he hadn't seen in so many years?

He needed to sort his feelings for Winona once and for all.

Winona didn't make it to the ranch until Tuesday morning, arriving in a cloud of snow she sent flying into the air, driving up Ty's long driveway faster than she should. She hadn't lost her taste for speed. Was she still reckless in the rest of her life? He hoped she didn't drive like that with his daughter in the car.

Ruby stared out through the living room window and said dully, "She's here."

"Yep."

"Why couldn't I stay here longer?"

"She said you had to come home. You're missing school."

"I'm smart. I can make it up by the end of the term."

"I believe that. For the record, I'd like you here longer."

Ruby met his eyes and smiled. The wonder of her still stunned him. "I wish I'd known you all along."

She threw her arms around his waist. "I love you, Dad."

Oh wow, this…this was something else. Did love really develop this quickly just because he was her father? Or was it an infatuation and as soon as the going got tough, the lovey-doveyness would be over. How did he know? He'd never been a parent before. One thing he did know was that he would spend the rest of his life doing his best by his child. "I love you, too, with all my heart, sweetheart."

He blinked hard so Winona wouldn't walk in here to find him crying.

Ruby, small and precious in his arms, asked, "I'm going to persuade Mom to stay for a few days. Okay?"

No, he thought, but he said, "Yes." He could get rid of her by the weekend, in three days, before Tammy arrived on Friday night. *If* there was a Friday night with Tammy.

They went to the door together. A statuesque blonde stepped out of the rental car. Winona didn't look much like the tough, savvy scrapper he'd been involved with more than a dozen years ago. She still took his breath away, though, nearly knocked him flat on his back.

She was all grown up and achingly beautiful, the promise of her all those years ago delivered in spades. Her clothes looked expensive. Through the open fur coat tossed casually over her shoulders were glimpses of cream wool slacks and a white sweater that looked softer than sin.

These days, Winona had money.

"Hello, Ty," she said, her voice even more sultry in person than it had been on the phone. "It's been a long time." She stepped into the house bringing with her a cloud of perfume. She wrapped her arms around him and kissed him on the lips, as though they had been old friends instead of brief, frenzied lovers, and had stayed friends over the years. If he thought that maybe her tongue had touched his lips, that must have been his imagination.

Words he would have never applied to Winona all those years ago came to mind…*refined, sophisticated, urbane. And still sexy. Hotter than hell.*

"How have you been, Ty? It's been too long."

"Not because of me."

He'd surprised her. She probably remembered him as a pushover. He had been way back when. He didn't plan to be one this time around. When she'd kept his child from him, she'd robbed him blind. He had never wanted to end their relationship. All of those years ago, he'd thought she was the one. *The One.*

She noticed Ruby standing behind him.

"Why did you leave, honey?" Her tone was harder than it had been with Ty. She was angry. Understandably so. Fear did that to people.

"Why do you think? You let me believe Kevin was my father for my entire life. How could you, Mom?" Ruby's face was red and she looked close enough to tears that Ty edged closer in case she needed him. "Did you lie to Kevin, too? Did he think all these years that I was his?"

"No. He accepted you as his daughter, though. He loved you like one."

Ruby did cry then and Ty wrapped his arm across her shoulders. "Dad— I mean, Kevin lied to me, too?"

"If it's any consolation, he didn't want to. From day one, he thought you should know the truth. I thought it would be best for everyone if we pretended we were one family."

"You hid the truth from me, too, Winona." Ty couldn't help how angry he sounded. Now that she was here, the wonder of having a daughter was replaced by fury. "You couldn't have called me even once? I would have been there for Ruby. I would have helped raise her. She was mine!"

"Ty, I'm so sorry. I fell in love with Kevin and I wanted a family unit."

"Is that the truth? Or was it just easier for you to leave me out of the loop?"

She didn't answer him, but turned to Ruby. "How did you find out about Tyler?"

Ty grasped her arm. "Answer me."

"Can we talk about how this affected you later? In privacy?"

"I'm old enough to understand everything, Mom. You might as well talk in front of me."

"Not about old loves."

Winona was right. There were some things that shouldn't be discussed in front of a young girl.

Winona pulled back one side of her fur and rested her hand on her hip. She still had a killer body. Despite his anger, old feelings swamped Ty. The attraction hadn't died. He tried not to look, but her pants fit her as though she'd poured on melted butter.

"What now?" Winona asked, but Ty didn't respond. She was talking to Ruby.

"I want to stay with my real dad for a while. I want to get to know him."

"Ty, how do you feel about that?"

"I want it."

Winona nodded. "Ty, can we stay for a few days?"

"Yes." In that time, he'd get to know his daughter better, but he'd also have the chance to sort out his feelings for Winona, to exorcise them.

"Yes!" Ruby pumped her fist.

"How did you find Tyler?" Winona asked.

"I went online," Ruby answered. "It was easy because he's sheriff of Accord."

Winona tossed her coat across the back of the sofa. Her breasts still took his breath away. Ty remembered them naked all those years ago, how he couldn't get enough of sucking them, and how big her nipples were and how they used to peak against his tongue. They looked more full and womanly than they had and made those hot, sultry, summer nights feel like only yesterday.

Damn, how could he have those kinds of feelings with his child standing in the room? His life was becoming more and more surreal.

"How come you came to get me?" Ruby said. "You know you don't really care about me."

Winona rolled her eyes. "Stop being such a drama queen. Of course I came for you. You're my daughter."

Ty should hate this woman. She'd ruined him for other women, even Tammy, whose only fault had been falling for Ty.

It was time for Ty to find out exactly who he was. That poor young sucker who could be manipulated? Or a man who'd grown up enough to know his own mind?

Trouble was, he'd never put the time into getting over Winona, and he'd lost a good woman because of it. Because he still lived in the past, because he'd never dealt with his parents' mistakes, let alone his own with Winona, Tammy would pay a price.

Was this the legacy of the Jordan brothers? To glide through life ignoring problems rather than dealing with them? Lord, it was time to change.

"Ruby, honey, can you get my bag out of the car?" Winona asked. "It's on the backseat."

"Okay, Mom, but later you're gonna have to tell me why

you kept me from my real dad." She pulled on her boots and ran outside.

Winona turned her full attention on Tyler. "You've grown up, Ty. You're a man now."

"I guess," he said. He thought of getting answers from Winona now, but Ruby would be back too soon.

Ruby ran in with her mom's overnight case, her cheeks red and a grin on her face. Winona stepped away from Ty and he said, "Come on upstairs. I'll show you to your room."

He hung Winona's coat on a hook by the door then gestured for her to precede him upstairs. Big mistake. He walked behind her, his eyes level with her firm, shapely ass. He groaned and tried to hide it with a cough.

He wasn't a horny teenager. He was no longer an impressionable college student away from home for the first time. He was a thirty-four-year-old man who knew his way around women.

Trouble was, the message wasn't getting through to his libido.

CALLIE HAD GIVEN herself one day to grieve—Monday. On Tuesday morning, she'd dragged herself out of bed and had called the mayor. Between them, they had organized a town meeting for Thursday evening. The mayor had proven to be as efficient as she was. He wanted this resort in his community.

Then she'd called Nick.

When Nick answered, he asked, "How are things there? Is Gabe ready to sell? Have you managed to convince the town that this is a good idea?"

"The first meeting is on Thursday night."

"Excellent work. I'm coming down."

What? "Why?"

"I've got the artist's renderings for the hotel. They're stunning. I think they'll sell the town on the project."

"Great. That will make the job easier."

"Are you okay?" Nick had always been smart. "Something's changed in you. What happened?"

"I've been looking into Gabe's business, as you asked me to."

"And?"

"And he's squeaky clean. He runs a great business. He's smart and ethical."

"There must be something we can use. Get out to the ranch and find out more."

"I can't spy again, Nick. It felt wrong the first time and I shouldn't have done it. I've already checked all of his files. Gabe caught me snooping. I'm lucky he didn't throw me in jail."

"So?"

"So, I won't do anything else for you that's illegal." She'd answered too hotly, but honestly. How much did Nick expect her to compromise herself?

"I can hire the best lawyers," he said. "I'd get you off."

"You're not listening. I won't break the law for you."

"Then find a legal way to do it."

"What's going on, Nick? You've never asked me to do this kind of thing before. Why is this so important to you?"

"That's none of your business. What *is* your business is getting what I need to seal this deal."

"I won't break the law. You can threaten to fire me all you want, but you can't force me to commit illegal activities for you."

"Get this job done, one way or another."

"I'll be a professional. I'll cajole and instruct. I won't break the law. Get used to it, Nick."

If he wanted to fire her, so be it.

After a moment's silence, Nick said, "I'll see you on Thursday evening," and disconnected. Callie threw her phone across the room. *Hell.*

Hell!

Her rage was cold. White-hot. She'd betrayed a man and her own ethics. All she wanted now was to finish this job and get home.

Since Tuesday morning, her life had been a whirlwind. She'd signed the papers to put the condo and house up for sale and had faxed them back to the agent.

She and the mayor had pulled this meeting together. Callie had had flyers photocopied and hand-delivered them to every resident and business in town.

She'd put a poster up in the window of any business that supported the idea.

She'd driven down back roads to deliver to farms and ranches.

Nick would bring completed architectural renderings for the meeting.

Sophie was having a lot of trouble with Mom. Callie needed to finish the job here and get home to Seattle to support both Sophie and Mom.

The push was on.

CHAPTER SIXTEEN

"LET'S HAVE IT, WINONA." Ruby was in bed. It was Wednesday night and the woman had avoided Ty's efforts to get at the truth.

"Why did you hide Ruby from me?"

"I already told you. I wanted a family unit. I'd fallen for Kevin and wanted to marry him."

"What about me?"

"What about you? We separated and I married another man."

God, the woman could be obtuse. "What about me getting to know my little girl?"

"I'm sorry, Ty. I thought it was better for Ruby to have a stable home with one father. Maybe I made a mistake, but Ruby would have been happy believing Kevin was her dad if she'd never found out otherwise."

"You're missing my point. *I* was her real father. I never got to spend time with her. I missed thirteen years. *Thirteen* years."

"I thought I was doing the right thing for Ruby."

They were going around in circles. There was never going to be a satisfactory answer for Ty.

ON THURSDAY EVENING, Gabe wandered aimlessly through the house, staring first at the floor in front of the fireplace where he and Callie had made love. He'd shared himself with her, his body yes, but also his soul.

He'd told her things he'd never told another human being. He'd thought that he'd finally found someone to listen to him, to understand him, to love him.

Was this fate's way of telling him that he really didn't deserve happiness? That life was just going to keep screwing with him as long as he went looking for more than he already had? That this land he loved so much was the sum total of his future, was *all* he would ever have.

He walked down the hall to the office. His objective mind understood that Callie had been doing what she had to do to keep her job. Yeah, he understood that, but he'd been about to offer her a way out. After he'd caught her, that option was no longer available.

She'd broken his trust—for his brother. Another woman lost to Nick.

Déjà-vu all over again. It hurt as much this time as it had the first. Maybe more so. This time he'd gone in with his eyes wide open.

He couldn't sleep. Rarely ate. His dogs, the children, kept him going, but he wished to hell Callie had never entered his life. He'd been drifting, yeah, but accepted his life exactly as it had stood.

She'd given him hope for the future and it had all been a lie. There was a lesson in here somewhere, but damned if he knew what it was.

His phone rang and he ignored it. He couldn't stomach talking to anyone. Two minutes later it rang again, and then again. Finally, he gave in.

"Gabe, you need to get to town. Fast."

Ty's voice on the end of the line sounded too anxious for Gabe's comfort.

"Get where, Ty? To the sheriff's office?"

"No, the auditorium in the school."

"Why?"

"She's holding a meeting."

Cold suspicion crept through him. "She?" But he was afraid he already knew. Callie.

"Callie and the mayor have called a meeting at the high school for seven this evening."

He would fight. He'd claw the bastards apart if they tried to build. No more Mr. Nice Guy. "I'll be there."

"Good to hear some spirit in your voice. There's something else, Gabe. I—I want you to meet someone."

"Who?"

After a long silence, Ty said, "My daughter."

Gabe fumbled the phone. "Your *what?*"

"I have a daughter, Gabe. I just found out on Friday night. She's beautiful."

"But, how? With who? When?"

"With Winona."

Gabe stifled the curse word he nearly used. He hated the woman, hated what she'd done to Ty.

"How old is the girl?"

"Thirteen."

"Are you sure she's yours? With Winona, you never know."

"She looks like me. She's mine. She's wonderful. I'm bringing her to the meeting."

Gabe needed to meet her, to confirm for himself that Winona wasn't pulling a fast one on Ty. The woman was a viper. Gabe wouldn't put it past her to try to pawn off someone else's kid on tenderhearted Ty. "I'll be there at seven," Gabe said. "Latest."

At a quarter to seven, Gabe hovered at the rear of the high school auditorium with his back to the wall beside the door, while townspeople filled the seats. He was here among them, but...apart.

He might have opened up to Callie, but here in town, his awkwardness came flooding back and he still felt...he searched for the right word…*gauche*. He thought that described how he felt. *Awkward. Unsophisticated.* Unable to gauge what his reaction to these people should be.

Yet he was determined in his purpose for being here. So fleeing wasn't an option.

In his panic, the room looked like an open field of land mines, of exposed IEDs—improvised explosive devices. Here, in this room, Gabe could identify every one. He saw too many people to whom he attached negative energy.

Billy's dad sat six rows from the front on the right. IED. *Bam!* Audrey Stone, Billy's sister, sat beside him. IED. *Bam!* Monica Accord sat on his other side. An IED if there ever was one. *Bam!*

Laura Cameron sat in the second row, more beautiful now than she had been at eighteen, damn her cheating heart. Another IED. *Bam!*

Callie sat on the stage at the front of the room. She was only doing what he knew she had to do, but she was going to ruin his life.

Maybe he should have made love to her more and kept her with him longer, to really cement a relationship with her. Maybe he should have asked her to live with him that morning before Nick called. Would things have worked out differently?

She watched Gabe from the stage, her face shuttered. He couldn't read her. She'd closed herself off. There wasn't a speck of animation in her expression.

She sat beside the mayor. No surprise there. Howard Walsh would sell his soul to bring money into Accord. He was the one who'd engineered all of the changes while Gabe had been away in Afghanistan. Gabe had come home to a different town, one that swelled with visitors on weekends and, during the summer, all week long.

No wonder he disliked coming into town.

Noah Cameron stepped into the room and nodded to Gabe.

"How're you doing, man? Haven't seen you in town in a while."

It was exactly this type of situation that left him flustered. He and Noah used to be buddies, but both Gabe and Nick had broken Laura's heart—Nick when he'd seduced Laura and left town, and Gabe when he'd said incredibly hurtful things after finding them together, and had left town to join the army.

Laura was Noah's sister.

So, was Noah friend or foe? Gabe didn't know, but he appeared to be friendly. Gabe could either ignore the guy, or he could take him at face value.

"Hey, Noah." He couldn't find anything else to say and Noah stepped forward and pumped Gabe's hand in a solid handshake.

"Good to see you, Gabe. You planning to sell your land for this resort?"

"Nope."

"Good." Noah grinned and left to sit down.

Thank God for tree huggers.

Ty stepped into the room in his sheriff's uniform. He took his sheepskin jacket off and threw it into an empty seat in the back row.

Gabe noticed right away that something was wrong. Normally, Ty would never wear a wrinkled uniform shirt. His eyes roved the audience with an avid gleam until he spotted his target and hunger was replaced by despair. Gabe followed Ty's sight lines until he saw Tammy Trudeau sitting in the front row.

Gabe glanced back at Ty. Ty turned and Gabe saw his face, shocking him with the depth of change in his little brother. Judging by the dark circles under his eyes, the man hadn't been sleeping, that was certain. Ty was a good-looking, easygoing man women loved. Even as a small boy, girls used to follow him home from school.

He didn't look easygoing now. He looked troubled, almost haunted.

Gabe noticed a young girl standing quietly beside him. His daughter.

"Gabe," Ty said, "this is Ruby. Ruby, my brother Gabe."

By the look of her, she was Ty's. No doubt about it.

A gangly young teenager, Ruby stared up at Gabe with something like hope in her eyes. What for? What on earth did Gabe have to give a young girl?

"I've heard all about you."

She had? What would Ty have told her about him?

Gabe didn't know what to do. He knew that he *wanted* to wrap his arms around this pretty, soft girl and welcome her into the family.

Was that appropriate? Would he scare her?

Frozen by indecision, he didn't move. She looked disappointed. He hated that he might have made her unhappy.

Slowly, he reached out one hand. When she didn't flinch away, just stared at him with expectation in her eyes, he settled his hand on her shoulder.

"Hi," he said. So lame. "Welcome to the family." Too formal. Too stilted.

It didn't seem to bother her. A broad smile lit up her face and crinkled her pretty gray eyes. She had Ty's eyes.

"Can I call you Uncle Gabe?"

He smiled. "I'd like that."

Ty motioned for Ruby to sit in the empty seat beside his coat. Gabe dropped his hand from her small shoulder and she sat. When Ty's avid gaze watched everything she did, his frown softened.

Ty looked miserable and Gabe's heart sank. "What are you going to do when Tammy sees Winona?"

Damn. Winona had run circles around the sweet boy Ty had been. Barracudas were nicer than Winona. The woman was a bottom-feeder. She'd trampled Ty and had left him heartbroken. It had taken him a few years to recover.

Gabe had often suspected Ty of dating Tammy because of an uncanny resemblance to Ty's first love. Looks like that problem might come back to bite his butt tonight.

"Winona's staying at the ranch." Ty took off his cowboy hat and twisted the brim in his hand.

Oh, good lord above. "Are you out of your mind?"

"I think so, Gabe. Something's happening between us."

"*Something?* What?"

"I don't know. I'm…confused."

"Yeah, I'll bet you are. Take my advice. Boot that viper out of town and then march up that aisle and haul Tammy home and marry her."

Gabe glanced down and saw Ruby watching him, biting her lip. He didn't think she could hear him, but maybe she had. He lowered his voice. "Winona's trouble, Ty. Always has been. Always will be."

Another worry struck. "Have you slept with her?"

"No."

"But you're tempted, aren't you?"

Yes. Bam! Gabe had never been disappointed in his younger brother before, but Ty was in danger of making a doozy of a mistake that was going to blow all his hopes and dreams to smithereens.

"And Tammy?" Gabe stabbed a finger toward the front of the room. "What about her? What about when she sees Winona?"

"She won't. I convinced Winona to stay home." Ty said no more, but sat beside his daughter and stared straight ahead, his expression unreadable.

Sitting in the row in front of where Gabe stood, Ruby slipped her small hand into one of Ty's. Ty had a daughter.

Gabe was an uncle. It was the best shock he'd received in a long time. It was flat-out awesome.

He rubbed his chest above his heart. He had a niece.

Someone at the front of the room called the meeting to order.

A commotion at the door had the audience all turning to see who it was.

Nick entered, shocking the hell out of Gabe.

He approached, his expression neutral.

"Gabe," he said, but he might as well have been greeting a stranger for all the warmth his voice held.

Gabe nodded and left it at that. What was there to say? They had a history that was about as toxic as it could get between brothers. Dad would be so disappointed in them, not that Nick would care. He had been only five when Dad died, and firmly attached to Mom.

Gabe thought of those years before Dad died as heaven, though, when all three brothers had got along, when Dad's absences had been mitigated by the fun times when he'd been around. Surely Nick could remember hints of those good memories?

At any time over the years, if Nick had called to apologize for what he'd done to Gabe and Laura, Gabe would have forgiven him. He couldn't honestly tell what kind of man his youngest brother had become, but if sending a woman to pull the land out from under Gabe's feet was any indication, Nick hadn't grown one iota.

At this rate, there would never be peace between them.

Tyler stood, reached across the back of his chair and shook Nick's hand. Gabe wished he hadn't, but he couldn't ask Ty to take sides in brotherhood. He'd already asked him to take sides in the resort issue.

Asking any more than that of Tyler wouldn't be fair.

Nick strode up the aisle to the stairs that led to the stage, seemingly oblivious to the murmurs around him and the audience watching him.

He'd gained a presence with age, almost an indifference to his surroundings. He was his own man and the rest of the world be damned. To Gabe's eye, he appeared older than his thirty-two years. He looked tired. Overworked.

Nick had chosen his road. If it aged him prematurely, so be it.

When Nick reached the stage, a woman in the second row stood and stumbled over seated men and women to get to the aisle. Laura. It looked like she couldn't get out fast enough.

Then she hurried down the aisle toward where Gabe stood in the back of the auditorium and his breath caught in his throat.

He'd gone out of his way to avoid her in town until now. After he'd found her and Nick in bed together, he'd never talked to her again.

Now here she was and she'd grown up so well, a beautiful, endowed and sensual woman who was too exotic for small-town Accord.

As anger surged, he swore under his breath. She should be here as his wife. They should have already been married for a dozen years and had a bunch of children who looked like the two of them. If she'd remained faithful, he would have never joined the army, would never have gone to Afghanistan, and his best friend, Billy, would never have died.

He moved as though to leave, but the back of the room had filled up and the doorway was blocked. The air became thin and the walls and people closed in on him.

Laura almost ran into him. He grasped her shoulders to hold her at arm's length. He didn't want to touch her, didn't want to remember how good she used to feel in his arms.

She was so distressed she'd walked right into him. "I'm sorry, I—" She looked up and gasped. *"Gabe."* No sound came out, only the shape of his name on her full lips. Her wide hazel eyes drank in the sight of him, cataloged every detail of his face.

Then, as though remembering that they were no longer lovers, no longer friends, she deflated and whispered, "Gabe, I—"

She didn't seem to have anything else to say.

What else could she say? Nothing would ever be right between them again. How do you make peace after a betrayal that was profound enough to hurtle him away from town and into war?

He'd avoided her since returning home. He hadn't wanted to see her, to meet her, to have any kind of scene.

Now, Nick's presence spurred on a need to clear the air. He wanted to talk. He wanted to know everything, but this was neither the time nor the place. He let her go.

Laura slipped past him and left the building.

Mayor Walsh cleared his throat. "Good evening."

A full audience of heads swiveled to face the front of the room again, releasing the glare of the spotlight that had paralyzed Gabe.

CHAPTER SEVENTEEN

AFTER MAYOR WALSH introduced Callie, she stood to speak. Knowing that Gabe was at the back of the room listening made the job more difficult. But not impossible.

She'd lived through so much in life.

She would live through this.

"As many of you know," she began, "one of your own, Nick Jordan, has plans to build a resort on the land he grew up on. More than anything, he would like the town's support for this project."

For a half an hour, she outlined exactly what a resort of this size could do for the town. How the businesses would profit and prosper. How it was a natural extension of the town's revival. How it could boost the town's growth into a new level.

How it could provide much-needed jobs and keep the young from leaving by offering them careers.

She unveiled the drawings that Nick had carried in with him, to gasps from the audience.

Callie was impressed. The architect had done an amazing job. All clean lines and spare minimalism, it sat in and among mature forest growth. A few of the tall pines appeared to grow up through the center of the building.

Her last pièce de résistance?

Nick would pay for anyone graduating from Accord's high school interested in a career working for him at the resort to attend college to study the hospitality and tourism industry and/or culinary arts. In return, upon completion, he would expect them to work for him a minimum of two years. Little enough time to trade for a few years of education.

The crowd broke into applause and Callie knew she'd won the town over.

She threaded her fingers together and squeezed, ordering herself to hold in all of the complex emotions bedeviling her. Not only were the two most important men in her life in the same room, the situation was public.

To a man as private as Gabe was, this must be hell—to have his land discussed as though it were owned publicly by the town.

I'm so sorry.

A bead of sweat ran between her breasts and yet, she felt a chill.

She'd lost Gabe.

She'd lost a beautiful thing.

She felt worse for Gabe than she did for herself. On many levels, she was stronger than he was, but then, she hadn't been betrayed as he had, and she hadn't gone to war, as he had. She hadn't survived a bombing while her best friend had died in front of her. She'd had so much less to deal with in life.

Throughout the Q-and-A part of the meeting, she listened to what Nick and the mayor said with only half an ear. The presentation over and done, she was tired.

In a few minutes, she would have to mingle outside the room and become her most professional, persuasive self. With an effort, she rose above her own heartbreak and rallied her thoughts.

Nick ended the evening by urging the townspeople to convince Gabe to sell. "For the greater good."

Gabe, I'm sorry.

Nick turned to her. "You did well."

His praise rang hollow.

She left the stage and started the long trek through the

crowd toward Gabe, to get this over with, to let him say whatever he needed to say to her so she could get on with her work.

He stood talking to his brother Ty and a young teenage girl.

Before she could reach Gabe, Jeff Stone did. "Sell, for God's sake. Think of someone besides yourself for a change."

Callie watched Gabe retreat further into himself.

Nobody noticed when she approached.

A soft voice beside Callie said, "Hi, Ty. Ruby."

"Tammy." Ty stared at her with hunger, but also something more. Guilt, maybe?

Tyler noticed Callie and introduced her to Tammy. Tammy was friendly, but there was something going on here, some tension permeating the atmosphere, that Callie didn't understand.

Tammy walked away. When Ty and the teenager moved on, there was only Gabe left in front of her.

He'd reverted to mountain-man recluse mode, watching her warily as he had that first day she'd knocked on his door. She missed the man he hid inside. She missed his arms around her. She missed the physical and emotional intimacy they had forged between them.

She'd ruined it and had no idea how to get it back when her job, her livelihood, her mother's safety, depended on this ski resort coming to fruition.

She touched his arm, frantic for some small sign of affection, of attachment.

He placed his hand over hers and she basked in the warmth of his touch. Under his anger and disappointment in her, she saw a hint of something she thought was concern.

"You play with someone like Nick and you get burned, Callie. He has no conscience. You remember that. Don't trust him."

"I have to for now, Gabe. You know that." She stepped aside to allow someone to pass. "I'm more sorry than I can say that you are stuck in the middle. I wish Nick had chosen another piece of land outside of another town to develop. I wish he hadn't sent me here to betray you."

"What's done is done," Gabe said.

"That's philosophical of you. If I were you, I'd hate me."

Like she hated herself. She stepped away from him and set off to mingle and answer any questions that needed answering.

She could use a drink, or two, or three.

She could use oblivion.

She could use a Gabe Jordan hug.

LATER, CALLIE RAN into Nick in the lobby of the B and B.

"Are you staying here?"

He nodded.

Kristi called to them from the living room. "Can I interest either of you in a glass of wine?"

It was nearly eleven and Callie had as much energy as a wrung-out dishrag.

"I'm heading up to bed. Thanks anyway."

Nick followed her. "A word in your room, Callie."

Once she closed her door, he said, "You slept with him."

She kept her lips shut. It was none of Nick's business.

"I only guessed, you know. Looks like it was a good guess."

He stepped close. "I don't care if you screw Gabe left, right and center as long as you deliver what I need."

"I know who I work for. I'm a professional." *But you haven't behaved like one.*

"Are you, Callie? Have you managed to maintain your professionalism?"

No. She'd fallen for Gabe hook, line and sinker. He was better than any man she'd ever met, and she'd blown it big-time. The second she'd realized that she was falling for him, she should have walked away. She certainly shouldn't have slept with him, not when Nick had the power to hurt him so badly.

Callie lobbed a question back on Nick. "This isn't one of your normal business deals. This one's dirty. It has the emotional stamp of revenge all over it. Are *you* maintaining your professionalism?"

Nick's jaw worked.

"What's this *really* about, Nick? It isn't about money. If you never worked another day in your life, you would still be rich. Why do you need to destroy Gabe? Because he embarrassed you in front of Marsha and her father when you were young? How petty is that?"

He loomed over her and pointed a finger in her face. "You be careful."

"Oh, back off. What is it with you Jordan boys that you think you can intimidate me with your damn size?"

"Don't fall for him," Nick warned. "Do *not* fall for my brother."

Too late. She'd already fallen like a ton of freaking bricks, and she was lost. The only course of action left to her was to behave like the professional that she was and get the townspeople to convince Gabe to sell and then leave town.

"Don't worry, Nick. *Nothing* will get in the way of me doing my job."

Nick left the room, slamming the door on his way out.

Callie slumped onto the bed. She wanted her mother, wished she could still call and talk to her as she used to do when she needed advice.

Johanna was gone, though, so Callie had no one to rely on but herself.

Callie curled into a ball on the bed, cold and alone and aching for Gabe.

In a little while she dried her tears and sat up.

She reapplied her makeup, put on her coat and boots and walked downstairs. She found Kristi in the parlor.

"Callie, that was an exhilarating presentation." Kristi turned to her with a smile. "The ski resort sounds wonderful. I can't wait for it to come true. We'll all have to work on Gabe until he agrees to sell."

Oh, Gabe, what have I done? I brought a blight to town and you're going to be the biggest loser. You're going to be hounded until you give in.

"Kristi, do you have any of that baked custard left that you served after dinner?" It had wild rice in it and golden raisins and some kind of liqueur. Callie had never tasted anything so good.

"Yes, do you want another piece?"

"Could I have two pieces? To go?"

Kristi seemed to pick up on Callie's somber mood. "Of course. Give me a minute."

She returned five minutes later with a bag that she placed into Callie's hand. With a serious look, she said, "Tell Gabe to do what he needs to do for his own good. He doesn't need all of us bothering him."

"Thank you, Kristi. You're a gem."

She got into her car and drove out to Gabe's house. Once there, she stared at the warm glow in the one front window. When she stepped out of the car, she smelled wood smoke on the air. He had a fire going.

She knocked and waited.

The door opened and Boo stepped out and licked her hand. Gabe stared at her without a word. There was an awful lot of somberness going around tonight, as though the whole world were crying.

He didn't move.

"May I come in?" she asked.

"You can't think— You can't want—"

"No, Gabe, I don't want to make love. I mean I do. Desperately. More than anything else, but no, I don't expect that we will." She stepped inside, forcing him to back up. She slid past him and he shut the door. "I thought you might be feeling alone tonight. I'm the last person you want to see, but I think I might be the only one in town thinking of your welfare."

Only the fire lit the room and Callie greedily drank in every detail of the ordinary, unimpressive, wonderful space.

Behind her, Gabe touched her shoulder. Afraid of splintering, she slipped away from his touch. She couldn't get through this if she let him touch her before she had her say.

"Can you get a couple of plates and forks?" She looked up at him.

He left the room and she heard him making noise in the kitchen. She took off her coat and draped it across the back of the sofa, then sat on the floor in front of the fire and hugged her knees to her chest, staying there until Gabe came out with a tray. She scooted back to lean against the sofa and patted the floor beside her and Gabe sat down. He set the tray aside.

"What's going on, Callie?"

"I came to say goodbye."

She felt Gabe still. "You're leaving?"

"Yes. No. I mean—" She closed her eyes and gathered her thoughts. The clock in the kitchen ticked away the minutes. Other than that, there was little noise. She wasn't sure Gabe was even breathing, he was so contained, had turned so deeply inside of himself for protection.

He shouldn't have come to the meeting.

"I mean," she said calmly, "I will be leaving, yes, but not for a couple of weeks. I doubt that I'll see you again. You don't come to town and I won't be coming back out here."

She took his hand. "But, Gabe, you were *such* a pleasure and I couldn't resist. It isn't much of an excuse for the pain I caused you. I deeply regret that you got hurt."

He opened his mouth to speak, but she raised her hand to forestall him. "One more thing. I did *not* sleep with you because I wanted to seduce you into selling."

"I know."

"You do? I was afraid you might think that I had. I wanted to make sure you never believed that."

"I did for a minute. Then I thought about who you are and it didn't fit."

She curled her legs under her and scooted sideways so she could see his face. "I'm sorry, Gabe." She touched his cheek. "You'll never know how sorry."

He stared into the fire.

"Are you okay?" she asked.

"I'm fine."

He wasn't about to open up to her. Why should he?

"For the record," she said, "you're a better man than Nick will ever be."

His laugh sounded rough. "For what that's worth. He still always gets the girl, one way or another."

"No."

"What?"

"No. Nick doesn't 'have' me, not in the way you do."

Gabe wouldn't look at her.

"I'll miss you," she said. Her hand gripped his and then she stood.

He stood, too. "What did you bring me?"

"Kristi's custard. Comfort food. I thought you might need a little comfort tonight." She left the bag on the side table.

"I did," he said. "I do."

She didn't know what to say to that. Was it an invitation to stay?

"I'm going to visit Laura in the morning and get some answers from her."

"Oh, Gabe, that's such a good idea. It's the right thing to do."

They were talking like friends, as though a sweet fledgling friendship were developing. Even though Callie knew it couldn't go anywhere after her betrayal, she treasured these brief moments, held them close to take out for examination later when she knew she'd have trouble sleeping.

"Kristi wanted me to tell you to do what you have to do for *you,* and not do what the town wants."

"Billy's father wants me to stop being selfish and sell."

"Everyone in town will be selfish in trying to persuade you to sell. Everyone has an agenda, Gabe."

They hovered in a weird tension, as though suspended in gel, neither one wanting to be the first to end the night. Callie had started this meeting so it was up to her to end it.

She leaned close while Gabe seemed to hold his breath. She rested her lips against his, closing her eyes to savor every drop of this last kiss. He smelled familiar and clean and manly, and so Gabe.

She pulled away and didn't dare look at him, but left without a word.

WINONA BRUSHED AGAINST Ty again, too close to be another mistake.

They were in the kitchen. Ruby had just gone up to bed, tired after the night's meeting.

Winona actually thought he bought her little apologies, that he didn't realize these close meetings were contrived, that he believed they were innocent. Had he really been so naive that he'd bought into Winona's manipulations when he was young?

She leaned across him to get a spoon from the cutlery drawer and her breast touched his biceps.

"Stop," he said, grasping her wrist. Her pulse beat beneath his thumb. "Winona, don't do this."

"Do what, Ty?"

"This." He gestured between them. "Come so close and then pretend you touched me by accident."

Winona chuckled and it was low and throaty. "Okay. You got me. You've grown into a beautiful man, Tyler." She brushed her fingers along his jaw. Fire trailed her red nails along his skin. "I still find you attractive. What's wrong with that? I'm a signature away from divorce."

"You were sleeping with Kevin while you slept with me, weren't you?"

She sobered. "Yes, I was."

At his raised brows, she said, "I've learned to tell the truth, Ty. I made mistakes in my past that I can never take back, but I'm trying to make them right now. I used and abused your heart. I would never do that again." As if to swear to that, she rested her hand over his heart.

Ty absorbed her honesty. "That's good, Winona. You really worked me over. I'm glad to hear you've changed."

She stepped to the refrigerator and pulled out a bottle of white wine. She poured two glasses and handed him one. "Are you with someone?"

He sighed. "Not anymore." The wine was tart on his tongue and turned to acid on its way to his stomach. He set it aside.

"Then what could possibly be wrong with us acting on our attraction?" Winona stayed close and he could feel the heat of her through his shirt.

When he didn't respond to her question, she stepped close. "If you can't answer right away, then you're tempted. I'm going to be as honest as I can be here, Ty. I want you. Yes, I betrayed you, but I kicked myself many times over the years for choosing the wrong man. Believe me, I paid a price." She raised her glass to her lips and drank. "I'm single now, Ty, and I want you. We're here now. We have no ties. We're a man and a woman who want to do what comes naturally."

She kissed him, tasting like wine, and lingered on his lips. She'd always been a great kisser. That hadn't changed.

He grasped her around the waist and pulled her to him. Her breasts full against his chest and her waist small in his big hands, she didn't feel the same as Tammy.

Tammy.

What about Tammy?

He pulled away slowly. She nipped at his bottom lip to keep him close.

"What is it, Ty?"

"I—" He didn't know. Tammy was gone for good. Wasn't she? *God, Jordan, get your shit together.*

She leaned into him, smelling thick and exotic and expensive, like the bath oil his bathroom smelled like now. Heat poured from her in musky waves. She bit his mouth without mercy this time, wanting and taking and the hell with resistance. She plundered with her tongue, making Ty dizzy with her aggression. It should be him.

She wanted aggression. Fine. So be it.

With both arms across her back, he pulled her against him hard enough to leave bruises, and bent her back over the kitchen table. She wrapped her legs around him.

The blouse that had some kind of funny knot at the front fell open and her breasts spilled out, still perfect fourteen years later.

"If we do this, Ty, no regrets." She all but steamed in his arms, her nipples already peaking, her desire blatant. His groin throbbed. She ran her hands inside his shirt, her fingers through the hair on his chest.

He breathed heavily. He would have regrets. He knew it. He no longer wanted Winona outside of this crazy lust.

He wanted Tammy. Even if she was no longer his, having sex with Winona would feel like he was betraying her yet again. Dating her because she reminded him of Winona had been bad enough. Sleeping with Winona now would be so much worse.

Ty pulled away from her and lifted her up from the table. Underneath the lust, he didn't feel a damn thing for her. There was nothing about Winona that he liked aside from her body.

And that body, and sex, wouldn't be worth how low he would feel in the morning if he gave in tonight.

CHAPTER EIGHTEEN

Ty SHOWED RUBY how much grain to put in the buckets, then hooked them onto his small tractor. He got on and she sat behind him and they drove from the barn to the bison enclosure.

"This is so cool," she said.

Ty smiled. Every day, every hour, every moment spent with Ruby was a revelation.

Her interest in the bison and ranch life was fathomless.

He showed her where to fill the bins the bison ate from. "It's important to keep them clear of snow. That's why I was out here so long on Sunday as soon as the storm stopped. To clear the couple of feet of snow from the feed bins."

"Do they have to eat every day? Like us?"

"Yeah. I'm raising these animals domestically. They're no longer free to roam the range so I'm responsible for their food."

Hirsute wandered to the fence.

"Can I pet him?"

She reached a tentative hand.

"Go ahead. He won't bite."

"His head's so big!"

Ty laughed. "Yeah."

She petted Hirsute for a while then said, "His eyes are so small for his head. He's really warm. His fur's uneven. It's shaggy."

"That's winter fur to keep him warm."

Ty watched her and smiled. Man, she was precious. He

planned to make her a fixture in his life, one way or another. He had a lot of time to make up for.

"Dad?"

He liked the sound of that, but her voice was hesitant.

"Yeah?"

"Do you still love my mother?"

Out of the mouths of babes! "No. Not like I think you mean."

"Do you think you might ever marry her?"

Was that what Ruby wanted? Was she trying to be a match-maker between him and her mother?

Had she shown Tammy the photo of Winona to get her out of the way? Could Ruby be that conniving? He hadn't spent enough time with her to know.

"No," he said. "I won't be marrying your mother."

Ruby's *oh* sounded small and sad.

Without Tammy, Ty doubted he would ever marry.

Man, that hurt.

On Friday morning, Nick came to see Callie before he left. Unfortunately, she was still in bed.

The flu or whatever it was that Gabe had suffered through last weekend had hit her with a sledgehammer.

"Why aren't you up yet?" He stood in the open doorway.

"I'm sick."

"Do you need anything sent up before I leave?" He carried an overnight bag with him and his overcoat on his arm.

"Could you have Kristi send up a breakfast? She knows what I like. I don't think I can face the dining room this morning."

They were oddly formal with each other, as if they both wanted to forget the emotion of the night before and get back to their usual relationship.

"You can do this?" he asked.

She understood what he asked. "I can do the job. No problem. Ask Kristi for a quart of coffee. That and a shower and I'll be good as new."

After Nick left Callie released a long sigh.

She managed to eat the breakfast she didn't want but knew she needed. When she dressed, she made sure to be careful with her clothes and her makeup. Just because she felt like crap didn't mean she had to look like it. She was heading out to Sweet Temptations, where she knew a lot of people congregated every morning. This particular morning, she needed to take the pulse of the town.

At the bakery, she ordered orange juice. She'd had enough caffeine for the day. Two cinnamon buns sat in a tray. "I'll take both of those."

Really, Callie? Two pastries? Your pudding belly doesn't need the calories.

She bought them anyway.

Every table was full. Time to glean everyone's reaction to the meeting, to gauge how many leaned toward Nick's side of the issue. She chose a table full of older men. They looked retired. She guessed they would take the most persuasion. In every town and city, for every new project Nick had proposed, there were holdouts, people who wanted nothing in their world to change.

"May I join you?"

As one, they nodded. One of them jumped up and found a chair for her.

"What did you think of last night's meeting?" she asked. No doubt they had already covered every point but were ready and eager for another go at it.

She listened while they argued, surprised but also depressed to find almost all were in favor of the resort. Surprised because she'd expected more resistance from a bunch of old guys. So much for making assumptions based on looks. The depression came from her worry for Gabe.

She reached for her second cinnamon bun but found that it was gone. She'd eaten both already?

Mindless eating. *Bad sign, Callie.*

She'd been blue before in her life. She would get over it. But the more tables she visited in the bakery, the more stores she visited, the more townspeople she talked to throughout the day, the more depressed she became. There was a groundswell in the town who welcomed tourist dollars, who *wanted* the resort.

Times had been hard for a few years. Their summer tourism trade had given them a taste for steady employment and an even steadier paycheck.

With an updated, flourishing town, maybe fewer of the young people would leave. As one woman said, "Our young have been bleeding out of town for years. It's time to stop the bleeding, for them to stay home."

Jobs would keep them here. Nick's generous offer of an education would appeal to a lot of parents who wanted their children to succeed.

She'd done her job well. With this kind of almost universal support, it wouldn't be hard to get local government approvals, to somehow get Gabe's wishes overridden and for her to get her bonus.

She could get Mom into a home earlier than she'd thought, no matter how long the condo or house took to sell. She had breathing room.

On Friday evening, falling into bed exhausted that night, Callie's last thought was *Oh, Gabe, what have I done to you?*

GABE NOTICED CALLIE sitting with a bunch of men at one of the tables in Laura's bakery. Her kiss last night had been sweet.

He wasn't here to see Callie. He was here to settle a score with Laura.

She stepped out from a back room with a tray of baked goods in her hands. When she saw him, she stopped and stared. A strong-willed woman, he didn't think she was often at a loss for words. Then again, she'd never seen Gabe in her bakery before and, after last night, maybe she could guess why he was here.

He approached the counter. "Can we talk?"

She handed the tray off to a young woman and said, "Follow me."

He did. She took him into a kitchen that looked so unlike Laura with its big bold stoves and countertops and walk-in refrigerator. Laura was warm and sensual while all of this was cold. The smell was something else, though, heavenly and spicy and lush like the woman.

They could have been so good together.

She faced him quietly today with none of last night's panic. "Well, Gabe? Let me have it."

"Have what?"

"Give me hell."

"That's not why I'm here."

She cocked her head. It might have looked coy on another woman. On Laura, it was all about curiosity and caring.

"I want answers. The biggest one is why?"

"I wish I could tell you, Gabe. I asked myself that for a long time. I don't know what came over me that night with Nick."

"Did you love him more than me?"

"No! Never."

Thank God. He didn't know why that had been so important to him.

"Not love. Lust, then?"

She shook her head, clearly uncomfortable talking about it. "I don't know." Her lips compressed and then she said,

"I'm going to change that answer. Of all the people I know, you deserve the truth. It was lust. I'd been attracted to Nick for a long time, but I ignored it. I could handle it. I wanted you, Gabe. I loved you, not Nick."

"And what happened that night? You couldn't control yourself?"

"Nick came on to me so strongly. He— I'm not sure what he did. He kissed me and the next thing I knew we were in bed together and you were there."

"He seduced you."

"Yes, but I can't absolve myself of all responsibility. There were two of us in the bed that night and I was a full participant."

She passed a hand over her eyes. "I couldn't stand the way you looked. It was the biggest mistake of my life, not just because I'd lost my chance to have a family with you, but because of how much I'd hurt you."

Gabe wanted to punch something. He'd lost Laura because of one night of lust. The senselessness choked him.

"I'm angry at the moment. One of these days I'll forgive you. For what it's worth I've always blamed Nick and been disappointed in you."

He turned to leave.

"Gabe."

He stopped.

"You didn't deserve what we did. I hope someday you can find the happiness you do deserve."

He walked away then, unsure of what had been accomplished outside of finally talking to Laura after so many years.

When he stepped into the café Callie was no longer there and he was absurdly disappointed.

ON MONDAY MORNING, Gabe answered the phone on the second ring. He'd been on the phone most of the morning, ordering dog food and supplies for the business.

The number didn't look familiar. He answered.

"Gabe? It's Kristi Mortimer." From the B and B.

"What can I do for you?"

"I'm worried about Callie MacKintosh."

His blood thrummed. "Why?"

"She went up to her room late Friday night and I haven't seen her since."

"That's only two days."

"I know, but she should have come out at least once or twice."

"Maybe you've just been too busy to notice her around." What did it have to do with him anyway? Callie's visit on Thursday night after the meeting had been a goodbye if ever there was one.

"Gabe, I don't have any other guests right now." Kristi made a noise that sounded like exasperation. "I'm cooking meals that no one is eating. She doesn't come out of her room. I haven't heard the shower running. She isn't using the fireplace."

"I'm on my way."

At the B and B, before he had a chance to say anything, Kristi ran up to him.

"I've been listening at her door. There've been no sounds." She ran for the stairs and Gabe followed. "What if she's dead?"

"She's not dead, Kristi. She's a young healthy woman."

"People have heart attacks. Aneurysms. All kinds of strange things."

"Have you tried knocking?"

"Yes! There's no answer."

"Maybe she left without telling you."

"Without her car?"

He took the stairs two at a time and stepped into Callie's room.

She lay on her back on the bed with the covers thrown aside. He stepped over clothes on the floor.

He leaned close. "Callie?"

She opened her eyes slowly, her focus on him sharpening even more slowly. "Chewbacca?" She reached out and touched his beard. Her focus shifted to the ceiling and the room around her and then back to him. "What are you doing here?"

"Came to see you. Heard you've been sleeping a lot. Are you sick?"

She sat up. Her hair was dirty and mashed against one side of her head. "No. Just tired."

Her ashen skin, the lack of fire in her eyes, her dull demeanor worried Gabe. Where was his bright, colorful girl? Where was that joyful energy he'd found so attractive?

He turned to Kristi who had followed him upstairs.

"What do you have in the kitchen? What can you make for Callie?"

"Anything. What does she want?"

Callie sat on the edge of the bed staring at the carpet.

"I don't think she knows what she wants," he said. "She needs nutrition."

"I have a root vegetable soup. Or beef with barley."

"Soup is good. Bring a mug of each. Do you have any more of that custard?"

"A fresh batch. Are you going to take care of her?"

"I'll stay as long as I need to."

"Callie took custard to you last week, didn't she?" Gabe heard a smile in her voice. "Should I bring up a slice for you, too?"

"Yeah, I'd like that." Maybe not everyone in the town was his enemy these days. Hard to tell by the number of phone calls he'd received from people arguing that he sell the land to Nick. He'd stopped taking calls and had let the machine take them, then weeded through the messages for anything relating to the business.

He squatted on his haunches, putting himself into Callie's line of vision. "What's going on?"

"Nothing serious, Gabe. Sometimes I just need to sleep."

"For two days? That sounds like depression."

"It isn't." She stood up and walked to the bathroom. "I'll be out in a sec."

A minute later, Gabe heard the toilet flush and the water run, then she came back out.

After one look at his face, she said, "Don't worry. It's nothing serious. Remember I told you about my closet sessions with my mom and how much they used to freak me out?"

"Yeah."

"This weird thing happens to me sometimes. When I feel overwhelmed by life, I curl inside of myself. I have to shut out the world, unplug the phone, make myself a haven and sleep."

"For two days?"

"Usually only for one."

"What triggered this?"

"Nick's success. The town is all over the resort. They love it. They love what it will do to the town. It's a shoo-in."

"Except that I haven't sold."

"You're going to become a pariah. Everyone's going to hate you."

She touched his cheek. "I've fallen for you, Gabe."

His heart rate kicked into the stratosphere. She'd fallen for him. How could a few such simple words make his heart, his hopes, his dreams take flight?

"I was never going to make both brothers happy, but now that Nick has won, I'm sick that you will lose, in one way or another. And I helped to make that happen."

"Don't beat yourself up, Callie. Please. Let me worry about myself."

"I can't."

"Would Nick have come after me if he'd had a different assistant?"

"Of course."

"Right. This was always Nick's deal from the start with or without you. You did your job. You earned your salary. You didn't set out to ruin my life. Nick did."

Gabe stood up. "I'm going to run you a bath."

"I can do it." She didn't move.

"I'll do it."

"You don't have to take care of me. I'm perfectly capable."

"I want to."

He found a basket of spa items beside the claw-foot tub. Looked like they were compliments of the B and B. He poured body wash under the running water. It smelled like roses.

He called Callie to the bathroom but she didn't respond. He returned to the bedroom and picked her up from where she still sat on the edge of the mattress.

"*Whoop!* I'm not sick. I can walk."

"I know. I feel like taking care of you."

Back in the bathroom, he stood her on her feet and turned off the water.

"Undress," he said.

At a knock on the exterior door, he said, "That will be Kristi with food. Wash yourself and then come out."

He took the tray from Kristi and put it on the small table bookended by two chairs. "This smells good."

"I added a pot of tea. I thought she might like that. Let me know if she needs anything else."

"Thanks."

He set up the food on the table in the sitting room. "Hurry up. There's soup and tea. Don't let it get cold."

By the time she came out in a bathrobe, he had a fire going.

"Sit."

She took one chair and he took the other. Her hair was still wet. She smelled like roses.

He poured her tea from a china pot with roses all over it. Kristi had provided two china cups and saucers. He poured Callie's first and put a mug of soup in front of her with a slice of bread that looked full-of-seeds-and-nuts healthy.

"Drink."

She did.

"I don't like you this tired. I don't want you diminished," he said. "I want the Callie who stood up to me, like at the beginning. Quit your job."

"I can't. Someday, but not yet."

"You have to. It's making you sick. *Nick's* making you sick. You're compromising your ethics."

She didn't answer for a long time. "You're right."

"Good."

After a few spoonfuls of soup, she said, "We both know I can't quit. Mom depends on me."

"We need to find a way around that."

"We? I'm not your responsibility. You have to stop taking care of me."

"You started taking on responsibility too young. You need to take a break."

"Look who's talking. You started young, too, and still take care of everything and everyone around you, including stray creatures."

Gabe hid a smile. She was coming alive in the argument. He doubted she realized how much she was eating. "I didn't start as an infant. I had a good ten years of nurture from my parents before I had to take on my brothers. You had none."

"But you seem to continue to take on responsibility."

"Because I found out it's in my character to like it."

"And it isn't in mine? Are you telling me I'm selfish?"

"No! Get real, Callie. I'm telling you that you're tired and you need a break."

She put down the slice of buttered bread she'd been eating. "Yes. That's how I feel."

"The first thing you need to do is get away from Nick. You need to quit."

She nodded. "I'll start sending out my résumé as soon as I get home."

"No. I mean now."

"That's not possible. I can't afford to quit now."

He couldn't believe what he was about to suggest, but he'd missed her. He wanted her. "You could if you came to live with me."

Her mouth dropped open. Then she snapped it shut. "My mom."

"Her, too."

"What kind of work would I do here in Accord?"

"You wouldn't have to work. You could help me with the business."

"I need more than that. I studied business administration. I liked it. I need to *do* something."

"Let's work on logistics later. Give us a chance. There must be a way."

He watched her weigh her options. "Not all business people live in the city. There must be something here for me." She pulled away from him. "Something bigger than the dog-sledding."

"We'll find it. We'll work it out."

"I've put my condo and Mom's home up for sale."

Suddenly, she sat up straight, her expression alarmed. "Oh!"

"What?"

"I've been asleep for days. I haven't called to check on Mom."

"Eat the other mug of soup. I'll call. What's her number?"

She rattled it off and he picked up the receiver from the hotel phone. When a woman answered, he identified himself and explained the situation.

"This is Sophie," she said. "I was wondering why I hadn't heard from Callie."

"She's feeling better and should be home in a day or two. She can explain what's happening when she gets there. How's her mother?"

"Up and down. Tell Callie no change."

Gabe relayed the message.

"Callie's heading home tomorrow."

"That's good," Sophie said. "Tell her I'll see her when she gets here."

Gabe joined her at the table. "That's settled. See whether you can get a flight out of Denver tomorrow."

He gulped down his cold tea. "Then call Nick and give notice. No. Don't. Just quit. As of today."

"On one condition," Callie replied. "Taking care of others can be admirable, but it can also have its downside. It can also become neurotic."

She was talking about him. He waited.

"You can't take responsibility for Billy's death any longer."

"I think it's more than that. It's tied in with his father's anger that Billy enlisted when I did."

"I know, I heard, but that wasn't your fault, either. He was a grown man." She set her teacup into the saucer with a firm click. "I'll call Nick and quit if you'll go see Jeff. Set him straight. Put your guilt aside."

"It's not easy, Callie."

She covered his hand with hers. "I know, but you have to do it."

"Yes." He placed his other hand on her cheek, where it

looked ridiculously big against her delicate head. "I'll do it. Call Nick."

As Gabe guessed, it didn't go down well. He could hear Nick yelling from across the room.

When she ended the call, Callie was pale again, but also defiant. Her eyes sparkled. "That felt good."

Gabe smiled. Thank God. She could live a better life now.

"Do you want me to come with you while you talk to Jeff?"

Gabe stood. "No. Make your reservation to fly home while I'm gone then pack your bag." He cradled her face. "Stay with me tonight? Leave from my place tomorrow?"

She leaned into his touch and closed her eyes. "Yes," she whispered. When she opened them, they were clear and clean. His Callie was back.

He drove straight to the house Billy had grown up in.

Jeff answered at Gabe's second knock. The smile the man had ready for whoever the company might be slipped when he saw Gabe. "What do you want?"

"We need to talk."

"No, we don't."

"Let me in."

"You're never setting foot in this house again."

"Fine. We'll do this on the doorstep."

Jeff tried to close the door, but Gabe slammed his hand against it, angry, needing to get this done and move on with his life with Callie. Today was the beginning of the rest of his life. "I've held this in long enough because I didn't want to hurt your feelings, but no more. I didn't ask Billy to join the army with me. I did everything I could to dissuade him. He wouldn't hear of it."

Gabe, man, we're best buddies. I wouldn't think of sending you off alone.

"I talked myself ragged trying to keep him here."

Jeff's jaw was set, his mind closed.

The thing is, man, I need to get away. I married Monica too young. I just wanted to get out of my dad's house. He's too rigid. Thinks he knows what's best for everyone. I'm sick of him bossing me around, but I just replaced one boss with another. At least with Uncle Sam bossing me around, I'll be doing some good instead of hanging out in my wife's house with my thumb up my ass. He'd grinned. *And I'll be getting paid.*

"He wanted to leave town. He wanted to see the world." In the end, Gabe couldn't bring himself to say, *he wanted to leave you.*

"I tried to keep him safe." Callie was right. It wasn't his fault that they had hit an IED that day. If it hadn't happened to them, it would have been the truck behind them. If Gabe hadn't cajoled Billy into coming out that day, he would have been in a shitload of trouble. He'd spent too many days pretending to be sick. The army only had so much tolerance for that kind of behavior. Gabe had known the truth, though. Underneath Billy's laziness there had been sheer terror. Poor happy-go-lucky Billy wasn't cut out to be a soldier. He was afraid of death. It had found him anyway.

Gabe spread his hands away from his sides. "Half of us in the truck survived that day and half died. I know you wish it was Billy who survived and not me. For these past four years, so did I, but no longer. I have a reason to live now. I can't take the blame for Billy's death anymore. He was a big boy who joined the army under his own steam. Live with it, Jeff."

Gabe left without looking back, because he really didn't want to see how much he'd devastated the man.

He called Callie to tell her he'd be a little longer. He had another person to visit.

He walked to the Palette. The place was empty of customers. Gabe barely noticed the art on the walls. Monica stepped out of a back room. Her face brightened when she saw him.

"Gabe, hi!" She spread her arms. "What do you think of the gallery? It's great, isn't it?"

He smiled, genuinely happy for her. Maybe she was starting to land on her feet.

He didn't know what he had to say to her that differed much from anything he'd said before, but one thing he could do was unload his guilt.

"Something's changed in you, Gabe."

"I've met someone."

Monica seemed to fight a battle and then smiled. "I'm happy for you, Gabe. You won't forget about me, will you?"

He pulled her into his arms and held her, breathing his newfound strength into her.

"Never."

Her smile looked a little sad, but she was happy for him. He could tell.

There were no pleas for his company, for him to change his mind about them, no neediness. Just acceptance. She couldn't have given him a better gift.

He left with a lighter heart.

Change was good and unburdening a body of guilt a gift for the soul.

Back at the B and B, Callie was packed, dressed and ready to go when he returned. He carried her suitcase to the car while she settled her bill.

He drove her out to the house and nothing in his life had ever felt better or more right.

ON MONDAY AFTERNOON, Ty waited outside the school for Tammy at the end of the school day. Activity teemed around him, but he had his eyes firmly fixed on that front door.

He'd called her on Friday and asked her not to come to the

ranch. Winona and Ruby were still there. Somehow, they had convinced Ty to let them stay a few more days. He couldn't bring himself to say no, to Ruby at any rate.

The kids cleared out, teachers left one by one or in pairs, but still no Tammy.

Maybe she was working on lesson plans.

Finally, he entered the building. He knew which classroom was hers.

He stepped through her door and found her at the back of her room pinning artwork to a bulletin board.

He approached. "Tammy," he said, his voice as rough as sandpaper.

She didn't jump, didn't flinch, didn't acknowledge him.

He moved to her side so he could see her face. Silent tears ran down her cheeks.

Gently, slowly so he wouldn't spook her, he took her in his arms. "I'm sorry," he whispered.

She remained stiff. *Give in, damn it, Tammy. Let me hold you.*

But she didn't. She pulled away and swiped her hands across her face.

"What do you want?" she asked, jutting her chin forward, her sadness replaced by defiance.

"We need to talk. About us."

"There isn't an us."

She might as well have hammered a nail in his coffin.

"I hoped we could work on us."

"And Winona?"

"She's not the woman I used to know."

"Do you still love her?"

"No, Tammy."

Anger flashed across her tired features. "How about this, Ty? I don't believe you."

"I don't blame you." In essence, his silence about Winona had been as damning as any lie. He'd broken Tammy's trust.

She marched up the aisle toward the front of the class but spun back around halfway there. "Why, Ty?"

He knew what she was asking. Why had he started dating her?

"The truth, Ty. Ruby showed me her mother's picture. It's obvious why."

The time for denials and silence was over. Time for him to man up.

"Yes, you looked like her. Like a dead ringer."

She took a deep breath and placed her palm on her belly as though to calm herself. "Did you ask me out because of that?"

He didn't need to say it out loud. By the pain in her eyes, she already knew the answer.

"Don't ever talk to me again. Don't come near me again."

"You're nothing like her. You're better."

"That's supposed to make me feel good?"

"I hoped so, yes."

She strode the rest of the way up the aisle and picked up her coat and purse from her desk, her actions jerky and not at all like the fluid Tammy he knew.

"I wish I'd never met you." She left the room, taking with her all of the air.

Ty couldn't draw enough oxygen into his lungs. His chest ached, burned. He doubled over. Was this how a heart attack felt? Or was it what having the organ torn from your body felt like?

Tammy was gone. For good. There wasn't a thing he could say or do to get her back.

He rested his hands on his knees and stared at the floor while he struggled to breathe.

He'd hurt a good woman. Badly. She hadn't deserved it.

How disgusting, how very appropriate to learn too late that he hadn't deserved her.

Maybe the kind of woman sitting in his home right now was as good as he would get, a little dishonest, a lot self-centered and not Tammy.

CHAPTER NINETEEN

TYLER CLOSED THE driver's door of Winona's rental car. He was sending her and Ruby home.

They were going to work out the details of joint custody over the phone.

Winona opened her window. "We can stay longer."

"No. Ruby belongs in school."

"But I can—" Ruby started from the passenger seat.

"Ruby, stop," Ty said. "You're going back to school." Man, this being a father business was hard when all he wanted to do was keep his daughter close to him for another week. Or month. Or year. As it was, he'd already smothered her with hugs before putting her into the car.

He wanted Winona out of his house. She'd tainted his space.

"Get home safely. Ruby, I'll come visit at Easter. Winona, I want her for the summer. Let's make that happen."

Ruby leaned across her mother and high-fived Tyler. "Yeah!"

Winona pulled onto the road and drove away.

Ty couldn't walk back into his empty house at the moment. Not without Ruby there.

She'd kept his loneliness at bay. When all was said and done, he'd wanted Tammy there, not Winona.

He wandered to the fence and waited. Gradually the herd of bison drifted over. He smiled remembering how much Ruby liked the big beasts. She said she needed to write some kind of history report this term. She was going to write about bison, with her dad's help.

That reminded Tyler. He needed to buy a computer and get on the internet and get Skype. He and Ruby were going to work on her project together long-distance. Ty was going to share his knowledge of keeping bison, of bringing them back to life after near-extinction. Ruby was going to research the historical details and fill him in for his own curiosity.

Ty spent time with his herd, giving them attention, scratching their hairy heads. Hirsute, he noticed, didn't come near him.

"I miss her, too," Ty said to the open air.

CALLIE TOOK ANOTHER dogsled ride with Gabe. They let the dogs out into the run and watched them.

"I feel like one of those dogs right now," she said. "Free. Ecstatic. Weightless."

Gabe took her face in his hands and kissed her deeply. Her mountain man tasted like fresh air and sunshine.

"I like having you here on my land."

"I like being here."

Their lovemaking that night was sweet.

They slept on the floor in front of the fireplace because that's what Callie wanted. There was something appealing about sleeping in front of a blazing fire, covered by nothing but quilts and Gabe Jordan.

IN THE MORNING, Callie put her purse over her shoulder and picked up her suitcase to take it to the car.

"Put it down," Gabe said. "I'll carry it out."

"But your knee is aching."

"That doesn't affect my ability to carry." He took the bag out of her hand and set it against the wall. "There's another storm coming in, but you'll get to the airport in plenty of time. Your flight should lift off before it hits."

"Okay."

He took her into his arms. "I don't want to say goodbye. I want you here forever."

"It's only a temporary separation. I'll be back soon."

He put her head on his chest. "Promise?" His deep voice rumbled in her ear.

"Promise."

They heard a car pull up outside.

"Lord, who is it? We only have a few minutes left together."

Someone banged on the door hard enough to rattle the front windows.

"Who the hell—" Gabe opened the door.

Nick stood on the other side, waves of fury and disdain flowing from him. He looked at Callie. "I thought I'd find you here, sleeping in the enemy camp."

Gabe stepped forward. "Back off, Nick. She's made her choice."

Callie placed her hand on his arm. "It's okay, Gabe. I got this. Nick, thank you for everything you've ever done for me and my mother, but I just couldn't do this job for you."

"Why not? Because you wanted to sleep with my brother?"

"Because I *love* your brother."

"Funny, changing one brother for the other."

"What do you mean?" Gabe asked.

"I mean, I wonder that Gabe can stand to sleep with a woman who's already screwed his brother."

"Nick."

She felt Gabe turn to her. She couldn't look in his eyes. She'd wanted to avoid this. She pressed her hand against her stomach because she felt sick.

"You slept with Nick?" He sounded rough.

She forced herself to meet his accusing glare. "I didn't want to tell you. I knew how you'd react. I wanted to avoid this."

She reached for his arm. "A long time ago. Only once. Before I worked for him. It didn't *mean* anything."

"Come on, Callie," Nick said. "Tell him the truth. We've never stopped sleeping together."

"Nick, stop!" Callie grabbed Gabe's shirt. His eyes had gone cold. She'd made Nick angry when she'd said their one night together hadn't meant anything. She knew him well. He would draw blood. "Gabe, it isn't true. Nick's messing with you."

She couldn't get through to him. Gabe was in some other place, knee-deep in misery and pain and grief. And anger. Maybe seeing another time and another woman with Nick.

Her happiness shriveled. She couldn't get through to him. She'd been so close to pure joy. Nick had just killed it.

"Rat bastard." She slapped Nick as hard as she could, then shoved him aside and ran out of the house.

She heard flesh hitting flesh but she didn't stop to see what was happening. The Jordan brothers could kill each other for all she cared.

She couldn't stay here, had to get away. She jumped into the car, turned on the engine and peeled out of the driveway.

Sucking in air, she told herself she would not cry.

She hoped Nick choked on his own bad intentions and croaked, and Gabe could…could what? She didn't know what to think about him and his lack of faith in her.

Where was the damn road to the highway? Gabe had told her which one to take. A sign for side road 93 appeared. That sounded familiar.

She turned onto the narrower road and accelerated. The car fishtailed and she slowed down. Why hadn't he told her it wouldn't be plowed?

She continued on the road, wondering how long the drive was. *Gabe, what did you get me into?* It was a terrible road, twisting and hilly.

A long gradual incline appeared in front of her. She drove up carefully, slipping a bit, but she finally crested the top... and caught her breath.

Ahead of her a long, steep hill led to a sharp turn at the bottom. Oh God. She slammed on the brakes but it was too late. The car was already sliding, turning, spinning, faster, faster, until she came to a stop with a terrible crash and grind of metal.

Her head hit the window and everything went black.

"SHE'S RIGHT," GABE SAID. "You are a rat bastard." He punched Nick. The satisfaction he felt didn't make up for the remorse that flooded him. How could he have believed Nick instead of Callie, even momentarily?

Because of past betrayals. But Callie wasn't Laura. Despite her snooping in his files that once, she was honest and pure. Gabe hated himself for his weakness where his brother was concerned. He'd gone insane for a moment, but he was back now in full force.

"Get off my land."

Nick picked himself up from the veranda floor and wiped his bleeding mouth. "That's a good punch you've got. Did you learn that in the army?"

"Go to hell."

"I don't like losing, Gabe. You should have remembered that."

"I know all about you, Nick. I know exactly who you are. Mom spoiled you rotten after Dad died. You think anything and everything you want should be yours, whether or not you've earned it."

"I've earned everything I own," Nick shouted. "I worked

my butt off for every penny. And don't you dare mention our mom. You couldn't be bothered to come home for her funeral. The army would have given you leave. She was a good woman. She deserved your respect. I'll never forgive you for that."

Gabe stared at the man. Was he really so detached from everything that happened here? Gabe had thought Nick would have heard somehow.

"A truck I was in drove over a bomb. I was injured and hospitalized. My best friend died."

"What are you talking about?"

"Billy Stone was killed that day. When I was in the hospital recovering I got word that Mom had died. After I recovered, I brought Billy's body home. What was left of it," he said bitterly. "Mom had already been buried by then."

He stepped forward. "I loved our mother every bit as much as you did. I would have been here if I could have. I take flowers to her grave every week."

Nonplussed, Nick said, "I didn't know."

"There's a lot you don't know. Take your head out of your ass and look at the people around you. Look at what you do to them. How you destroy them. There's more to life than chasing the next buck."

Nick stared at Gabe for a long time, but his poker face gave nothing away. "Maybe you're right about that."

He walked to the car that waited in the driveway with the driver's door open and the engine still running. He drove off and Gabe was left alone in the open doorway.

He didn't know what to think of that conversation except that the anger had felt good, cleansing, and clearing the air a relief.

He didn't know where he stood with Nick now and didn't much care.

Callie was gone. She would make it onto the plane and take

off just fine, but it would be hours before he could call her in Seattle to apologize. He'd grovel if he had to.

In the meantime, he had to feed the dogs and get them settled in before the storm hit.

CALLIE HAD NO IDEA how long she'd been unconscious. Her head throbbed. She looked through the windshield. The storm had started. The car had hit a tree and the front was smashed in. She wasn't going anywhere.

Her hand shook when she touched her temple. It came away wet with a little blood. She wrenched the rearview mirror sideways so she could see. Her head wasn't bad, thank God. The cut was small, but a bump had formed.

The wind howled around the car. Snow had already started to build up on the hood, probably three or four inches so far. She'd been out for a while.

She scrabbled around in her purse for her cell phone. She couldn't find it! Where was it?

An image of it sitting on the small table in Gabe's hallway flitted through her mind. She'd plugged it in to recharge before going to bed. She had no memory of unplugging it and putting it into her purse.

Her suitcase was back at Gabe's, as were her big coat and heavy boots. All she wore was her thinner leather coat and her dress boots that she'd planned to wear on the plane. She had no extra clothes with her.

She was so screwed.

Never leave your car. Wait for help to come to you.

Noah had given her sound advice, but she wouldn't have stepped out of the car to go anywhere in this storm. She had that much common sense.

She would have to get out to hang something on the car to make it visible. Surely someone would drive along soon.

The howling wind mocked her. No one else was stupid enough to be out in this.

Why hadn't she bought the neon tape to hang on the outside of the car? It would have shown through the snow. Her frugality had gotten her into a real pickle here. She'd been buying so much already, another ten bucks wouldn't have broken the bank.

She leaned her head against the steering wheel and sighed.

She couldn't hang out her clothing. Her bright blue mittens would show, but she needed them to keep warm. She needed every stitch to keep warm.

A thought struck. She didn't need her bra. Her very red bra.

She struggled with her coat and clothes, pulling her bra off while undoing as little as possible. She couldn't stand to lose even a fraction of her body's warmth through exposure. She got the bra out then buttoned everything back up.

Despite the ferocity of the wind whipping around the car, she managed to get the door open, then slammed it shut to preserve what little warmth there was inside the car. With one hand on the car, she walked the circumference of the vehicle until she found the antenna. She tied her bra to it, tightly enough that the wind wouldn't claim it, then made her way back to the driver's door.

Back inside the car, she tried to start it, but nothing happened.

From the glove compartment, she took out one of the candles and a small metal cup and the matches.

Keep a window cracked so they don't use up all the oxygen in the car.

She leaned over and opened the passenger window half an inch. Since that side of the car rested against a second tree, the window might not be as exposed to the wind, so she wouldn't get as much snow blowing into the car.

She arranged the candle in the cup on the dashboard and

lit it. Pulling the emergency blanket from the backseat, she opened the plastic bag and pulled it out. About to toss the empty bag into the backseat, she halted. Maybe it could keep her feet warm. She tried to fit both feet into the bag, but couldn't. She did manage to wrap it around one foot. She'd have to transfer it from foot to foot to keep them warm.

It took a while but gradually a sliver of warmth from the tiny candle flame replaced the cold trickling through the open window.

Snow had blanketed the windows. The only light inside the car was that flickering flame. Callie took deep breaths, determined to keep that old fear of the darkness at bay.

Breathe, honey.

She breathed the way Gabe had taught her. She liked the way he called her *honey*. She wanted to hear it again. She would keep herself alive, damn it. This storm would *not* get the best of her.

GABE STARED OUT at the furious storm threatening to blow everything that wasn't tied down to hell and back.

The dogs were fed, the guy wires on the prospector's tent reinforced and doubled with more wires and the woodpile beside the fireplace could last half a dozen days if he needed it to.

Callie should be home by now. He dialed her cell number.

Something rang nearby. He pivoted and swore. Callie's phone sat on the small table beside the door, still plugged in.

He unplugged it and carefully set the recharger beside the phone. Did she have a home phone number?

She'd been in a state when she'd left. He needed to apologize.

He called directory assistance and got a number. No answer. He left a message.

He wished she was here, wished he could take care of her

again as he had when she was sick. She probably wouldn't let him, though. She'd only allowed it because she'd been ill. She had too much energy and independence to let him take care of her for long. He liked the way she popped up to do things, like a jack-in-the-box who couldn't sit still a second longer.

He stalked into the kitchen to make dinner. In the middle of building a sandwich he lost power. Following all of his foul-weather emergency routines, he soon had a few kerosene lamps lit along with a handful of candles. He took his sandwich to the front window and stared at his silent phone.

Ring, damn it.

SHE'D FALLEN ASLEEP. Callie hadn't even felt it happening. Just a sign of how exhausting the deep cold and stress were.

Her first thought upon waking was of Gabe. How was he? At home? Safe inside with the dogs already fed and watered? Hunkered down in front of a circle of warmth and light cast by the fire in the hearth? Asleep in a cocoon of quilts?

But then full memory returned. He'd believed Nick. *Gabe, how could you?*

She stared at the candle that had burned down three-quarters of the way and imagined it as Gabe's fire.

She wished she were there with him, so they could talk through their differences. No, that wasn't true. She didn't want to talk. If she had him here, she'd kiss the ever-loving piss out of him and then hold him, just hold him, so she could feel the strong beat of his heart against hers. She'd found this awesome, stubborn, tiresome man, but he believed his brother over her.

Does that really matter, Callie?

No. Again, only the truth would do. They could get past that conflict, somehow, but how many times would Nick continue to come between them?

How long had she been asleep? Noah had said the candles

lasted about eight hours each. It was down three-quarters, so she'd already been here at least six hours, since the time she'd awakened after the collision. That made the time about ten at night.

The wind still howled, greeting her like an old friend. At least there was that sensation. Without the wind and the small candle, there would be nothing but a vacuum.

She wanted to jump out of the car and run so badly, do anything other than sit here trapped like this, but she couldn't.

The cold inside the car grew more profound.

She started to get sleepy again. What the heck? This was ridiculous. Her mom had always said she had too much energy. She shouldn't be this sleepy. After making her decision to quit working for Nick, her energy had bounced back.

She glanced at the passenger window. In the slight glow of the candle, it looked like it was closed again. How could that be? She leaned closer. Snow filled the crack she'd left open for oxygen. No! How deep was it?

She wrestled her way out of the cocoon she'd made of the thermal blanket. Forcing her stiff limbs to work, she crawled across the passenger seat and unrolled the window far enough to stick her mitten through the snow. A bunch of it tumbled into the car. Her mitten hit more snow. Then more.

She had a choice. She could extinguish the candle. She shivered. The only meager light in the car, it was also the only heat—and meager didn't begin to describe how little it felt.

No, she did *not* want to blow it out. It freaked her out to consider spending the rest of the night in profound darkness.

Think, then, what can you do? You don't know how thick that snow is.

She opened the glove compartment. There wasn't much in there.

Wait!

The rental company had provided a map of Colorado. She

pulled it out and opened it. Her fingers didn't want to cooperate, but she forced them to roll it into a tube and pushed it through the snow.

Nothing.

Carefully, she eased it back into the car, leaving the hole intact, and dumped a bunch of snow out of the tube. Gently, and with patience, she threaded it into the hole. She pulled it back and dumped out more snow two more times until coolness rushed in onto her cheek. Fresh air. Yes! She'd done it.

Her shivering increased and she crawled back into the thermal blanket, but she'd lost valuable heat. As carefully as she could, she tried to move the candle closer, but the dashboard humped up over the wheel and there wasn't enough room between the dash and the window for the candle. She didn't dare put it on her lap or the passenger seat. What if she fell asleep again and it fell over and started a fire?

She toyed with the idea of lighting both candles at once for more heat, but in an hour and a quarter or so, she would need to light the second one to get her through the night. She would need that full eight hours of burning the second candle. Once that second one burned down, what would she do? What if the storm raged for another couple of days?

SHE OPENED HER eyes slowly to a black world, to profound darkness. The second candle had died out. So had the storm. Here in a car covered in God knew how much snow, Callie could see nothing.

Worse, she could hear nothing.

Her nerves protested. *Give me sound.* Noise. Anything but this vacuum. What if this was the end of her life? No! She wasn't ready to go yet. *Give me life. Give me laughter.*

Give me Gabe's laughter.

She refused to die.

The cold, though. More profound than the silence, the cold

could kill. The silence wouldn't. She would use Gabe's techniques and come to terms with life's silences. First, though, she had to survive the cold.

The thermal blanket was no longer enough. Her thoughts drifted to thick, down-filled duvets. If she didn't somehow devise a way to keep warmer than she was, she would die here.

What could she do? The way she felt right now, she needed at least a dozen blankets to keep her warm. She thought of Gabe's dad on top of Everest. How had he felt at the end?

She had a vague memory of someone saying that, at the end, the body shuts down and the person "falls asleep." She didn't want that. Had to fight it. Had to protect what little heat she still had in her core.

She tested her arms. They still worked. She wasn't too far gone yet. She reached into her purse, her actions slow and stiff, and rummaged for her Swiss Army knife.

There might not be any more blankets in the car, but there was material—the fabric of the seats and the foam inside.

Easing one mitten off, by feel, she opened each of the tools until she found the knife.

Oh lord, it was tiny. She suppressed a sob.

It would do no good to cry.

Move! Get on with it!

She kept her eyes closed, because it was less disturbing to consider that she couldn't see anything because of her eyelids than because she was surrounded by profound darkness.

Pulling her arm out of the blanket and reaching as high as she could, she brought her arm down hard onto the passenger seat and felt the knife sink into fabric. She tugged until she felt the knife move, probably no more than a fraction of an inch, cutting the smallest bit of fabric.

It was a start.

She did it again. And again. And again.

And again.

Her arm ached, but she didn't stop.

Her blood started to move again, to feel less like a solid and more like a liquid. So, even if she couldn't pull apart enough of the seat fabric and foam to keep her warm, for these moments while she worked, she sent blood back out to her extremities.

She felt them come alive.

Yes!

She didn't know how long she worked before she was able to tear the fabric from the seat. Deciding to cover her bare head first, she wrapped the cloth turban-style around her head, her hands shaking from the cold.

Her teeth chattered.

Next, she started on the upright portion of the passenger seat, front first and then the back, in the same routine as for the seat. Once finished, she loosened the blanket from around herself and wrapped the fabric around her feet.

Her actions slowed until she was barely moving. She couldn't afford to stop, though. That would lead to giving up and freezing to death in this sensory-deprived hole. No. She refused.

Awkwardly, she managed to turn around and climb between the front seats onto the rear bench seat. Again, she raised her arm and brought it down full-force into the seat. Inch by painstaking inch, she cut off the fabric and wrapped it around her calves. The next piece went around her thighs and, the next, across her torso.

The last pieces from the back were meant for her arms, but not wanting to limit her range of motion didn't put them on yet. She tossed them onto the passenger seat.

Now came the hard part. She struggled to breathe, to force herself to use the last of her strength to carve chunks of foam out of the back of the bench and toss them into the front.

When she'd carved out as much as she could, she stumbled

back into the driver's seat. With no idea how long she'd taken to accomplish her task, undoubtedly hours, and whether it was day or night, she settled the blanket underneath herself as well as she could.

Reaching around blindly, she located a piece of foam and molded it to one foot. She did the same with the second foot then snugged the blanket tightly around them.

Another piece of foam went across her legs and then the blanket was snugged around them. Foam went across her stomach and chest and, again, the blanket came over.

A piece of foam went over her head.

Next, she wrapped the last pieces of fabric around her arms, picked up the last piece of foam and tucked it around her hands, then as best she could, pulled the last bits of blanket across herself.

Done.

Her breath came in angry shallow huffs and her body protested everything she'd just put it through, but that was okay. She was still alive.

Now to wait.

With all activity over, the silence came crushing in on her, landing heavily, palpable, a weight against her chest.

Panic set in.

No. God, stop.

Gabe's voice drifted into her consciousness.

Listen. There is always something to hear, even if it's only your own heartbeat. That will never fail you.

Oh, but it might, Gabe.

If someone doesn't find me soon, my heartbeat might fail me.

No! No negative thoughts.

She concentrated on the thin pulse of her heartbeat and thought of Gabe.

WHEN CALLIE STILL wasn't answering her phone the mornin
after the storm ended, Gabe worried.

At ten, he called Nick.

"No, I haven't heard from her. Not that I care."

"Well, I do. She left here angry and in shock yesterday
without her phone or her luggage."

Nick hung up without answering.

Gabe checked the flight she was supposed to have been o
and contacted the airline. She hadn't flown out. Not good. /
crazy dance skittered in his belly.

He phoned the B and B. No service. Damn. Somethin
had been knocked down.

He bundled up then waded through two feet of snow t
feed the dogs. He planned to harness them to his sled, rid
into town to the B and B and give Callie a piece of his mind
If she had lied about flying to Seattle yesterday, he'd neve
forgive her for the tension she'd put him through.

When the dogs heard him heat the pots of water he'd fille
yesterday, they jumped up and shook snow from their backs

They yipped for their food. Given that the water was froze
solid in the pots, it was going to take a while to heat it. Th
temperature had dipped dangerously low last night.

Callie, where are you?

He raked snow from the top of the prospector's tent, the
opened the flap and pulled out the coolers. Finally, the wate
boiled and he tossed in some chicken.

While he followed every step that needed to be done t
care for the dogs, Gabe strained against the restriction, agains
taking the time to do it, when he'd never once in his life re
sented caring for his dogs.

But a balloon of foreboding filled his chest and grew large
by the minute until he could barely breathe.

The dogs were fed. The pots were clean. The dogs wer
harnessed to the sled, ready and willing to run.

Amid their yipping and howling, Gabe shouted "Hyah!" and they took off. His dogs never disappointed him.

He turned them onto the road past the house. They didn't balk. He'd driven them on the road before on rescue missions for people caught in the storm. When cars couldn't get through, sled dogs still could.

Snowplows hadn't been out here yet. They would do the main highways first. It would take them a long time to get back here.

He rode straight into town until he stopped in front of Accord House. He set the brake and ran into the hotel.

Kristi Mortimer came out of the living room to see who had entered. When she saw Gabe, she smiled. "What are you doing out and about? Are the roads passable?"

"I need to talk to Callie. What room is she in?"

Kristi frowned. "She hasn't been back since the day she left here with you. I thought she was flying to Seattle."

"So did I. She never made it onto the flight." Gabe swore. "You haven't heard from her?"

"Not a word. The phones are down, though."

Gabe ran to the cop shop down the street. He knew in his bones that Callie was out there somewhere stuck in the snow.

He thought of how he'd awakened in the middle of the night to the unearthly stillness and darkness of a storm that had spent itself. She would be terrified.

He needed to get to her.

If she'd been trapped in a car on the road somewhere, that silence would have killed her.

He pushed the station's door open so hard it banged against the inner wall.

Tyler jumped to his feet, his hand reaching for his gun. "What the— Gabe!"

"I need the inhalation rewarmer."

Ty's eyes widened. "What's happening?"

"Callie's missing. She left for the airport early yesterday but never made it."

Tyler unlocked a cabinet, pulled out the machine Gabe needed and shoved it into his hands. "Just a sec."

He ran to the back of the room and opened a cupboard door. Rows of bottled water lined one shelf. He took out a couple and ran to Gabe.

"Take these."

"Distilled?"

"Yeah. Where are you looking for her?"

"I'm on the sled. I'll check the side roads in to my place from the highway."

"I'll check the highway. It's been plowed." Ty wrestled into his rancher's coat and cowboy hat while he slammed the door shut behind him. "She might have been found by now. I'll radio the hospitals for news. You have your cell with you?"

Gabe nodded.

Ty jumped into the SUV parked at the curb and took off.

Gabe rushed the dogs back to the house and parked them in the front yard. While they yipped their impatience, Gabe ran into the house and packed a bag of blankets and his warmest mittens and put a cup of milk into the microwave and filled a travel mug with hot chocolate.

Ten minutes later, he was back outside and on the sled, turning the dogs north.

He flew down to Sideroad 98. That was the one he'd told her to take. Maybe she'd gotten stuck there.

The dogs ran their hearts out for him until they reached the highway, but it was slow going with the new heavy snow on the road. No Callie.

He phoned Ty. "Any news from the hospitals?"

"She isn't listed in any of them."

"Keep me posted."

He traveled along the shoulder of the highway until side

road 97. Maybe she'd taken the wrong one. When he reached the end with no sign of her, he cursed.

He took the dogs across 96 and 95 and 94. The dogs' energies were flagging.

"Sorry, kids. We can't stop. Find Callie. Where's Callie?"

As though they understood him, they took off again, down 93. He took it slowly because it was a bitch of a road. That's why he'd told Callie to stay clear of it.

He had to check, though.

At the top of a steep hill, he pushed the foot brake into the snow so the sled wouldn't barrel down the hill over his dogs.

Something hulked in the ditch beside a couple of trees, something unnaturally large under a foot of drifted snow.

His pulse thundered. Oh dear God.

He caught a glimpse of red. He pulled closer and stopped. A couple of inches of red satin peeked out from the snow.

He set the brake, brushed off the snow. She'd hung a red bra out so she would be found. His breath caught on a rough laugh. Who else but Callie would do something like that?

His blood beat hard in his neck. Callie was inside this tomb of snow on the side of the road.

He brushed snow from the top of the car and down the driver's side, terrified of what he would find inside. The door opened with an effort and there she was—pale, still, eyes closed, deathlike.

He pulled off his glove and touched her cheek. Too cold.

"Baby," he whispered. "Callie, honey." His voice broke.

He touched her neck to find a pulse. He located the carotid artery. Yes! A pulse. Faint. Barely there, but there, damn it.

He placed his hand over her nose and a faint brush of air tickled his palm.

Only then did he notice what she'd done. His smart, determined Callie had cut all of the seat cushions apart to mummify herself in foam blocks, including carving one out to fit over her head, most likely saving her life.

He parted the foam, tossed it off her and lifted her into his arms with utmost care. Depending on which stage of hypothermia she'd entered, it was crucial that he move her as little as possible to avoid shocking her body into afterdrop—an even further drop in her internal temperature than she already had.

As well, he needed to render her limbs immovable so cold blood from her extremities wouldn't pump back to her heart.

She made a small sound. He pushed his parka hood off with his shoulder and lifted her higher in his arms until his ear was against her mouth.

"You came," she murmured in barely more than an exhalation of air.

His eyes misted. She was conscious and coherent.

When he passed Daisy, she leaped against him. Shy, recalcitrant Daisy wanted to see Callie. Carefully, Gabe bent his knees and Daisy touched her nose to Callie's face and whimpered.

"She'll be okay, girl. I'll make sure of it."

Gabe wrapped her in the blankets he'd brought. If she had severe hypothermia, they wouldn't prevent her core from further cooling. He needed to get her to the hospital stat. But first…

He took the inhalation rewarmer out of its bag too forcefully.

Calm down.

He needed his wits about him. The first thirty minutes treating a patient with hypothermia, whether in the field or at hospital, were critical.

Don't screw up.

With every exhalation, she lost more of her body's heat. He needed to arrest that process. The rewarmer, which heats and humidifies oxygen, would gently warm her head, neck and thoracic core.

He opened the distilled water and poured it into the inlet port. He attached the airway to the other port and the power cable to the portable battery to warm the water.

Gently, he strapped the head harness and mask to her face. She watched him quietly. Calmly. She was one in a million.

"I'll get you to the hospital."

When he kissed her forehead his lips came away cold.

He didn't bother unpacking the hot drink he'd brought. She was too far gone for that. She might choke on anything he tried to get into her.

Daisy turned around and howled then leaped forward, chafing to leave, to get Callie inside. The sled moved an inch but the brake held.

"Hold on there, Daisy. We'll go in a minute."

He wrapped the blanket up around Callie's face until only her nose showed. He hated putting her into the darkness but he needed to protect her.

He jumped onto the back of the sled, pulled the brake and set the dogs moving smoothly. The sled inched forward and they were off, slowly, with Gabe steering his dogs over the twists and hills of the road to the nearest hospital, even while he wanted to give the dogs their head and race on wings. He had to pull up and park the sled on the side of the road because the hospital lot was still being plowed.

"Stay." He lifted Callie out of the sled, in her bed of thick blankets and wearing the warmer that sat on her chest, parted the blankets so she could see and carried her to the front doors of the building.

A nurse ran over. "What happened?"

"Hypothermia. She got caught in her car in the storm."

Staff took over, putting her onto a gurney, and when she

was gone Gabe felt the loss of her in his arms. He wanted her back.

He had a general idea what they would do with her. They would take her temperature to determine which treatment was required. He suspected they might be able to get something warm into her, and warm her slowly starting with her trunk. As well, they too would monitor her to watch for afterdrop. Hypothermia sufferers often collapsed because of a further cooling of core temperature after removal from the cold environment.

Gabe wanted to be the one doing all of it for her, but it was out of his hands now. Because of Colorado's winters and its proximity to the Rockies, this hospital had experience dealing with stranded motorists and lost hikers.

He trusted them.

He wanted the process rushed so he could hold her, but there was no rushing coming back from hypothermia. He couldn't sit here to wait because his dogs sat on the side of the road.

He left the hospital, retrieved his sled and ordered his dogs home. They were exhausted. Once there, he followed his normal routine of getting the dogs off the traces and onto the spans. He took a shovel and the awl out onto the creek and made a hole to collect water then made broth for his pooches.

When he distributed it, with Daisy being the last to receive it, she didn't drink right away. She lay with her head on her folded paws and stared up at Gabe. A whimper emerged from deep in her throat.

Gabe took off his glove and rubbed her ears. "She's getting care now. She'll be fine."

She had to be.

"Drink." He tipped the bowl closer to Daisy and she drank obediently without her usual antics.

Callie had wiggled her way into Daisy's heart.

She'd wiggled her way into his heart.

It was long past time to make Callie his; the hell with anything Nick tried to do to separate them again.

TYLER GOT THE CALL from Gabe and breathed a sigh of relief. Thank God Callie was okay. That whole business had scared the bejesus out of him.

What if it had been Tammy?

He wanted to talk to her.

He hadn't spoken to her since that day at school. He'd seen her drive past the office once.

He drove to the shop her aunt had left her. She had a pair of women run it for her. At the moment, it was closed. Everything on Main was.

Tammy lived above the shop.

When he stepped out onto Main Street, wood smoke scented the air. Most folks would have their woodstoves and fireplaces running. He loved that smell. It reminded him of home—where he wanted to be right now. With Tammy.

He walked down the side of the building to her apartment door, his footsteps silent in the snow but his heartbeat marching heavy boots through his veins. He rang her bell.

Through the small window in the door he watched her legs come into view. She wore sweatpants with thick heavy socks—her cocooning gear. She'd probably been curled up, reading a book.

When she saw who it was she stopped, not quite all the way to the bottom of the stairs, and stared through the window. Disconcerted by the wariness in her eyes, he tried to smile, but failed.

He wanted to drag her out of there and back to the ranch. He wanted her to smile, to laugh, to be his happy Tammy.

She opened the door. "Is there a problem?"

Her scent drifted out to him and he wanted to gulp his lungs full of it.

He shoved his hands into his pockets so he wouldn't touch her. He didn't need to be a genius to know she wouldn't appreciate it. "Does there have to be a problem for me to want to come see you?"

She took her time answering, measuring her response. He wanted her sassy quick wit back. "These days, yes." He didn't like her so subdued. So quiet.

"Tammy, there's stuff I want to talk about."

One sharp shake of her head denied him. "How is Ruby?"

"We're getting to know each other."

"That's good. A man should know his children." She bit her bottom lip. "Is she still at the ranch?"

"No. I sent her home, with her mother."

"Is she still in your life?"

"Winona?"

Tammy nodded.

"Only as much as I need her to be to keep Ruby available to me. I don't want her in my life."

"Well, that's good." She started to close the door and he straight-armed it to stop her. She jumped back. He didn't blame her. The action had been violent.

"We should talk," he bit out.

"There's nothing more to say."

"Tammy, please." Too much of his life was slipping out of his control and he didn't know how to get it back. He reached a hand toward her, but she flinched so he dropped it.

He took off his hat and scrubbed a gloved hand across his head. "Okay. We won't talk."

He heaved a sigh. There was nothing left to say.

Quietly, Tammy closed her door and locked it.

He trudged back to his car. He was damned glad that Gabe had found his woman safe and sound.

If only it were as easy for Ty to find his woman in the emotional blizzard that had wreaked havoc with his life. How did he thaw Tammy? How did he chip through the emotional wasteland she was trapped in right now? The same one that isolated him and made him fumble and grasp at the smallest gestures of warmth?

Better to not come back, to give her time. A small avalanche of snow fell from the roof and coated him. He shivered. What if he never got Tammy back?

CHAPTER TWENTY

GABE PLANNED TO stay at the hospital that night. Before entering, he called Ty.

"I'm staying near Callie tonight. In the morning, can you go out and feed the dogs? The road should be plowed by then."

He'd had a hell of a time driving his truck away from the house to the highway, slipping and sliding every which way. He'd fed the dogs their evening kibble.

"Sure, I can go out in the morning," Ty replied.

He sounded terrible. "You okay, buddy?" Gabe asked. "What's up?"

"I went to talk to Tammy today. She won't have anything to do with me."

"Boot Winona off the ranch."

"I already did."

"Good."

"I gotta go. I'll see to the dogs in the morning. Don't worry."

Ty hung up and Gabe closed his phone, torn. He'd never heard his brother so low, other than when Winona had dropped him all those years ago.

In Gabe's opinion, Ty had made a mistake of mammoth proportions when he'd let Winona back into his life. Gabe wondered whether he should talk to Ty. But, no. He was a grown man now, and had to find his own way. The time for taking care of his little brother was long over for Gabe.

He entered the hospital. Callie was in intensive care. He

couldn't go in to see her, but he could watch her through the glass. She slept deeply. He watched her for an hour. She didn't move. She could have been dead.

A shiver shattered his composure. He swung away from the window. One of the nurses approached. "Go get yourself something warm to drink. Not from the machine. Go down to the cafeteria. The coffee is brewed down there and will taste better."

When he hesitated, she said, "I can page you if there's any change."

He didn't need to give her his name. He recognized her from school even though she was younger than him.

"Do you want anything?"

"No, we have a kettle in the back. Thanks."

He came back twenty minutes later and Callie looked the same.

When he stood at the window staring, the nurse came back to him. "Go sit down. You won't be of any use to her if you get sick. I can set up a cot in a quiet room for you if you want."

"Thanks, no. I'll sit."

The morning, and a quietly rousing hospital, found him still sitting there. Every half hour, he'd got up to look in at Callie. Nothing had changed overnight.

The nurses did their rounds. Breakfast was delivered to the regular patients.

Just before she went off duty, the nurse checked Callie one more time. She came out smiling and beckoning to Gabe.

He ran over.

"She's awake. Go on in. Don't be too excited with her. Stay calm."

"Thanks. I appreciate it."

"See you on tonight's shift. She'll likely still be here."

Gabe stepped into the dim room.

Callie didn't move but her eyes followed him into the room.

"How do you feel?" he asked quietly.

"Good. Happy...to...be...warm."

She was tired. Her body had been strained to the limit.

"You didn't lose anything to frostbite," he said. "You still have all your fingers and toes."

"Lucky."

"No. It wasn't luck. It was you. You used your brain and kept yourself alive. The foam you cut up saved your extremities. I'm so damned proud of you."

"Don't...cry."

He touched his cheek. His fingers came away wet. He hadn't cried since Dad died.

"I can't help myself," he said. "I thought I'd lost you."

A team of doctors came in and Gabe had to leave.

"Go home and rest," one of them said. "You look beat and there are a bunch of things we have to do with Callie for a few hours."

Gabe kissed her forehead and left.

At the house, as tired as he was, he knew he wouldn't sleep for a while. He wandered outside to his dogs. Ty had obviously been around and had fed them and cleaned up after himself.

Gabe wandered up and down, talking to his dogs, petting them, drawing comfort from them.

At last when he felt he could sleep he went into the house and lay down. Four hours later, he woke up again, feeling better but needing to get to the hospital.

He'd live there if he could, until they released Callie.

He ate, called Ty about giving the dogs their evening kibble and then drove to the hospital.

Callie was doing better. Responding better. She could talk now, but she seemed withdrawn. Still tired, he guessed.

He stayed all night again, but she slept most of it. This time, Gabe dozed in the chair. He needed to get his schedule back closer to normal so he could spend the day with her when she was awake.

In the morning, when her doctor came in, he asked when she could go home. She should be good to go later in the day.

He went home and took care of the dogs. Fed them. Took the ones who hadn't gone on Callie's rescue for a dogsled through the woods, with the big sled loaded with goods, and then a half hour in the run. Then he finished the long ride and returned to the clearing.

Later, in the afternoon, he returned to the hospital.

Callie was sitting up, dressed and waiting to go home.

There were dark circles under her eyes, but she was whole and in one piece and alive.

She was silent on the drive home.

"I want to see the dogs."

"Tomorrow. You need to rest tonight. You don't look strong yet."

Inside, he carried her suitcase to his bedroom.

"No," she said. "Here."

Gabe laid out the quilts on the floor and built up the fire.

He fed her soup and bread and Kristi's custard that he'd picked up on the way to the hospital.

She ate it all.

"Hospital food was that bad?"

She smiled and nodded.

He cleared away the dishes and cleaned up then returned to sit beside her.

"You're quiet." He ran his finger under her chin. "Too quiet."

"I did a lot of thinking while I was trapped in that car."

"That sounds ominous."

Callie stared into the fire for a while before she answered. "I need to know that you trust me. I need to be sure that Nick can't come between us again."

"He won't. I won't let him."

"How can I know that, Gabe?"

"You have to trust me."

She bent her legs and rested her chin on her knees. "I want to."

He didn't know what to say. There was nothing that Nick could ever say that would make him lose faith in Callie.

"Can you tell me what happened between you two?"

"We slept together. Once. Years ago. I realized he wasn't my type. I broke it off. He hired me to work for him. End of story."

Gabe nodded. "Okay. That's the end of it, then."

She leaned toward him and kissed him. "Let's make love."

Gabe lay on the quilts and took her down with him. He undressed her slowly, revealing her lovely pale skin inch by inch, kissing every spot he uncovered.

When she was naked, she rose above him and did the same for him, her lovemaking quiet and deep and strong. While she kissed all of his body, he watched firelight play over her skin.

When he was naked, he pulled her to him. She smelled like smoke from the fire. Her skin felt like warm cream. He suckled her full perfect breasts while her soft nipples turned to hard little nubs on his tongue.

He rubbed his beard across them and they peaked some more.

"Someday," she whispered, "I want to see you."

He rose above her, supporting his weight on his arms. She stroked them from shoulder to wrist and back up again.

"What do you mean?" he asked.

She cradled his beard in her hands. "I want to see *you*. No more hiding, Chewbacca." She smiled, but he thought he detected a hint of sadness. Why?

Their lovemaking was slow, and sweet and long, lasting

hours. Callie brought him close to climax then backed off and loved his body some more, then straddled him until he came.

Twenty minutes later, she started loving his body again, bringing him close then backing off, touching every inch of him with her fingers and her mouth.

Then she moved away from him and touched only his mouth with her lips, kissing him for long minutes.

When he tried to enter her, she held him off.

"Not yet. I want more loving."

"Then let me love you for a while."

"Yes."

He did, paying homage to her breasts and her stomach and her pink core.

He turned her onto her stomach and kissed the length of her spine then sucked her buttock. Maybe he left his mark. He bit the backs of her knees and she trembled. He gently nudged her legs apart and aroused her with his fingers until she was so wet he couldn't hold himself back, almost mindless with desire for her, her musk inflaming his need, his erection too painful to bear any longer.

He knelt behind her and raised her onto her hands and knees and entered her, her passage exquisitely tight and silken. She cried out and arched her strong back. Her hair glowed brilliant red in the firelight.

He moved and she hummed to his rhythm.

Taking them down onto their sides, he tucked his arm under her leg and brought it up and away, giving him even greater access and depth. He put his other arm under her head, so he could feel her spine and full bottom against him. She reached a hand behind her to cup his face. He cupped her breast.

Still he moved, in and out of her. Still he held back his release, sensing that she needed this night to last.

She sighed and gasped and made erotic little animal noises. With one hard thrust, he sent them both over the edge.

WHEN GABE LEFT the house to feed the dogs, Callie pretended to sleep.

They had still been making love when dawn arrived. Gabe rose, built up the fire, covered her with a quilt and showered.

She heard him in the kitchen. She smelled toast. She heard him at the back door getting ready to go outside.

He came into the living room and bent to kiss her cheek, checked to make sure that she was sleeping then left the house by the back door.

She opened her eyes. Her body ached, hummed with sated pleasure. She'd never loved a man as she loved Gabe last night. She'd never been so thoroughly loved.

She rose and showered, then got clean clothes from her suitcase and dressed.

At the front door she put on her coat and boots and picked up her suitcase and the keys for Gabe's pickup truck from the small hall table.

She let herself out, started his truck and left.

Deep, deep inside she knew that Nick would always come between them. She didn't have the strength at this time to fight both Nick and Gabe. Nick would interfere in their lives. Callie couldn't cope right now. She needed a rest.

At the airport in Denver she bought a ticket for a flight home, left a message on Gabe's home machine telling him where she'd parked his truck at the airport then turned off her cell phone.

She hadn't had the heart to tell Gabe that last night had been goodbye.

CHAPTER TWENTY-ONE

GABE HAD BEEN looking for Callie for a month. Still nothing. No trace.

He was down to his last resort. Nick.

He was in Seattle, in Nick's office building. He found the number of Nick's office and stalked past the secretary's desk.

"Hey!" she yelled. "You can't go in there. Who are you?"

He heard her pick up the phone. "Security!"

Without waiting for whoever was about to come along to drag him away, Gabe exploded into Nick's office. Floor-to-ceiling windows on two sides flooded the room with light. A corner office. Surprise, surprise.

Two men jumped up from chairs in front of Nick's desk.

Cool as a cucumber, Nick looked up from the document he'd been signing, took his time setting his pen down, leaned back in his chair behind his massive desk and stared Gabe down.

Gabe didn't blink.

"Gentlemen," Nick said. "I'm afraid I have to end our meeting early. May I ask you to leave?" He handed them the document he'd just signed. "Linda will book an appointment for me at your leisure, and at your offices, where we'll finish our business."

Gabe stepped aside so they could leave then filled the doorway again. A second later a couple of security guards burst into the outer office.

When they grasped Gabe by both arms, he resisted.

"That's enough." Nick stood. "It's all right. I can handle this."

"Are you sure, Mr. Jordan?" one of the goons asked.

"Yes." He added, his tone repressive, "He's my brother. Close the door on your way out. Linda, thank you for calling security. Hold my calls until Mr. Jordan leaves."

Gabe stepped in and the guard closed the door behind him.

The silence in the room teemed with unspoken resentments on Nick's part. Gabe might have come here in desperation, but he didn't come to fight. His battles with Nick were over. Old grudges weren't worth losing Callie over.

Nick sat back down.

Gabe remained standing.

"What do you want, Gabe?"

"Where is she?"

"Who?"

Gabe didn't bother to respond.

"Why would you think I would know? She quit working for me, remember? Was that your influence?"

"You were making her sick," Gabe said quietly.

When he'd found her and his truck gone that day after a night of the most profound lovemaking of his life, he'd beaten himself up. He knew it had somehow been his fault.

It took him close to a week, and a night of drinking at Ty's house, to figure it out.

He'd told her she could trust him, that Nick could never come between them again, and then he'd asked her about her affair with Nick.

She must have known then that whatever had gone on between her and Nick had mattered to Gabe. He should have left it alone.

He'd sensed that sadness in her. He should have known

what he'd done. Before leaving though, she'd given him the beautiful gift of her love.

And now he couldn't find her.

Nick stood and walked to the window behind his desk where he stood with his back to Gabe. "How?"

"What?" He'd lost track.

"How was I making her sick?"

"By demanding that she compromise her ethics."

Nick was quiet for a long time. Without turning around, he said, "I know where she is."

"She contacted you?"

"Only because she had to as her former employer."

"Where is she?"

"It will cost you."

Gabe took a step forward. "Why?"

"Because it's costing me."

"Because you had to find a new assistant."

Nick turned from the window. "Yes. That's exactly right. Because I had to hire a new employee."

There was something happening here that Gabe wasn't getting.

Nick walked to a walnut cabinet against the wall. He opened a door and took out a bottle of Laphroaig. He poured it into two cut-glass tumblers and returned to his seat. He handed one to Gabe.

"No, thanks."

"Take it." Something in Nick's tone caught his attention, a subtle shift, a reluctant camaraderie.

Gabe took the glass and sat across from his brother.

"Cheers," Nick said and drank.

Gabe sipped his drink. He'd never tasted anything so expensive. "There's something to be said for money."

Nick chuffed out a laugh. "Trust me, there's a lot to be said for money."

He held his glass up to the light and studied his Scotch. "I find that in the oddest way history is repeating itself."

"What do you mean?"

"Years ago when I was in high school, my older brother starting dating the sexiest girl in town. She wasn't the prettiest or the most sophisticated, but she had an earthy sensuality that drove me to lust after her. Then she became engaged to my older brother and I went away to college."

"Laura."

Nick sipped his Scotch. "Laura."

Gabe grunted. He hadn't known Nick had wanted her.

"When my brother embarrassed me in front of my future father-in-law, I came home and screwed his fiancée blind."

Gabe didn't rise to the bait. The past was truly done and gone.

"So how is history repeating itself? Are you lusting after Callie?"

"Lusting? Yes."

That took Gabe by surprise. Nick had had a lot of years to do something about it and hadn't.

Nick leaned forward. "Let's get down to business. You want to know where Callie is and I want that land. Sell me your third."

"Done. Have your lawyers draw up the paperwork and I'll sign. Where is she?"

After a protracted silence, while Nick stared at his desk, he asked, "Are you going to marry her?"

"Yes."

"Don't invite me to the wedding. I won't come. Callie is in my bad books. I don't forgive easily." He set his glass down on his desk with a hard click. "You know that."

He opened a drawer of his desk and pulled out a sheet of paper with his company letterhead on it. He jotted something down and handed it to Gabe.

An address. "Is this here in Seattle?"

"Yes."

Gabe stood and put his glass down beside Nick's with a restrained click. "I'll be back here in one week. Have those papers ready."

He opened the door, but just before leaving the office he glanced back. Nick was staring out the side window, his face in profile, and what Gabe saw there shocked him.

Nick Jordan loved Callista MacKintosh.

GABE RETURNED TO his hotel room and got ready to see Callie by shaving off his beard and moustache. She'd told him to stop hiding. She was right. It was time.

He took a cab to the address Nick had given him.

It was a low-rise apartment building. It didn't look like the best area of town.

He ran in behind a tenant and took the elevator to the fourth floor. Down the hall and around the corner he found 403. He knocked.

The door opened and there she was with her alabaster skin and red hair and green eyes. They misted over.

"Invite me in," Gabe said.

Her throat worked as though she was having trouble speaking. She stepped aside and he entered and closed the door behind him.

He took her into his arms and lifted her off the floor. She wrapped her arms around his neck and held on. He crushed her so hard it was a wonder she could breathe, but she didn't complain.

He gulped in the scent of her, drank in her essence, and

cupped her fragile head in his big hand. He'd missed her. He'd ached for her.

"Callie. Oh my God, Callie."

When he finally eased his grip, he let her down gently, by degrees, because he really didn't want to let her go. Ever again.

She touched his cheek.

"I see you," she whispered. "You're so handsome."

"Come home with me." The second the words left his mouth, he remembered that was no longer possible. "No. You can't. I sold it."

By the shock on her face, he might as well have shot her. "No, Gabe, no. Why?"

"Because I want to be with you. My home is with you."

"But—"

"Why aren't you in your condo?"

"I sold it. I sold my mother's house, too. We both live here now."

Gabe noticed what he hadn't until now, a woman sitting on a sofa watching them—an older version of Callie but with graying blond hair instead of red.

"She's younger than I thought."

"Yes," Callie whispered. "The Alzheimer's started early." She touched his face. "Gabe, why did you really sell?"

"Nick wouldn't give me your address unless I sold."

She swore.

"It's over, Callie. He no longer has any hold over me. I want to be with you forever."

"Are you sure?"

"Yes. Nick can do what he wants. I'll never be sucked in by him again."

Callie grinned. She believed him.

"Where are the dogs?"

"I have to go back to Accord and sort out all of that. I'll have to board them."

"Wait. Stop. What's the date?" Callie picked up a small desk calendar that sat beside her mother. "You can't be here. You should be getting the dogs ready to transport to Anchorage."

"I'm not running the Iditarod."

"Why not?"

"I've been hunting for you."

"No. You have to go. You *have* to. It's your dream."

"You are my dream."

"I won't let you give it up."

"You don't have a choice."

"When do you have to leave the house?"

"I don't know. I only just told Nick I'd sell to him an hour ago."

"Call him. Tell him you need two months. Make your closing date the end of April."

She picked up her phone. "Call him and tell him while Mom and I pack."

"Pack? Where are you going?"

"To stay with you at your house while we get ready for the Iditarod."

"Are you sure?"

"I've never been more sure of anything in my life."

She took his face in her hands, her palms soft against his bare skin. She kissed him senseless then ran to another room and started opening and closing drawers.

"Mom, come in here and help me pack."

By the time Gabe ended his call with Nick, she'd already carried one packed bag into the hallway.

The three of them flew home to Accord while Gabe got to know his future mother-in-law.

The quiet shoosh of the sled's runners echoed in the still air. Gabe had been riding across a silent plain for the past hour. Bright burning sunlight glinted off miles of white snow. There was no sign of the sled in front of his. At the next checkpoint, he'd pull the dogs over for a meal and a rest.

He'd lost track of how many days they'd been on the road. Even without racing to win, this was an endurance test.

He glanced over his shoulder. He couldn't see a soul. He might as well be out in this vast wilderness alone. This beautiful, stunning, humbling wilderness.

Despite being so far south of the north pole, he felt as though, if he took one wrong turn, he would fall off the edge of the earth.

Here be dragons. Were there? Should he be afraid? He didn't dare close his eyes or he might not wake up for hours.

In fact, he didn't know whether he currently slid over land or ice. All was white in every direction.

The dogs raced on, he hoped on target.

His mind slipped, thought of home and of Callie.

He felt close to Dad here.

He pitched forward, his fatigue so profound, he almost lost his grip on reality. Maybe he did. He could have sworn he heard his dad's voice.

"Dad?" He was hallucinating.

He'd been thinking about Dad for most of the trip. How could he not? Dad had instilled this sense of adventure in Gabe when he was just a toddler.

A small breeze kicked up, carrying with it the scent of water.

Gabe looked around, disoriented. He kept on, doggedly aware that to stop now would be dangerous. He had to make it to the next supply dump or the dogs would go hungry, never mind his own hunger.

Next year, he would know how to plan differently.

The scent of water became pronounced and Gabe panicked.

"Haw!" he yelled and the dogs turned, yipping against the leaden momentum of the sled moving forward. Again, he yelled, "Haw!" and they pulled harder, turning, and Gabe put a foot down to help them, but it hit nothing and came up wet.

Jesus. What the hell?

They had just about ridden straight into a stretch of open water.

He pulled the dogs to a stop and they stood panting.

Gabe panted, too, and waited for his heart to stop racing. If this was open water, somewhere along the way, he'd gone off course. He should be south of here.

He leaned over the handle of the sled and tried to catch his breath.

Gradually, he calmed and drove the sled around in a huge arc until they were heading south. Even up here when Gabe tried to control as much of the adventure as he could, there was danger.

There would be no race next year.

He wouldn't do this again. He wanted to get home safe to Callie and the babies they would make. She, and the family they would make, would be his adventure now.

They rode on to the next checkpoint. He settled into appreciating every molecule, every second, of his last big outdoor adventure. Gabe felt his father's presence around him. A sense of profound love streamed through and over him. Dad had taught him so much.

"I've missed you," he whispered, his throat sore, his voice raw.

"Dad!" he hollered. "I've missed you."

At that moment, Gabe knew, Dad had never really abandoned him. He'd always been there.

In Gabe's memories.

In the way Gabe treated people, in how he lived his life according to the morals and ethics Dad had taught him.

He hadn't resented his dad for abandoning him. He'd resented him for leaving such big, big shoes to fill. A man who could risk his own life to try to save another was a hero in any language, anywhere on earth. How was Gabe to measure up? He hadn't even been able to save Billy.

Hush-sh-sh, be at peace, the wilderness seemed to whisper.

Gabe thought of all he'd done in his thirty-seven years. After Dad's death, he'd raised his brothers while Mom worked. He'd persevered through a lonely adolescence, driving himself through his responsibilities, but missing having a dad to talk to. He'd survived Laura and Nick's betrayal.

He'd dedicated those years of his life to the military, doing what he'd been raised to believe was a little good in the world.

He'd lost Billy, but Callie was right, the only one responsible for Billy's life—and death—had been Billy himself. Time to lay down that heavy mantle of responsibility, to set aside the guilt once and for all, and to take care of people because he loved doing it. He'd been born to love and support those around him, and wasn't that a noble character trait?

He was worthy.

Peace finally settled over him, cloaked him with the urge to live a full life, to become all that he was meant to be. And to stop hiding.

Life, or fate, or God, or whatever, had gifted him with Callie.

Dad hadn't been able to save himself or that other climber

on Everest despite a heroic effort, but he'd left his son a valuable legacy.

He rode on to the next checkpoint where he pulled in at dinnertime. He fed the dogs, ate a meal himself and then they settled in to sleep for hours.

He lay on his back and thought of Callie waiting for him at home, of how lucky he was to have her love.

He lay gazing up at the firmament and thought of something Kant wrote. *Two things fill the mind with ever new and increasing admiration and awe...the starry heavens above me and the moral law within me. Neither of them need I seek...*

He worried about Nick. There'd been no love lost between the brothers for so many years, and Nick's latest antics might have killed their relationship for good, but Gabe knew that he couldn't have done much more to bridge the gap. He'd behaved according to his own moral laws. That was the most he could do.

Just before slipping into that blessed darkness of sleep, he thought, yes, this world fills me with awe. He'd followed his moral compass and had lost his home, but had found a life-long companion. Thinking in a different way, he'd lost only the physical manifestation of a home. He'd found his philosophical and spiritual home in Callie.

CALLIE ARRIVED IN Nome, Alaska, nine days after the Iditarod started. She knew Gabe wouldn't come in so early, but she wasn't taking a chance.

Throughout the night, she waited. She drank coffee and hot chocolate from vendors and had bacon and eggs in a small restaurant, smiling as competitors crossed the finish line to wild cheers and celebration.

No Gabe yet.

She knew that for Gabe this challenge hadn't been about winning. It had been a voyage of discovery.

Shortly after eight o'clock two mornings later, on a mild sunny winter day, Gabe rode into Nome with a weary smile on his hirsute face. His beard had grown again since he'd left home.

He looked like a mountain man again. She was happy to see his dear lovable face, hairy or not.

When she glanced at the dogs, though, her heart stopped. Only one dog led the others. Where was Daisy?

Gabe ran the dogs slowly to the end of the street and called for them to stop.

Callie ran to greet him. When he saw her, his smile broadened and cut through the fatigue in his eyes.

"Callie," he breathed. "You're here."

He wrapped her in a bone-twisting hug. When he kissed her, she tried to crawl inside of him, to inhale him, to swallow him whole.

Gabe.

Every thought outside of his name flew from her head. She raised a hand to his cheek. His skin felt like ice.

She pulled away and smiled up at him, but couldn't see him through the blur of tears.

"Gabe. My beautiful mountain man."

He rested his forehead on hers. "The dogs."

"I know. I'll help." She stepped away. "Where's Daisy? What happened?"

"She twisted a paw on a hunk of ice. She's in the sled."

"You go take care of the others. I'll see to her."

Callie approached the sled slowly, taking her time to come around from behind it so she wouldn't startle Daisy.

When Daisy saw Callie, she barked and tried to untangle herself from the blanket Gabe had wrapped her in.

"Shhh. I'll help."

Daisy let her open the blanket and look at her swollen paw. Callie felt the bones. She couldn't feel any breaks. A vet could tell them more.

Callie lifted her out and set her on the ground. "Stay."

Daisy lay down in the snow. Callie sat buddha-style on the ground beside the dog and watched Gabe feed and water the others. They had come through for him.

"Any other injuries besides Daisy's?" she called to Gabe.

"Not a one."

Of course not. Gabe would have taken care of them. She was so proud of him.

Later, they lay on a duvet in front of the fireplace in the small room she'd been able to secure on short notice. It wasn't much, but it didn't matter. She was here with Gabe and *that* was what really, truly mattered.

"When did you decide to come?" Gabe asked.

"Immediately after you left. I knew I wanted to see you cross that finish line."

"What about Johanna?"

"I called Sophie to come stay with her until I get back."

"What about the rest of the dogs?"

"Ty's taking care of them."

Callie stretched, a full-body spine-popping stretch.

"You know what I'd like to do someday?" she asked.

"What's that, sweetheart?" Gabe stopped nuzzling her neck to ask.

"Make love in a bed."

Under her ear, she felt a laugh rumble in Gabe's chest just before he picked her up and deposited her on the bed and picked up the duvet from the carpet.

"Aahhhh," she said, but not because of the soft mattress. Because of Gabe's big body covering hers.

Six months later

CALLIE SETTLED HER mother onto the sofa in the solarium. A local business had donated the furniture. It was bright and colorful and comfy.

She'd begged, borrowed and stolen until she'd filled this big old building with enough furniture to bring in her first clients.

The town of Accord had agreed with Callie six months ago when she presented them with a proposal for a long-term care facility for senior citizens. The town needed something like this.

"Sophie, when everyone finishes dinner can you bring them in here to spend time with Johanna?"

Sophie had been the first employee Callie had hired.

Gradually, all eight of their current residents returned to the solarium after lunch.

Right on time, Gabe showed up with the new Husky puppy he'd got a month ago.

He set Billy on the floor—yes, he'd named the puppy after his friend—where he ran in circles then approached Johanna and stretched up to put his paws on her knee. Johanna laughed. The residents loved Billy's regular visits.

They stayed and visited for an hour and then Gabe and Callie and tired little Billy went home, leaving the residents to Sophie and her staff to get into bed for the night.

Home for Gabe and Callie was a prospector's tent on a piece of property they'd bought outside of Accord, using the money Nick had paid for Gabe's portion of the Jordan land.

While Callie worked every day at Accord Home, Gabe worked on building them a house they'd designed together.

The first requirement? A fireplace that straddled the living room and their bedroom.

Callie used the outdoor toilet and brushed her teeth. Both she and Gabe showered at the old folks' home. He drove her to work every day, showered, then went home to take care of his dogs and to build their home.

She entered the tent. Gabe had turned on a kerosene lamp and started a fire in the stove.

While he used the washroom, she stripped and lay on the old quilts in the middle of the tent.

Went Gabe returned and saw her naked, he grinned.

"Chewbacca?"

"Yes, honey?"

"Turn out the light."

* * * * *

Don't miss Nick Jordan's story!
Look for HOME TO LAURA by Mary Sullivan
available from Harlequin Superromance
March 2013

SPECIAL EXCERPT FROM

HARLEQUIN®

super romance

An Act of Persuasion

By Stephanie Doyle

One night, Ben Tyler broke his own rule about mixing business with pleasure. And it cost him, because Anna Summers quit. Now he's ready to do almost anything to get her back.
Read on for an exciting excerpt!

She was here. Ben Tyler felt a deep satisfaction watching her walk through the country club.

It had been twelve weeks since he'd last seen Anna Summers. Three months since he'd heard her voice. He preferred not to think too much about the fact that he knew down to the minute when she'd last spoken to him.

"Hello, Ben." Anna looked different to him. Softer maybe. Her red hair still shifted about her face, and her freckles were still scattered across her face, but there was a change. Or maybe he'd simply missed seeing her.

"You changed your cell-phone number." The words were out of Ben's mouth before he could stop them. He hadn't meant to start with accusations. He'd intended to be agreeable before asking her to come back to work.

She shrugged. "I guess I didn't want to talk then."

"But you do now?"

"Now I have no choice."

No choice? "Are you in some kind of trouble?"

"You could say."

"Whatever it is, I'll fix it," he said.

"Oh, you're going to fix it. Just like that. Snap and it's done." There was no mistaking the edge in her tone.

Ben sighed at his strategic misstep. "Can we go someplace more private to discuss this?"

She nodded. They left and were halfway to his house when she finally broke the silence.

"So what did you want to talk to me about?"

He'd hoped she would start. But that smacked a little bit of cowardice to him. He was a grown man who fully accepted his actions. "I wanted to apologize."

She shot him a look. "Exactly what are you sorry for?"

He struggled to find the speech he'd prepared, the one that recognized he should have taken her feelings into account, that admitted he'd been wrong to shut her out. But she spoke before he could say anything.

"I'm pregnant."

**Will the baby bring Anna and Ben together?
Or will it drive them apart permanently?
Find out in AN ACT OF PERSUASION
by Stephanie Doyle, available March 2013
from Harlequin® Superromance®.**

What if you desperately
wanted a family but had
given up hope it would
ever happen?

Award-winning author
Mary Sullivan
presents the follow up to
IN FROM THE COLD

Home to Laura

AVAILABLE IN MARCH

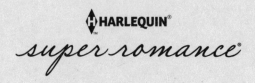

More Story...More Romance

HSR71837

Try a new author!

From debut author
Colleen Collins

The Next Right Thing

When attorney Marc Hamilton offers suspended private investigator Cammie Copello a chance to reclaim her career, she must weigh her secret love for him against following her lifelong dream.

AVAILABLE IN MARCH

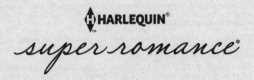

REQUEST YOUR FREE BOOKS!
2 FREE NOVELS PLUS 2 FREE GIFTS!

HARLEQUIN®

super romance®

Exciting, emotional, unexpected!

YES! Please send me 2 FREE Harlequin® Superromance® novels and my 2 FREE gifts (gifts are worth about $10). After receiving them, if I don't wish to receive any more books, I can return the shipping statement marked "cancel." If I don't cancel, I will receive 6 brand-new novels every month and be billed just $4.69 per book in the U.S. or $5.24 per book in Canada. That's a savings of at least 15% off the cover price! It's quite a bargain! Shipping and handling is just 50¢ per book in the U.S. and 75¢ per book in Canada.* I understand that accepting the 2 free books and gifts places me under no obligation to buy anything. I can always return a shipment and cancel at any time. Even if I never buy another book, the two free books and gifts are mine to keep forever.

135/336 HDN FVS7

Name	(PLEASE PRINT)
Address	Apt. #
City	State/Prov.	Zip/Postal Code

Signature (if under 18, a parent or guardian must sign)

Mail to the Harlequin® Reader Service:
IN U.S.A.: P.O. Box 1867, Buffalo, NY 14240-1867
IN CANADA: P.O. Box 609, Fort Erie, Ontario L2A 5X3

**Are you a current subscriber to Harlequin Superromance books
and want to receive the larger-print edition?
Call 1-800-873-8635 or visit www.ReaderService.com.**

* Terms and prices subject to change without notice. Prices do not include applicable taxes. Sales tax applicable in N.Y. Canadian residents will be charged applicable taxes. Offer not valid in Quebec. This offer is limited to one order per household. Not valid for current subscribers to Harlequin Superromance books. All orders subject to credit approval. Credit or debit balances in a customer's account(s) may be offset by any other outstanding balance owed by or to the customer. Please allow 4 to 6 weeks for delivery. Offer available while quantities last.

Your Privacy—The Harlequin® Reader Service is committed to protecting your privacy. Our Privacy Policy is available online at www.ReaderService.com or upon request from the Harlequin Reader Service.

We make a portion of our mailing list available to reputable third parties that offer products we believe may interest you. If you prefer that we not exchange your name with third parties, or if you wish to clarify or modify your communication preferences, please visit us at www.ReaderService.com/consumerschoice or write to us at Harlequin Reader Service Preference Service, P.O. Box 9062, Buffalo, NY 14269. Include your complete name and address.

Love the Harlequin book
you just read?

Your opinion matters.

Review this book on your favorite
book site, review site, blog or your own
social media properties and share
your opinion with other readers!

Be sure to connect with us at:
Harlequin.com/Newsletters
Facebook.com/HarlequinBooks
Twitter.com/HarlequinBooks

It all starts with a kiss

THE ONE THAT GOT AWAY

KELLY HUNTER

Check out the brand-new series

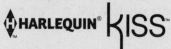

Fun, flirty and sensual romances.
ON SALE JANUARY 22!